The Stinging Fly

NEW WRITERS · NEW WRITING

'... God has specially appointed me to this city, so as though it were a large thoroughbred horse which because of its great size is inclined to be lazy and needs the stimulation of some stinging fly...'

—Plato, *The Last Days of Socrates*

The Stinging Fly
new writers, new writing
PO Box 6016, Dublin 1
info@stingingfly.org

Editor: Danny Denton

| *Publisher* | *Poetry Editor* | *Website Editor* |
| Declan Meade | Cal Doyle | Ian Maleney |

| *Assistant Editor* | *Eagarthóir Filíochta* | *Reviews Editor* |
| Sara O'Rourke | Aifric MacAodha | Thomas Morris |

Contributing Editors
Dan Bolger, Mia Gallagher, Lisa McInerney, Thomas Morris, Sally Rooney and
Nidhi Zak / Aria Eipe

© Copyright remains with authors and artists, 2021

Printed by Walsh Colour Print, County Kerry

ISBN 978-1-906539-89-4   ISSN 1393-5690

The Stinging Fly gratefully acknowledges the support of The Arts Council/
An Chomhairle Ealaíon.

NEW FICTION

GENERAL MECHANISM
[FOUR RESPONSES TO *IBM 1401: A USER'S MANUAL*]

FEATURED POET

NEW POEMS

COMHCHEALG

COVER ART

Lee Welch

COVER DESIGN

Emily Good

The Stinging Fly was established in 1997 to publish and promote the best new Irish and international writing. Published twice a year, we welcome submissions on a regular basis. Online submissions only. Please read the submission guidelines on our website. We are no longer seeking submissions for our Winter 2021-22 issue, which we will publish in November 2021.

The next general open submission window for fiction and poetry is from December 6th 2021 to January 10th 2022. Work received during this time will be considered for publication in our two 2022 issues. Please contact the editor with essay queries from November 2021 onwards.

Keep in touch: sign up to our email newsletter, become a fan on Facebook, or follow us on Twitter for regular updates about our publications, podcasts, workshops and events.

stingingfly.org | facebook.com/StingingFly | @stingingfly

By way of an editorial...

Welcome to our Summer 2021 issue. I really hope you enjoy the great new writing that's gathered here.

Towards the end of 2019, the small team of people who work on this magazine gathered together for a workshop on strategy development led by Janice McAdam. Janice had brought paper and pens, sweets and oranges. Also demands that we think and talk about stuff we don't often take time to think or talk about. Why do we do what we do? What is it that defines us? What do we believe in? What's it all for?

We spoke our thoughts. Janice made notes and took them away. And then over the course of last year we met several more times—at first in person and then on Zoom. It took time and effort to refine our thinking and to get the words right. We will publish our new strategy in full next month but we invite you now to read its main points across the page.

The key benefit of working on the strategy is that it allowed us to better understand the work we do and to express why we believe that it's important. I hope it will enable other people—including you, our readers and supporters—to understand what we do more clearly, too. And that you will be encouraged to continue reading the work we publish and supporting all the other work we do such as teaching, mentoring, writer development, etc. We want to build upon the spirit of community that exists between our writers and readers. And we want this community to be open and welcoming to everyone who seeks to join it.

The past year has led many of us to ask big questions. The Covid-19 pandemic has caused massive disruption to how we live our lives. I've no doubt we'll feel its impact for a long time to come. Hopefully, however, we have come through the worst of it now and we can start the process of recovery and renewal. The small team here want to get on with creating a more compassionate world through literature.

Declan Meade
Founding Editor & Publisher
May 2021

OUR PURPOSE

To enrich lives and deepen understanding through literature.

OUR VISION

Our vision is of a world made more compassionate through literature.

OUR MISSION

To seek out, nurture, publish and promote the very best
new writers and new writing.

OUR VALUES

Quality

We believe that writers and readers deserve excellence. In all aspects of our work—our publishing, our teaching, our mentoring—we push for outcomes of the highest standard.

Commitment

We believe that writing is a craft, a practice that demands discipline, dedication and time. We support our writers, nurturing their potential and furthering their ambitions. We make space for them to produce their best work.

Community

We believe that literature has the power to bring people closer together. Through our work we create loyal communities of writers and readers, within Ireland and beyond.

Social justice

We believe that writing matters and can be a force for positive change. We want to play our part in building a just society.

The Strange Kid

Glen Jeffries

He told me as we were by the front door readying ourselves to go outside. He was kneeling, his hands looped around the frayed lace-ends of his walking boots. 'Good news,' he said. 'I've just sent off for it.'

He looked up at me from his (perhaps strategically) subordinated position, searched my face for recognition and found what, I imagine, in truth, he was hoping to find: no recognition. He held the silence for long enough to let his point land, but not so long that it would require me to interject, and then clarified: 'The magazine. The old issue with that story in it.'

I should have remembered. He'd been talking about it for a while, since the spring probably. I still recall him arriving at my apartment and gingerly carrying his muddied bike up the stairs, his fluorescent green jacket marked down its back with a single, spattered, brown line, and declaring when he reached the hallway at the top (helmet still on) that he'd just listened to the best short story on his ride over here and that I should give it a listen, or a read, too.

The next time I saw him he'd printed it for me: 'Here you go. I couldn't fathom how to do double-sided but the font is the same as the original magazine so it looks pretty authentic. I underlined my favourite sentence. Don't skip to it—reach it in your own time; it's right near the end anyway.'

I read the story the following day when he'd left for work. I enjoyed the story, I did. The single sentence—just fifteen or so words about some woods becoming legendary—was underlined with a fountain pen and when I turned the page over I could see through its reverse three separate globules like little molehills of blue ink where he must have unintentionally pressed more firmly. It was just the sort of story I expected Will would like: a tale set in small-town America, involving unkind characters and wildlife. And there was a strange kid in it.

'I hope we have a kid like that one day,' he told me when we discussed the story. I didn't fully understand the aspiration, as the kid had bad skin, was bullied by a stepfather and told barefaced lies—something I can't abide—to pretty much everyone (including a police officer). But as a concession I told him I thought the kid had a strong imagination.

He suggested that I could, if I wanted to, place the print-out in my bookcase. By pure chance I slotted it on a shelf between *One Hundred Years of Solitude* and *The Adventures of Huckleberry Finn*. 'That's perfect,' he said, when he noticed where it ended up.

A few months passed before he mentioned the story again. 'Remember that story? The one I really liked and got you to read? It's on your shelf at home printed out.' I told him I did. 'Well, I decided to order the author's collection with the story in it. I couldn't find the edition here so it's coming from America. I guess nobody knows him that well over here.' It arrived a week or so later and he read it quickly, concluding that it was very good but there was probably no need for me to read it. It was summer by then and we were sitting outside at a restaurant having lunch and he had the book with him. Just over the other side of the fence railings from our table there was a full-service car wash and there would be loud, intermittent blasts as a powerful hose stripped off the dirt and for the next minute or so I watched tiny particles of mist and grime float towards us. 'There are no more strange kids or big wildlife in the other stories,' he added. 'Just some minor marine animals and cuckolds.'

Then about a month after that he brought the story up again: 'I was reading it yesterday, for the first time on my laptop, and the full-page illustration the magazine originally ran alongside it came up. I didn't see this before when I read the story on my phone. Must be a compatibility issue—the magazine should look into that. Anyway, the imagery and colours are so perfect. Brooding khakis. The animal poised. The kid lying down. I've started looking into how one might go about getting hold of old issues of the magazine.

There's eBay and second-hand bookshops... But better than that there's also a process out there to order old copies direct from the magazine publisher itself, through the mail from the US.'

He explained this 'process' as we were in my kitchen cooking with anchovies and the briny absoluteness of the aroma made by those dead, miniscule, silver creatures almost mocked the gargantuan complexity of the procedure he outlined. He had determined that although it would cost more to get it this way than, say, eBay, 'what with the cost of the magazine itself and the postage out to America and back,' it was worth it.

Only one question remained for him: 'Do you think I should include a full cover letter with the cheque, or just a slip of paper with the issue number I'm after?' I asked him what the process prescribed. 'The instructions remain silent on this point. A lacuna. I think I'll play it safe and write one,' he said, adding after a short pause that, 'The size of the paper I'll use for my letter will indicate clearly that this is an overseas order—in case the person in the department thinks 'UK' is a typo for 'AK'.'

October passed and by November there was still no sign of the issue.

'I have concerns, Clara. I should contact them and find out what's going on. Do you think I should write a letter or use the email address they provide on the website? I guess email would be much quicker but to email does seem to go somewhat against the grain of the whole procedure.'

He must have emailed, because some days later I went to his apartment and as I came in the door he explained to me excitedly that he'd had an email back from the magazine: 'Look! From a guy working in the relevant department. An actual human working on this. His email is a good one. Well-crafted; good spacing too. Look.' He turned the laptop screen round. I read the email and the reason for the delay was explained: Will had dated the cheque incorrectly; he'd not used the American date format so it couldn't be cashed until next month.

Buoyed now by the news that this was 'all in hand' (the term used by the department), he admitted he actually took delight in the additional interaction caused by his error: 'The address I sent the cheque and letter to was just for a

PO Box in some town in Kansas. I went on Google Maps and did a tour of the streets looking for warehouses—it must be a warehouse, right?—so I could get a feeling of what I'm dealing with. The town isn't that big but I couldn't spot anything that looked likely to be it so I decided just to imagine it and write that down instead. Want to see it?'

He showed it to me on a printout with a couple of his manuscript revisions remaining in the wide margins:

Single storey: this is a small town and therefore space is of little concern. Squat, regular, block shapes make it up, and they are painted an orange that in ordinary light looks faded but in the occasional winter glow of the full moon must turn beautiful. On either side of it, only parking lots and scrub unless you walk back across the road (into another parking lot) so on the right, out of the far corner of your eye, a Dairy Queen sign appears, rotating slowly, ceaselessly. The entrance, unsigned, is two wired glass doors blocking out any view of internal workings and is reached via a gentle ramp. If one were to venture in, along the hospital-scrubs-blue, easily-cleaned, lino-floored corridors and past various, orderly offices filled with efficient people (editor's note: like the guy who replied to my email), a main hall would be reached. The lungs of the building. In there, columns and rows of tall bookcases dated by year, then by month, and then further marked by issue number. All the colours and words within those magazines are hidden entirely. The only splashes of colour against the brown of the bookcases are the few red gate valves for the water detection system and the flashing lights of the temperature and humidity gauges.

He asked if I liked it. I told him I did and asked what he intended to do with it. 'Recycle it into my work maybe? Seamus Heaney wrote a great number of little prose description pieces and bundled them together and called them *prose poems*. Could do that if I get good at this stuff.'

Just before Christmas I went over to his apartment and saw that the magazine had finally arrived. It was there on the coffee table, and he'd lined it up precisely on top of the white envelope it had been delivered in, so precisely that around each edge there was an inch of white.

'There was no note or anything else with it in the envelope. Just the magazine. So simple,' he said, tapping the front cover twice with his index finger, as if with pride.

It lay there like that for a few more days and then one morning I walked past and it was opened. I saw he'd underlined that same sentence. Turning the page over in my hand gently, so as not to add any fingerprints or warping to the immaculate copy, I could see the ink through the thin paper connecting like a desire line through a forest of words.

Then, in the very first days of the new year, he told me to come over to his apartment and to bring pastries to celebrate (exactly *what* we were celebrating I did not know). I opened the apartment door, knelt down to take off my boots, my hands working loose the frayed lace-ends, and I saw hung on the wall directly opposite me a pinewood frame, and inside that pinewood frame three pages side-by-side. On the left, was the story's title page and illustration cut from the magazine. In the middle, the page with the underlined sentence also snipped from the magazine. Then on the right, a printout of the email from the magazine department explaining the delay.

'What do you think?' he asked.

I told him, and he responded: 'Some people have a mirror by the door to check they've not applied too much lipstick or missed something stuck in their teeth. Well, this is a bit like my mirror. My checkpoint. When I'm sat down there like you are now, fiddling with the matter-of-factness of boots and laces and finding keys and checking I've got everything I need, I'll look up, and see it, and think: God, I love that story, and that strange kid, and this one little sentence. What a way to be ready for the outside world!'

I pushed a loose strand of hair lightly back into place behind his ear and smiled encouragingly, and went into the kitchen to throw away my chewing gum. I saw in the bin the remains of the discarded magazine. It was twisted and scissor-cut and stained in places, marked wet and brown by coffee grounds that still clung to the pages like crumbs on a plate. I lifted it out and turned to find the pages of the story that remained. I read for a few paragraphs. It was the bit where the strange kid was talking to the police officer. There you are, I thought, lying, yet again.

A Full Study Of Darkness

January 6, 2021

Learning to live in the dark—
I can't help but wonder what's walking
out there, in the park, beyond my windows
and doors, far away from all my opinions.
Is there a world apart I will never belong to? I—
an idea dissolved in blue and black.
The green we remember seems faint
and far away. Music plays. We half-listen.
A teacher once told me, 'get far from here'
yet there she stood. I take comfort in that.
A will to remain. But her comfort isn't mine.
Today the weight of words defies all understanding.
Once, I might have used them, flung them up
in the air just to see the shapes they fell into.
Now words are stones. Without lightness.
Harsh and cold to touch. And I have dissolved
into many. Not a multitude, too difficult
to convey. But something less than promised.
Or maybe something more.
It depends on how you feel about standing still.

Jonathan C. Creasy

The Youths

Lisa Owens

They met at work. They were hired at the same time to assist two senior members of staff. They were nicknamed 'The Youths' because they were in their mid-twenties. She had a boyfriend at the time, and he had just come out of a long relationship that had involved a short period of cohabitation.

Initially, neither liked being lumped together as 'The Youths'. He thought it made him sound inexperienced. She didn't like the association with him. She thought his friendly demeanour was a façade; that he was secretly arrogant, not as clever as her yet more convinced of his cleverness. She felt he avoided tasks like photocopying and mail-franking; that he considered these things to be beneath him.

For the record: he did frequently make tea for anyone who wanted one, and even though sometimes she suspected this was a clever mode of work-avoidance, and a subtle play for popularity (thus, ultimately, power), it also contradicted her theory that he believed himself to be above mundane chores, so she gave him the benefit of the doubt; also, he washed up his own mug carefully, whereas most of the other employees, including those she otherwise considered decent, thoughtful people (including herself, initially, until she followed his lead) left their dirty mugs in stacks in the sink for the cleaner to do after-hours.

The Youths did not do anything so obvious as get together at the office party, but they did get drunk and advance the party beyond the office to a pub first, and then a bar, with ever dwindling numbers, until finally they were the only two left—and that night was when she first sensed he liked to be near her; that he would position himself close to her where possible, and gravitate back towards her when she moved away (in order to test the hypothesis that he liked being near her).

He remembered this slightly differently. He claimed he did warm to her that evening but purely on a 'friendship level'. Until that evening, he had perceived her to be more efficient and diligent than he was and—wary his more relaxed working methods would be compared unfavourably to hers—kept his distance. That evening, though, he realised he could make her laugh, and vice versa, but he knew she had a boyfriend and therefore the possibility of romance seemed remote. Anyway, he was enjoying being single and dating various girls after having spent his student days and beyond in what he referred to as a 'prematurely domestic' relationship (partly to underplay its importance in front of potential prospects, while also making clear that he was not after another cosy, traditional coupling, at least not yet).

She had a slight problem with the way he said 'girls', even though it was how she referred to herself and to her female contemporaries, because 'woman' felt too serious and matronly; or else too worldly—too whole-person-who-has-it-all-figured-out—whereas she considered herself to be more of a work-in-progress. But *him* saying 'girls' was borderline disrespectful. In his mouth, it made women her age sound silly and unserious, primarily objects of desire without substance or durability. She mentioned this the night of the office party, because she'd had a few drinks and felt powerfully certain of her position on this point, and of the point's towering importance. He countered that it was more complicated: there wasn't an equivalent of 'guys', which could cover any male up to 'at least forty-nine', and also had the advantage of grouping people together in a friendly, genderless bunch. He asked if she preferred 'women' and she claimed she did, but it didn't really sound right coming from him either, it sounded faux-respectful, therefore somehow worse than 'girls', so she wondered if he should just stick with 'someone': e.g., 'There's someone I like at work,' and he said, 'Who?' and she frowned, and said, 'No I meant—' and he said, 'I know, I'm joking,' and she resumed, 'At work—or *wherever*, until you were more serious, and then 'girlfriend' would be acceptable, or 'partner'.'

*

It was just after the office party that the Ginny Spiro emails started. Of course they had emailed each other many times before then, but this started out with a message from her, with the subject Ginny Spiro and the question, What's her email? He replied: why don't you check the database like everyone else, and his lack of punctuation or capital letters told her this was a joke, and not him being the brusque person she initially took him for pre-office party. So she said it's easier to ask you and then he gave her the email address, saying, I got that from the database by the way it's not hard and she said cool, could you send me Carl Miller's number too then, and he sent her only a number in reply. She thought that was a bit cold, and read back through the correspondence a few times, feeling defensive, but also stupid, wondering whether he was just being rude after all; but when she called the number he had given her, and after she asked the confused person on the end for Carl Miller a couple of times, she realised he had sent her the number for the Greek deli where they and their colleagues sometimes went for lunch, and then she blushed: out of embarrassment for calling the number in the first place, and also because when she looked up at him, watching her, she found in his grin the stirrings of some energy there. In fact, it was so intense she had to look away.

So the Ginny Spiro emails continued in that vein: one or two liners, a conversation really, hundreds and hundreds of emails back and forward, so many that if they ever scrolled down the chain (as they both did, occasionally) the very first emails had been marginalised to such a degree that you had to read them vertically, one letter at a time.

They reverted to the Ginny Spiro chain when they were emailing about anything not explicitly professional. Often it was commentary on their colleagues, or tortuous metaphors re: how long the day felt, or the status of their hangovers, and when the first Ginny Spiro email of the day popped up, he would feel a jolt or twist that made him need to stretch (usually with his arms) to exorcise the surplus tension. He especially liked the Ginny Spiro emails that referred to something going on in another email thread where they were both copied; one of them would take issue with the way something had been phrased, pasting only the offending words, for example, reach out or take the lead and they would go from there, each trying to outdo the other with increasingly absurd jargon.

*

Once, she asked what he thought Ginny Spiro would make of her involvement in their emails. He suggested that one day, someone would discover and publish the Ginny Spiro Emails, which would then be adapted into a movie. And she replied that Ginny Spiro would be played by Meryl Streep; that it would be the first Oscar ever to be awarded to an actor who never physically appeared onscreen, and he replied actually laughing.

They decided Carl Miller, who sometimes came into the office with his dog, would be a joint cameo by JK Simmons and the dog from *Marley & Me*.

For many months while the Ginny Spiro emails evolved, she was still in a relationship, but had begun to feel an itch of impatience with her boyfriend: that he did not seem interested in how her day was, that he took off his socks on the sofa and left them there like two grubby skins; that she could not suggest they do something different, like go to see an exhibition, without him teasing her for being pretentious. What she could not admit even to herself was that the boyfriend was not the issue at all, not really. The problem was that she wanted to change, but she did not want him to come with her. She was pouring herself, slowly, like thick syrup, into another mould: sharper, funnier, more serious. Happier. Or at least, on the way to being happier, some part of her suspected, but this was not something she could interrogate because to do so would be to admit that maybe there was someone else at the root of the impatience she felt; an impatience that graduated into annoyance, then fury and ultimately the end of the relationship.

It was a mutual decision. It was important to her that she maintained her dignity and moral standing in the break-up, because she considered herself honest, and she had always taken a dim view of people who cheated, and anyway she did not cheat on the boyfriend, not even slightly: if the boyfriend had read through Ginny Spiro, for example, he would not be able to find a single thing that he could reproach her for (except perhaps the sheer volume of emails, but that is natural, she planned to say, if this conversation ever took place, between two people who work together every day and sit near each other and have the same, she would insist, semi-terrible job).

The break-up was never referred to by The Youths in person or via Ginny Spiro, but instead he learned about it some weeks afterwards, through one of their colleagues, who joked, with hand motions, that she was 'finally up for grabs'. He responded, 'You can't say things like that,' but he laughed so the colleague wouldn't take offence. Since the office party night, when she had taken him to task over how he said 'girls', he had been making a concerted effort to be more careful in the way he spoke about women, and this frequently caused him tiny moral quandaries when in exclusively male company, because it would be far easier to just let things go, to laugh, even agree; and sometimes, honestly, he did let it go, when he sensed that saying something would change the atmosphere. That was how deep it went, that stuff: preserving the fragile ego in front of him was, when it came down to it, worth more than making things a bit awkward in the name of enlightenment—and who was to say which is the kinder thing in any case: the taking of the moral high ground, or the going easy on the guy who didn't know any better? Anyway, this time, he did make the effort to say something, and not solely, but mainly because it was about her, and he wanted his credentials where she was concerned to be impeccable, because on hearing the news that she was no longer in a relationship, his heart rate had shot up, and he'd felt the blood pulsing in his ears, which he knew had turned red.

The fact she hadn't told him about the break-up was not at all hurtful or strange—conversely, it made him more confident that there was something between them, because if there wasn't, she would definitely have told him about the break-up, and if she had done so on Ginny Spiro, it would have breached the unspoken, intricate but utterly clear-to-both-parties terms of Ginny Spiro, and ended whatever it was that might have been going on between them right there and then.

In the months after the break-up, Ginny Spiro continued, but their in-person interactions became fraught. If they ever happened to be, for example, in the kitchenette at the same time, they would have bright, inane, palindromic interactions: 'You alright?' 'Yeah, alright thanks. You?' 'Alright, thanks, yeah'—as though they knew each other as well as two colleagues who did *not* email each other non-professionally all day long. On the one hand, he was moved by how instinctive this behaviour was; how complicit and committed they both were in maintaining their two realities, how compatible they must surely be to shift gear between the ease and camaraderie he found on the screen and this show of polite awkwardness. But he was frustrated too because as time went on, he wondered whether the emails were the 'real' thing at all, or merely a proxy for intimacy—if she was using him to satisfy some perverse need with no concern for what he might have needed. So whenever she asked him to join a group of them for lunch, casually, in front of everyone, as though he were exactly as unimportant, or important, to her as the others, sometimes, to maintain this illusion, he would join the lunch party and spend most of it talking to someone else; but other times, when he was feeling especially frustrated, he would claim he had to work through lunch, knowing she would be annoyed at the rejection of her own insincere invite. How was lunch he would ask, and she would take a long time to reply, but she always would eventually, with something terse like fine but quickly followed up with, hope you got your extremely urgent work done and he would respond, yep you can sleep easy tonight, and she'd say that's a load off and they would be back on track.

He was still going on dates all this time, and occasionally going home with the dates afterwards, but the experiences felt very external to him. He had started to view himself as 'internal' and 'external': 'external' did things—went to work and on dates and to the gym—while 'internal' was a buzzy state of low-level excitement, at once mildly stressful and extremely enjoyable—when he was emailing her at work, for example, or simply aware of her proximity. He could hold entire conversations with people that he later would be unable to recall, as he had been studiously *not* watching her, while knowing exactly where she was in the office at all times. Photocopier, meeting room; he felt almost omniscient. Some days, it was a genuine relief to go home and decompress in his own space, away from her.

She did not know whether he was dating anyone, because of course he would never mention it to her, but sometimes she imagined that he was, to see if she minded, and found she was mainly amused at the idea, because he couldn't possibly correspond to someone else the way he corresponded to her, and she ended up feeling sorry for the theoretical person, even responsible for their emotional welfare.

Then, one afternoon, she was pulled into a meeting—she had 'dropped the ball' on a minor issue that had, owing to her ignorance, escalated into something bigger—and after, had returned to her desk close to tears. He emailed (too rapidly to pull up Ginny Spiro), everything ok and she replied, because she did not want to fully break down at her desk, tell you later and he wrote, before he could think about it too much, beer after work? and she said haha 'beer' ok 'buddy' and he said sorry out of my depth here and she paused, not breathing, before she typed sorry and then, quickly, a beer would be good.

For the rest of the day he couldn't do anything. He would start a task but kept clicking back to their exchange to check whether he had imagined everything, whether in fact he had misread her right from the get go and all that was happening was a friendly drink between two colleagues.

When it was six o'clock, he went over in his coat and said, 'Shall we?' and instantly regretted it, fearing she might not see that by saying 'Shall we?' he was really communicating that he was in fact, *not* the sort of person who would say 'Shall we?' sincerely. But she, who had been trying to look as though she was still working, with a sufficient degree of absorption to belie the fact she'd been thinking about this moment all afternoon (she had been to the toilets already to sort out her hair) smiled while she clicked 'send' on the email she had already finished—but deliberately left unsent for this purpose—and said, 'Let's!' She switched off her monitor and followed him out of the office with her coat folded over her arm.

In the pub, she couldn't stop chewing the inside of her mouth, and one of his calves was so tense he worried he had pulled a muscle. It was the first time they had been properly alone since the office party, a fact that went unspoken, yet seemed incredible to both of them.

Their conversation was less fluid than their emails because they had the physical fact of themselves and each other to confront—there were eyes to look at, or not look at, hands to put somewhere. Things to talk about. The deadpan, affectless tone of their correspondence was not viable in person.

They drank wine. They sat on the same side of the table, leaning away from each other to begin with, but now and then each would shift position, ostensibly for comfort reasons, until their shoulders and knees were touching. A couple of times, she laughed energetically, moving forward and away with the effort of laughing, and when she came back to the original position he did not flinch, and had not moved: he was there waiting for her.

*

They spoke about their families mainly, trying to sound mostly ordinary, yet also slightly extraordinary, making reference to character-shaping circumstances or minor hardships, while omitting the darker traumas they nursed, saving them for when they were on surer footing. They got hungry and ordered chips, politely deferring to each other regarding salt and/or vinegar before agreeing to liberally douse them in both; then they ordered another portion, to soak up the wine, which they kept buying by the glass. A bottle would have been more economical, but it seemed too bold and certain a statement, as though the delicate premise of the evening might buckle under the weight of such a commitment.

They stayed past last orders, until the bar staff turned up the stools all around them and started wiping their table. By that stage they were holding hands, a development that had gone unacknowledged, had happened by such minute degrees that letting go felt crude and hurtful, but she did, standing up to put her coat on, and he decided he would not let it happen again unless she actively sought it out.

Outside, they stood by the road, and she rocked back on her heels, raising her eyebrows and pulling her face into a deliberately awkward grin, and he said, 'What?' and she said, '"What" what?' and he said, '"What what" what?' and she said, 'Stop it.' She felt so nervous she might be sick, while he was surprised by how calm he was, and he brought his face close to hers but waited to see if she would initiate the kiss.

Later, much later, she wondered if this was the very best moment of all, when their desire and hesitancy about destroying the desire were absolutely equal, when neither had yet put a foot wrong in the context of their whatever-it-was-at-that-point. Where their intellectual attraction and physical attraction peaked all at once, when nothing else in the world—their future children, their existing parents' eventual declining health—mattered more than their being together, at that moment. When they were simply two people who wanted to be with each other and no one else.

His impression was that he had tuned into a crystal-clear frequency while twiddling through static: sudden, surprising and surprisingly easy, so easy it almost spooked him when he (in years to come) thought about how it just as easily might never have been.

They tried to keep the relationship a secret, not because they thought it would be a problem at work particularly, but because they both loved the secrecy, the intimacy it afforded them. But soon, they had friends and family to answer to, flatmates and yes, colleagues, who sensed (and didn't like the sense) that they were being excluded from something. So The Youths let it be known, slowly, gradually—though, once the facts had been established in the office, the news took one single morning to spread.

They spent every night together the first six months, and then the next six months, and when the lease on her flat was up, they moved in together to a one-bedroomed place above a hairdresser. He stayed at the company, and was promoted; she took a new job (and pay cut) at a start-up, because she was ready for a change, and together they decided it would be good for them to be apart at least some of the time, to 'fill their cups' so to speak, in the world beyond their world.

They had sex every night for eight months: she believed she always initiated it. He believed that too, but with the caveat that it was the way they had always worked, that he was there and ready for her the second she made the move. Then, one night she didn't make the move, and he didn't either. She was privately hurt, and he was privately relieved that he could go straight to sleep because he had had a long day, and was tired, nothing more than that. When she brought it up a few days later, he said that he had intuited she was tired and didn't want to put her in the position of having sex unwillingly when it was clear she hadn't wanted to make the move. And she said, 'Why do I always have to make the move?', and he said, 'You *don't* have to,' and she said, 'Oh, OK then.' And just like that, they were in a fight, their first real fight, and they didn't have sex even though he then tried to make the move, because she said he was only doing so to prove a point, he had had his chance several nights ago and it was quite clear he didn't want to, and he said, 'I give up,' and they turned away, silently reviewing and honing their arguments, and with each pass, each grew more certain of their own position, before they fell asleep.

*

They moved on, they had less sex, they became more comfortable and less intense, though she always held on to that first rejection as proof that he didn't desire her unreservedly, that he was holding some part of himself back, for himself or for someone else, she would have to wait and see. He forgot all about it, except for the belief—reinforced through arguments to come over the years—that she leapt to incorrect assumptions, and that even when he did explain himself, and she accepted his version of events, the stain of her initial assumption remained, faded but indelible.

They married. They had a child, and then two more.

It was hard. She had known, rationally, that it would be, looking back on her own childhood, which was secure and full of love, certainly; but also boredom, tears, fighting, chaos. The dreary, messy, thick of it—the toileting, washing, feeding, whining—was, for her, nothing like the hopeful, precious days of earliest new-parenthood, where they would reverently gaze at the baby and at each other, a trio cast in almost divine relief. He was an only child, and had an orderly, relatively peaceful bank of memories, infused with a longing for rambunctious rough-housing with siblings. He did not find the children tiring in the same way she did—an exhaustion approaching bone-marrow-draining. He could make them laugh and shriek, even at their most cranky, and come up with endless games that would have everyone upside down or piled on top of each other while she stood with her back against the kitchen units watching, arms folded, wanting—but too tired—to smile.

He would have had more children, if she were up for it. He would have had five! But she was not.

On weekend nights, after the children were in bed, they would sit in the kitchen and drink wine. He looked at his phone so much she joked that he had a secret girlfriend. She knew he didn't—as far it was possible to *know*—and she felt almost sad for him that he didn't, that he just wanted, or needed, to look at his phone when he was with her, and then she felt almost sad for herself too.

He didn't have a secret girlfriend, but he was involved with several work-related women over the course of several years: nothing that ever came close to being *technically* inappropriate, by any *tribunal* standards, or to being detected by her, beyond the occasional intuitive frisson that she always decided to leave unexamined, or by anyone other than the women themselves, who even, when it came down to it, might feel a bit delusional if they ever confided in their friends about him. He was not an idiot: he never communicated with the women by any means other than in person; there was never any physical contact that could be construed as romantic—just longer-than-typical unbroken eye-contact, and intense, rangy conversations when he was working late, and a sick-hungry feeling in the pit of his stomach while he was contriving the having of the conversations. While they spoke, he would feel like he was glowing softly: as though a lamp had been switched on inside him. He did not want to sleep with these women, or kiss or even touch them: what he found himself craving was their clear and unfettered investment in him, their attention to him as a... soul?... a mind? just as she had invested in, and attended to him, in the beginning. Sometimes, after these conversations, he would return home to his wife—to her—and reach for her with a keen desire, and she, sensing some shift within him, would meet him in kind.

She had one long, tortuous situation with a local father, a married man with four children—two in school, plus twin toddlers—who she met at the playground, and was on nodding and eyebrow raising terms with before graduating to smiling and eventually droll comments about the challenges of young kids. They spoke freely and warmly about their partners—what brilliant parents they were, how supportive, how hardworking. This made the persistence of their interactions completely above board, she felt, because there was no question either would ever act beyond the bounds of their respective families. She spoke to him exactly as she would another mother—the content of their conversations was no different—but why then did she feel she had to look at the ground so often, why did she feel not just pleased, but excited, when she saw his shape in the distance—and why indeed was she so good at making *his* particular distant form out, distinct from all the other forms? Why did she sometimes, having spotted him, turn and go in the opposite direction, muttering half-baked excuses to her outraged children? Why did she blush when he said, jovially, 'We missed you guys!' after she'd been on a family holiday? She was not interested in any of the things he seemed to like. He was earnest and practical and wore things like hiking boots, and a technical-looking jacket that struck her as ridiculous in the suburban context of the playground. She held certain assumptions about him that she never verified, but entertained to herself like an in-joke: for example, that he had been a Scout, and a keen one at that. So he was not a credible threat to anyone's safety, nothing ever happened, nothing close to anything, but that didn't stop her, wide-awake, in the deep night, from imagining scenarios where their respective spouses had benevolently vanished and she and this other person, this… *ur-dad* unified with all their children to form a wholesome super-family.

She realised some time later, when the man had moved away (they had said goodbye with a self-consciously clumsy hug, the kind where both jostled a bit to make it less intimate, and the tough thread from the reflective patches on his technical jacket scratched her cheek, and her son asked loudly several times after, why she had 'cuddled Ted and Rudy's dad') and she experienced a wretched pining for him that made her feel foolish and embarrassed, that perhaps the reason she had let her heart to him for however long, however innocently, was that he was the first man she had encountered as a mother, who knew nothing about who she might have been before, who simply saw who she was right there in that moment—tired, fraying, trying, falling short— and yet still found her company tolerable.

But he, she had to remind herself—her husband—had known her before, *and* known her after, and still he was there, by her side, and that had to count for something too.

They argued more than they had ever argued, and the arguments grew more knotted, arose more quickly and were harder to resolve, because each was part of a history, each a palimpsest of arguments past. She, who had, at one time in her life, considered herself to be a controlled person, found herself exploding at him in public: in cafés, on the street, in restaurants, and what surprised her most was not that she could not contain herself, but that there was no longer anywhere *to* contain her fury when it arose, because she had no private life anymore: for her, the domestic was now everywhere.

He, who considered himself easy-going and anti-confrontation, retreated into himself, absorbing her rage into a bedrock of resentment and guilt. He knew he could not make her happy as he had once made her happy. They could not enjoy each other in the slow, selfish way they had at first, and he did not know how to square the disparity between them-now and them-then. He wondered: shouldn't she try too? Couldn't she see he was vulnerable also, lonely, exhausted, that he might be capable of such clichés as weeping in the shower, or punching a wall, or pressing his palms and forehead to a rain-streaked window?

Lately, she had started to feel like 'a woman in a film'. Sitting in the waiting room at the doctor's, or at the kitchen table, sipping tea while the children caterwauled around her, she could vividly see how the frame would be composed, her form statuesque, her face 'saying it all'. She wondered if this was the kind of thought that, if she mentioned it during a check-up, would cause her doctor to look at her—though she knew she would never say it out loud, and anyway, what was 'a woman in a film', if not simply, a woman? An attempt at saying: 'This is how it is, don't you think?'

Things became easier, in some ways, as the children grew independent by infinitesimal degrees. The Youths started accepting, finally, that this was it; this was their life, the one life they would have, the one life they had chosen—unless either of them would be bold enough, reckless enough to break it down and start again. They argued still, but as the children grew more sensitive to conflict, they learned to swallow the lesser things, to distil the anger into a look, or the sudden departure from a room, a firmly closed (but never slammed) door. Instead, they saved up their grievances, nurtured them, *cherished* them, until they'd got dressed up, spent a fortune on a babysitter and dinner—made an effort, in other words—to really get into it. 'We can't be trusted', they would say after each disastrous date, after the inevitable tears and then the inevitable sex, when they would vow never to go out again, 'We can't be trusted to behave like real people.'

Soon, he would be forty. Forty! She had a harder time coming to terms with his turning forty than he did. She had cried when her own mother had turned forty. She had thought then that forty was the beginning of the end, and now here it was, about to take him too, and she wasn't far behind.

There were things they knew for certain: there would be illness, there would be loss. Their own parents would die, one by one. The children would cause them despair and concern that would make them long for innocence; their innocence, their children's, the sleepless, squalling infants that were really quite straightforward after all, despite the heavy weather they had made of things. There would be a gradual loss of faculties, if they were lucky. One of them would end up alone, if they stuck together. Sometimes this knowledge overwhelmed him; made him wonder whether—knowing what he knew now—he should have kept his distance all those years ago, sent her Ginny Spiro's email address straightforwardly, without comment, let her stay with the boyfriend or some subsequent person, while he drifted on, maybe or maybe not finding someone else, someone he did not like quite so much, and with whom the stakes would not be so high.

The Youths were at a dinner party (another fortieth, weren't they all?) hosted by the parents of one of their children's friends from school. The talk turned to how each couple had met, and when their turn came, they smiled at each other and into their drinks. She, chin propped on fist, said, 'At work,' but he, expansive from the wine, said, 'Well—yes but,' and the others clamoured to hear more. They tried their best to describe it: the preamble, the silent drama—the magic, really, that had compelled them together. They spoke over each other, amending and rephrasing, but they soon gave up, sensing that it did not translate, and anyway no one else really cared: 'at work' would have sufficed after all. It didn't matter. It had happened, and there, better and worse, they were—shoulder to shoulder, knee to knee, hand in hand at the table.

A Story Of Our Time: Notes on Kafka's 'The Judgement'
Cathy Sweeney

September 22, 1912 is one of the most famous dates in twentieth-century literature. On that night, in one sitting, Franz Kafka wrote 'The Judgement'. In a diary entry the following day, he gave a detailed account of the experience: 'Only in this way can writing be done, only in a context like this, with a complete opening of body and soul.' The short story was dedicated 'to Miss Felice Bauer', a woman Kafka had been introduced to a month earlier, and with whom he had initiated a correspondence that would last five years and involve two marriage proposals and much heartache.

As with all of Kafka's work, 'The Judgement' has been subject to a myriad of interpretations—from a personal exposé of Oedipal angst to a parable about political conformity—but for many, most notably Elias Canetti in his book *Kafka's Other Trial: The Letters to Felice*, it is a means through which Kafka explored his conflicted feelings about embarking on a relationship with Felice Bauer. It is important to remember, however, that when Kafka wrote 'The Judgement' he was twenty-nine years old and living in the family home in Prague. After five years studying law at the university, he had secured a job as a lawyer in an insurance company, later embarking on a business scheme with his brother-in-law. 'The Judgement' may have been written in a matter of hours, but it was the fruit of many years of dedication to writing in a world that was hostile to any occupation that did not involve the making of money. A world Kafka was all too familiar with.

By 1912 capitalism was the dominant political and economic system of societal governance in Europe. As the child of ambitious parents who ran a fancy goods shop at the heart of the Austro-Hungarian empire, Kafka was a product of this system. His formative years were dominated by dinner-table talk of sales targets and profit-and-loss margins. In both school and university, the education he received was that of the production-line model in which vast amounts of knowledge were inputted into a young person with the aim of producing efficiency and compliance, rather than intellectual curiosity. As an adult, most of Kafka's time was taken up with his job as an insurance lawyer and the responsibilities that came with being part-owner of an asbestos factory. And yet, under the stolid veneer of the man who got up early every morning to go to work, was a writer whose heart was consumed with one thing, and one thing only—his failure to write as fully himself.

Torn between the desire to write and the demands of making money, Kafka is obsessed in his fiction with uncovering the site of tension between the 'unreal' world, of imagination, fantasy, creativity, and the 'real' world, of work, family, social engagement. Again and again, in his stories and novels, he puts an unprepossessing everyman figure into a nightmare landscape where they squirm and writhe until they can bear it no longer. Josef K. in *The Trial*; Gregor Samsa in *Metamorphosis*; a man from the country in *Before the Law*; K. in *The Castle*; the travelling researcher in *The Penal Colony*: all discover the tenuous nature of reality when they unwittingly cross into what Freud called the 'unheimlich', a German word that means both 'familiar' and 'unfamiliar'. This site of tension—the unheimlich—is a place where 'norms, limits, boundaries and foundations are neither natural nor fixed or stable', as Fred Botting describes it in his book *Gothic*. The 'real' part of Kafka's world may have been built from the sturdy bricks of capitalism, but the 'unreal' was constructed from the subterranean, murky world of the subconscious. It was on the night of September 22, 1912, when he sat at the desk in his bedroom while the rest of the house slept, and in one sitting wrote 'The Judgement', that these two worlds first crashed violently into each other.

On the surface 'The Judgement' is very much a 'real' story. It has a setting: a Sunday morning in spring. It has characters: an adult son and his father, both involved in the family business. It even has plot: the breakdown of the relationship between the two men. But its power lies in the fact that, underneath this flimsy surface, all is 'unreal'. There is no logic in the way the plot develops. The reader gets no insight into character motivation, no clues as to how to interpret the disturbing interaction between the two men. And the resolution, in which the son rushes off to kill himself by drowning, is shocking.

At the beginning of the story, Georg Bendemann is sitting by the window in his study on a Sunday morning at the height of spring. He has just finished writing a letter to an old schoolfriend who lives in Russia, and the task has put him in a mood of reflection. On first impression, he appears a rather benign character, a typical petit bourgeois, absorbed in the details of his life circumstances. We discover that his mother died two years previously and that since then his elderly father has taken a backseat in the family business, allowing Georg to come to the fore, with the result that the business has 'unexpectedly boomed'. He has also recently become engaged to a 'young lady from a well-off family'. The only uncomfortable dilemma that he's had to face—whether or not to tell his struggling friend in Russia about his good fortune—is resolved in the writing of the letter. And so, in a mood of self-satisfied confidence, he makes the journey across 'the little passage' to inform his father of his actions.

'As an entrepreneur of its own self, the neoliberal subject has no capacity for relationships with others that might be free of purpose,' the philosopher Byung-Chul Han writes in *Psychopolitics: Neoliberalism and New Technologies of Power*. Georg Bendemann is such a subject. As was Kafka's father and, it could be argued, Kafka himself, prior to the fateful night of 22 September, 1912. Georg has a market value mindset. As a perfect capitalist, he measures everything. He is Nietzsche's 'last man', a man who takes no risks and seeks only comfort and security. It is easy to imagine him updated for the twenty-first century:

suit by Hugo Boss / shirt by Marks & Spencers / tie by The Tie Bar / watch by Apple / tan loafers by Ben Sherman / gym membership / dry January / Tinder account still active despite engagement / books on bedside locker by Steven Pinker and Antony Beevor, both abandoned about ten pages in / Audi A8 in driveway / hair receding at brow…

Crossing over the hallway, Georg finds his father reading a newspaper. The room is 'unbearably dark' and when his father gets up his dressing gown falls open. Despite these small ripples of disturbance, Georg proceeds to inform his father of the letter he has written to his friend, going so far as to pull the envelope a little way out of his pocket, before letting it slip back. His father's response is bizarre. He refers to certain 'unlovely developments' that have taken place since the death of Georg's mother. He questions the very existence of a friend in Russia. He then alludes to a collusion between himself and this friend behind Georg's back, and finally, he disparages Georg's relationship with his fiancée, calling her a 'disgusting slut'. During this barrage Georg maintains a discourse of reason, tucking his father into bed and observing that he requires more care, even resolving to take the old man to live with him and his future wife in their new home. Then suddenly, overwhelmed by his father's taunts, he is unable to refrain from shouting, 'You play-actor!' Georg wishes his father would fall and break into little pieces, but in the end, it is he who breaks, rushing off to carry out the sentence that his father has passed on him, death by drowning. The transformation of Georg, from a rational man to an irrational one, is inexplicable. Is it he who has been acting all along? Playing the part of the good son, the sensible businessman, the wholesome fiancé?

This holding of oppositional realms in tension—the 'real' and the 'unreal'—is rare in fiction, particularly contemporary fiction. In uncertain times, we like our stories to play out on solid ground. On the one hand, this perhaps explains the current upsurge in popularity of true crime and horror, and, on the other, the deluge of novels branded by publishers as 'up lit' (life-affirming stories of hope, kindness, empathy and love). Readers, it seems, prefer to be firmly rooted in one world or another. Fiction reflects the values of the society that creates it, and a late capitalist society that strives to abolish thresholds with hypervisibility and transparency, inevitably produces fiction that is easy to classify: real or surreal, good or evil, thrilling or comforting, what's hot and what's not. This is especially true now as more and more of us (dressed in leisure wear, sitting at Ikea desks) spend our time online, in a world where everything is on display, and personal, even intimate, disclosure is normalised. But no matter how hard people try, it is not possible to eliminate the transgressive desires of the subconscious. The more we push darkness to the edges—denying it any legitimacy—the more we intensify our dread of it, and thus the power it holds over us. An insistence on positivity is wearying and the banal sentimentality of 'up lit' can be as dispiriting as incessant newsfeeds. The novelist Thomas Bernhard wrote that an idealistic literary work may produce disgust in the reader and lead them to 'fall back into negativity', but the real danger is that, in the name of clarity, accessibility and inoffensiveness, we will find ourselves living in a world where writers whose work is difficult or 'problematic' will no longer be read, or even published.

In the irruption experienced by Georg Bendemann in 'The Judgement', the most startling element is the way in which his appetite for life switches so suddenly to desire for death. Having 'raced' toward the river, he swings himself over the rails, 'like the excellent gymnast he had been in his early years' and, as he 'let[s] himself' drop into the river, he calls out, 'Dear parents, I have always loved you.' But, while he is a literal writer, death in Kafka's fiction should not be seen in purely literal terms. This rupture from one world into another is suffused with a powerful negative ecstasy. It is a deliverance from the terrible pressure of individuation, that conveyer belt transporting us endlessly towards personal optimisation. Death for the characters in Kafka's fiction is an erotic release from the tension of simply existing.

In our late capitalist world, the outward performing self—the 'play-actor' as Bendemann puts it—likes to believe that endless consumer choice equates with freedom. But all the while the subconscious nurtures a powerful desire to be free of this freedom we profess to love. We survive, quite comfortably for the most part, distracted by food or sex or work or new shoes or babies or drugs or football matches or holidays, but from time to time we become aware of a sensation of strain. Usually, we find a way to go on. But sometimes— like Georg Bendemann, or our updated version with his Marks & Spencers shirt and receding hair—there is an overwhelming desire to plunge into the abyss. In the introduction to Tristan Garcia's book *The Life Intense: A Modern Obsession*, the translators observe that 'a seemingly insignificant instant ... can suddenly leap out and give us a feeling of epiphany like a shock of electricity. This shock once again exposes us to the intensity of real life and pulls us out of the mire of routine which we have sunk into without even realising it.'

The writer and critic Walter Benjamin wrote, 'There are two ways to miss the point of Kafka's works ... One is to interpret them naturally, the other is the supernatural interpretation.' I have no idea what 'the point' of 'The Judgement' is (which makes it so brilliant) but I do not read it as a mystical story and there is more to any writer's work than biography (what their childhood was like, who they did or did not sleep with). Perhaps in 'The Judgement' we find something closer to ordinary, day-to-day life; the experience of being caught in a web of socio-economic expectation which, every now and then, the subconscious would like nothing more than to violently destroy. On that night of 22 September, 1912, I picture a tall thin man, dressed in black, hunched over a wooden desk, his entire face, lit by a lamp, in a state of rapture, especially his beautiful dark eyes. I wonder if he knew then, at 6 am, when the maid walked through the anteroom, and he said to her, 'I've been writing until now', that so much had been destroyed: (1) his chance of getting up early to go to work the next day, (2) the possibility, despite his subsequent prevarications, of entering into marriage, with all the constraints it would entail, and (3) all pretence of being an upstanding citizen. Did he know that the rest of his short life would be spent seeking to recapture the experience of writing 'The Judgement' … 'a complete opening of body and soul'?

Leaving Musée Picasso

How gold the light

off those wet streets,

light of some long day

ending, a day that began

back before math, before sweat,

fields in every direction. Clean.

Maybe that's what I recognised.

How clean those streets

could look after a rain

I never saw happen. I had emerged

into what could not be proved.

Jill Osier

On Passing

after Baudelaire

Your step was light but you looked sad to me,
unbearably, your beauty clothed in darkness.
A storm had lit the quay and turned the streets
to noise and water. A gust, up whips

your hem and I see lace, and Marilyn, and leg
and leg and leg. Your quick hands
pressed your wet skirt down and held it.
You saw me stare, I saw you clocking me—

a flicker lights your face, you vacillate. Rue Boucharel
your calf-length rain-black skirt still held in check.
In that bright flash a part of me long crushed

inflamed and opened. And then you ran.
My hands were wet with rain I feel it still.
I wonder if you wonder if you hadn't.

Paula Cunningham

We All Go

Liadan Ní Chuinn

1

My parents were hijacked before I was born, just two nights prior, and I think it's important. I don't know why.

They were driving out of the city on a road that got suddenly narrow, a bad artery, and then they were stopped in the road by a clot: people with masks and crowbars.

My dad was driving so it was my dad who braked.

The people in the road yelled: GET OUT OF THE CAR.

My dad said: Paula. (That was all that he said. He wasn't good at reassurance; when the dog died, he was supposed to break it to us gently, but we said: How is she?, and he said: Dead.)

The people with the crowbars yelled: GET OUT OF THE FUCKING CAR.

My dad got out. One of the people took his wallet and checked his ID. (They wanted to be sure they were only hijacking Catholics. His license said Michael Madigan so they took the car.)

They said: What's she doing?

My dad called: Get out of the car, Paula! (I think this is funny: if you can't beat them, join them.)

My mum hadn't got out. She was pregnant with me. The seatbelt had locked tight against her, and she couldn't find the belt's plug in the darkness. Her breathing was horrible. She was very scared.

My mum maybe said: Michael, or maybe: I'm stuck. She didn't say anything that could be heard.

The men with the masks moved in close. They smashed the windscreen. My mum didn't scream but tiny bits of glass got stuck in her face and her neck. She thought she might never move again but then the seatbelt finally gave and she moved like she was melting.

My dad took her over to the side of the road. They stood by the hedge (where blackberries grow; where badgers' bodies rot).

The guys with the crowbars drove off in the car.

My mum and dad stood in the dark. The night was very cold. It was before mobile phones but my mum wouldn't let them stop at a house to use someone's landline. She was too scared.

I was born two nights later. In the photos I am pink and Michael Madigan is smiling and my mum has those cuts all over her skin, just scabbing (like co-ordinates/freckles).

My dad told us about the hijacking. (He died when we were starting to be proper people: Bernie was eight and I was twelve.) He said it was because of tensions at the time.

The Orange Order wanted to march through Catholic areas and the people in those areas didn't want them to. He thought that this was what it was about because of the timing/location/target.

My mum's never mentioned it. If it were up to her, we wouldn't know.

But I think it's important. I don't know why.

I feel it in things, as though it's not over. Mum's something distant/something scared. If it were up to her, we wouldn't know about anything, like she thinks that's progressive, like she thinks we'll be safe. She won't let me wear GAA stuff; she's made Bernie do hockey. She talks about how ugly Irish is. She says things like: they're completely different down there, saying *down* meaning ROI, meaning *Free State*, meaning (depending on where we are): East, South, North, West.

It bothers us both but Bernie's more straightforward. She says: You're a partitionist, Paula!

It affects us both but I see that hijacking everywhere. I feel it in the way my mum loves Bernie (fervid, uncomplicated) and the way she sees me (holds me apart).

She says, suddenly: Jackie, do you have a girlfriend?

She says over the TV: Jackie, are you still eating meat?, and she waits for the answer because she doesn't know, she hasn't noticed, she can't tell.

I don't think that she blames me. That would be stupid. But I wonder about it. I think it's important.

If she hadn't been pregnant, she could have got out of the car. The glass wouldn't have cut her. She wouldn't't've bled. If she hadn't been pregnant, she wouldn't have been stuck on her own in the dark, watching the men in the masks come closer. She wouldn't have seen Michael Madigan get out of the car and leave her in it.

I've tried to tell Bernie. She doesn't care. She says: Oh my *fucking* god, Jackie. She says: You can't psychoanalyse everything. She says: See if you say this is why you can't pass your driving test—

Bernie doesn't hate me for it, but she wasn't there.

2

We have lectures called Housekeeping. It's hard to find the way to Anatomy because they want it hidden. (People have tried to steal bones.)

I don't know that I like the people I'm with. I let what they're saying move over me until I can decide. We sit together, stretched out in rows. Everyone has a laptop. The people in front of me are biting their nails.

The professor's name is O'Brien. He has the letters of eight qualifications after his name. He has a PowerPoint of photos of different tools/instruments: pincers, surgical scissors, scalpels on a steel tray. The colours are bleached coming through the projector.

He talks about the importance of Anatomy. He shows us sketches from da Vinci's notebook. He says these are crucial; he says these are key. (I saw his sketches in the museum. They were horrible: he drew sketches of Travellers as predators, as thieves. Nobody in the museum seemed to think this was bad. They framed them and labelled them, printed on thick expensive paper: 'A Man Tricked By Gypsies'.)

O'Brien says the most important thing is respect. He says that if we miss a session, we'll be disciplined. He says that what we'll cover in the sessions is vast. He speaks in abstracts, vague definitions. (Nothing he says means much at all.) He says that he once had a student expelled for coming to Dissection chewing gum.

This is when the people I am sitting with poke me. The girl named Rachel, sat at the far end, grins, and when we have all turned, like sunflowers, she blows a bubble with pink slabbery gum.

The others think this is great. I am so embarrassed to be with people who find this funny that I start to sweat. After the lecture, they stand together in a group, making plans. I don't want to dislike them so soon (it's Week 2), so I keep my distance. I start walking home.

I get in well before Bernie's back from school.

I turn on the TV. I don't care who's talking.

I get bored.

I log onto Blackboard on the computer. There're videos that're compulsory to watch. O'Brien said he'd refuse admission to anyone who hadn't seen them, and that Blackboard can tell him that information. (Bernie would say: A surveillance state.)

The videos are three minutes each. Whoever filmed them has chosen an over-the-shoulder angle, so they look a bit like Facebook Tastemade videos. They show: pale hands holding a scalpel, turning it round as the voiceover explains certain features; pale hands and the scalpel moving to the flat surface below them, getting closer as the camera picks up freckles, hair follicles, and the surface is skin; the scalpel slicing through skin as though through soap; substituting scalpel for pincers to peel back the first thin layer.

I don't mean to lose focus, but the video is slow and unreal. There's glare all over the computer screen, fingerprints and marks from where Mum's tried to wipe them.

I check my phone (the first sign of lack of respect).

There's a notification from Mum. She forwards me and Bernie stuff she's sent on WhatsApp: weird jokes, clips, 2-minute-long videos ('The Ulster Fry'). There's always that warning above, *forwarded many times*.

She's sent these things by people she works with, some people she's still in touch with from college/school, and she forwards them on because they all do. WhatsApp is, for her age group, what chainmail was to me and Bernie when we were small: pictures/animations/stories sent on and on and on, jumpscares, Thinking Of You prayers, badly spelt, long-winded threats: *send this to fifteen people or the Killer Clown will be above your bed when you wake up—*

That was when Michael Madigan died.

They're not really connected, him and the chainmail, it was just the same era.

Me and Bernie sat at the computer, pushing the back out of the swivel-chair, and our mum sat on the sofa minding Michael Madigan, syringing things through the RIG tube to his stomach: pain-relief, water, pastes that could feed him.

She cleaned around the RIG twice a day. She did it very slowly because Michael Madigan couldn't say when it was sore. It was always infected, the skin always raised, the pus always yellow, and the nurse used to say, as though shifting blame: this doesn't happen with RIG tubes. I've never seen this before.

She used to poke it. She called it Proud Flesh. *An excessive formation of granulation tissue.*

She used to say things to my mum like she wanted her to fight back, but my mum used to say: I don't know, Karen, I'm not a nurse.

Karen/Liz/Alison/Carla/Linda/Susie/Helen/Barb.

I don't know, Sandra. I'm not a nurse.

Michael Madigan needed course after course of IV antibiotics and Mum thought we were too small to leave at home by ourselves so she drove us all to the hospital and wheeled him in.

At home she sat beside him on the sofa in front of us, wiping his proud flesh with sterile alcohol pads.

It sounds bad, that the RIG was always infected, but if he hadn't had it, he'd have starved a lot sooner. He lost fat from places I didn't know you had it.

When Auntie Shauna had her boys, and they were tiny babies dressed in blue, everyone said things like, ohmygod, aren't they mini, and it seemed so impossible that everyone once was that size, that everyone's grown up from something so tiny, but by the end Michael Madigan was so skinny that it made perfect sense; he was nothing but bones making a frame, and it seemed like if you only folded him up right, he would still be the size of those premature babies.

Flesh melted off Michael Madigan's wrists and hands and fingers until his wedding band couldn't even stay on his finger, and that was *with* the RIG, with the pre-packaged feeds going through it.

His body hated them, though less than solid food. His body was always trying to send the liquids back: he vomited and vomited (which was horrible, and dangerous, because he couldn't always swallow).

Jackie, says Bernie.

She makes me jump.

You left the front door open, she says. Not wide open, but like. Still.

I log out of the computer.

She goes to the kitchen and puts bread on to toast. She stands against the counter on her phone, waiting for it.

I say, Do you remember Rowan?

She doesn't want to look up, but in the end, she says, The dog?

She says, Is that why you look like that?

There are big stretches between her sentences.

I say, I was thinking about Dad.

Bernie says, About Michael? Why?

She puts spread on the toast. She only eats Flora. She says, Are you in again tomorrow?

Yeah. 9 to 4.

Gross.

She lays down on the sofa and eats her toast. She looks sorry for herself, that she's had to come home to this (me). She looks at her phone. She doesn't get up.

Mum gets in later. She's not in bad form.

She says, I could eat a *horse*, which means she's going to eat toast.

She says at my bag on the table and my boots on the floor, It looks like a bomb's gone off in here, Jack.

She sits on the sofa and crunches on toast. She says, Bernie, love, any bizz?

Bernie says something about teachers. She builds to a punchline and my mum cackles.

When there's a pause, I say, See this weekend, I'm going up to Shauna's. I want to see the farm.

The atmosphere changes so fast it feels physical.

Bernie says, *Why*?

My mum stands up. She brushes crumbs from her workclothes. She says, Well, Jackie, you're a big boy now. You can do whatever you wish.

She goes upstairs.

Bernie's looking at me like I'm a freak.

I snap: What?

She says, What are you doing? But she doesn't want an answer, she's only answering me.

The stairs in this house are so steep that they're dangerous. My mum going angrily upstairs still has to take her time. She fell down the stairs when they first moved in here, down a whole flight, and she broke her ribs. They can't set ribs like another fracture. Even now, sometimes, she'll groan when she's moving.

When Michael got sick, he couldn't even try them. He was grounded on this floor (like Rowan the dog used to be). Mum got him a bed by the sofa. Sometimes Mum slept down here with him, and sometimes, when she was too tired, she went upstairs by herself.

When we were little, she used to say she could feel something on the landing: a presence, a person who used to live here. She said they were friendly and we shouldn't be scared.

I never felt it. Bernie said she did, but she just meant she was afraid.

Nobody said it again after Dad died. Ghosts are only interesting if you haven't any yourself.

3

We've been emailed group allocations. I'm second. At the lockers, we put on coats and IDs, and the first group comes out through the big double doors.

I see Rachel. She's started going out with your man she was sitting beside in the last lecture. She says to me, going past, It's really good!, and she smiles with teeth that are visibly wet.

There's a graduate who checks our IDs at the door. She scans us in with a barcode reader. She says, Grab a seat, as we're going past her, and people take stools at workbenches, as though the benches don't have yellowed chunks of person on top.

Harris sits beside me. He's almost my height. He says, YalrightJackie?, all one word.

Our workbench has a laminated label: STATION 8.

There are questions on Harris's side: kidneys/their survival; sympathetic/ parasympathetic nervous supply; blood vessels, lymph, their sources and drainage.

On my side is somebody's whole abdomen. It's dry/embedded with silicon. It's old, so some of it is coming off in plasticated flakes. It smells.

Harris puts his face down close. Whatdyouthink? he says, Renal Artery? Yeah?

I breathe through my mouth (in and out, in and out).

STATION 6 is someone's leg, cut off at the thigh and running down to their shin.

STATION 11 has questions about salivary glands but what it is, on the table, is somebody's head.

One half of the face, split down a vertical line, is hollowed out, to show the glands, but the other half is just normal, just a cold waxy face: a scrunched-up nose, an eyebrow, eyelashes, nose hair in the nostrils, their naked scalp from a head shaved.

Harris picks up the head.

I have my stomach pushed tight against the table.

He asks me a question.

I say, I don't know.

O'Brien said in the lectures, in the series called Housekeeping, that every body in this Department was given as a gift. People thought about the Uni and gave us their bodies.

I know this. I know what O'Brien said. But it doesn't feel like that now I'm here, looking around.

Did they know they weren't going to stay whole? Did they sign that it was okay to saw their head off at the neck? Did they know the Uni'd display their scarred ovaries beside this cut torso, sit them by a penis (pubic hair still intact), by limbs and digits, yellow and flaking, that they'd be split over benches with laminated pages and questions (a Treasure Hunt)? Did they believe that their gift would cure cancer?

I mean, they can't tell me. They just lay there. People my age (hungover/ flirting) lean over them, try to answer questions they don't understand. Nobody knows anything.

The time drags on. People start to leave early.

There's a girl snapping bones together. Her partner asks a question and she says brightly: I'm just playing!

Harris asks me if I want to get lunch when this is over. I say, No.

4

I know things, but not the people. So they're not stories to me, they're just Things That Happened, facts one-line long: my dad's dad Jackie and his older brother Felix were interned. Jackie died seven years later. Felix managed eleven.

I've looked online so I know some of the things the British Army did to the hundreds of civilians they took away and held captive, held without charge: water-boarding, injections, electric shocks, mock-executions, starvation, sleep-deprivation, sensory-deprivation, harrassment by dogs, dragging people behind vehicles.

I don't know that all of these things happened to Jackie and Felix, but I know they were interned and then they were never the same. I know that they died (seven/eleven years later).

I don't know what these things did to Michael Madigan.

Felix was one year older than Kate, who was two years older than Michael, who was four years older than Shauna. So when British soldiers came through the door and dragged out Jackie (who was forty-three) and Felix (who was eighteen), my dad was fifteen and Shauna was eleven and Kate was seventeen (but she emigrated, so what's she to us now?).

I know that Felix died when he was twenty-nine.

Their dad died before, when they were all still so young (though not as young as me and Bernie were when Michael Madigan died). Their dad died seven years after the raid/internment. Shauna was still in school. My dad was in Belfast, at the Tech. When Jackie died, Kate went to America and never came back.

This is all I know (flat lines, small words, Things That Happened, black typed on white).

I send Shauna a message on WhatsApp. She still lives near where they grew up, and it's she has the farm and what's left of its house. Her husband Roy has cattle on some of the fields that are turning to rushes.

She messages back pretty fast. She says: O hello my gorgeous nephew! it wld be brill to see you & Bernadette!, though I didn't mention Bernie.

She says I can go, so I'll go.

Bernie comes up to my room. It's late. She lies down on the bed as though it is hers.

I messaged Shauna, I say.

So you're going, she says. She rolls over so her back is to me.

You can come if you want.

Yea, she says. I know.

Sounds come out her phone. There are people shrieking on Instagram stories and noises from dances/TikToks/reaction videos. Then she puts the phone down, and it all goes quiet.

The room's dark. Her breathing sounds vaguely asthmatic.

She's asleep.

I can't be fucked to wake her. She'll get cold in a bit.

Bernie snores. She talks in her sleep. We shared a room for a stupidly long time because Mum didn't want to change Michael Madigan's study, with the computer and the vinyl and all his beloved DVDs. Sometimes Bernie used to say my name and it woke me up.

Once Mum found her out on the landing with her eyes wide open. Mum said, Bernie, love, what are you doing?, and Bernie said: Who are you? Why am I here?

Mum said the normal things you say to someone sleepwalking: Come on, let's go, you're dreaming, back to bed, but Bernie was angry and stressed and upset. She said, Where am I? Who're you? Leave me alone!

Mum brought her back into the room. She said, Jackie, don't get up. She sat on the bed with her and said, You're alright. Shh, bird, you're alright.

Bernie sounded like she was crying. She said, I don't understand. Leave me alone.

Mum sat there until Bernie was quiet and then she went to bed.

5

Today is the first day that we have Dissection. Before was Prosection, where somebody else had done the cutting for us. I see Harris at the lockers. He looks hungover. Rachel passes us when we're getting our white coats on. She's with her boyfriend and a new group of people. It's 8.57am. I focus very hard on buttoning my coat and holding my ID card at the right angle so the barcode hits the scanner, and standing at an okay distance from the person in front of me but when all of that's done, I have to go into the room like everyone else and the chill of it makes me sad and afraid.

The room is huge. It has a very high ceiling, like a vault, and it's cold as a fridge. In front of us, in rows, are stainless steel tables on wheels, each one holding up a shape covered with plastic sheeting. It looks like a morgue/a nightmare and it smells like a butcher's but with chemicals mixed in.

Professor O'Brien is here, though he says he's not staying long. He's going to pass us over to his assistant, Golda. He says, If you feel strange, you can leave, and I start to feel stressed, like I am going to do something I can never undo.

Golda says, Everyone find a table. She motions for us to move ourselves over to the stations, to attach ourselves to the bodies, their masked/hidden outlines, in groups of, she says, No more than five.

I go with Harris to one in the far corner. Two other boys come over. They obviously know each other from before, from school. They have their ID cards stuck to their white coats' breast pockets. They've both used photos of themselves from Sixth Form, with their hair permed into curls on top and shaved short at the sides.

I feel as though there's something pooling up in my lungs. I want to bite my nails but we're all wearing these thick blue gloves. I think of the video I watched, of fingers holding scalpels.

O'Brien says: Everyone, pull back the covers. He demonstrates his intention on the table nearest to him. He pulls back the covers, three layers of different plastics, and he shows us a naked body with the top half of its head completely gone, that is: with none of its brain or the skull that held it.

Harris pulls back our covers.

We meet a naked woman with half a head.

The Professor says something to Golda. They say quiet things to each other, so people at the bodies start talking to each other, too. Harris says to the other boys: What school did you go to?

Inst.

Professor O'Brien leaves. Golda takes his old spot in the middle. She's tall, taller than a lot of the boys in this room. She's wearing a white hijab, and a white coat with her initials sewn into the breast-pocket, and thick blue gloves that ride right up her arms. Okay, she says, Everyone relax.

She says, Slowly, now, just whenever you're ready, I want you to *touch* your body, and she presses against the skin of the body closest to her.

The Inst. boys look at each other. I know that they're going to touch the woman first. They press on her forearm (first gently, then hard) and they kind of laugh.

Harris touches the woman's shoulder. He rubs his gloved fingers together. He says, Does this remind anyone else of Granny In The Graveyard?, and the Inst. boys laugh hard.

They're not looking at me but I know that they know I don't want to do it. I push my finger against the woman's upper arm. Even through the glove, it feels hard and strange. Her skin is like leather from the embalming.

Golda is talking about scalpels.

She is cutting into the man's skin, peeling away layers, working her way down into adipose tissue. The people near her bend their necks in round the body, wanting to see everything that she does. Already people are like that: dying to be ahead.

Golda picks up a large metal bowl, stainless steel like the table, and says, This is very important! Is everyone listening? Everything you take from your body must go into the bowl at the end of your table. Have a look! Every table has one, you see? You must put everything from your body into your body's bowl because the contents of these bowls get returned with the person to their family. It is absolutely critical that all their tissue is kept together and not mixed up.

Then she places skin in her body's bowl. She drops in white fascia and curds of yellow fat.

Harris's stomach rumbles and the Inst. boys piss themselves.

I look at the woman. She only has half a face but there's enough left to see her nose, which is broken, bent to one side from the weight of her body lying down on itself for however many months it was before she was ready.

One of the Inst. boys says, I've heard all the fluid gathers in certain places. Like wherever there's fat gathered, it completely liquifies in the embalming, so when you cut in it's all fat and formaldehyde, liquid together, and you cut in and it hits you with splashback. Swear to god. It hit my brother in the eyes.

That's all for today.

Golda watches us go.

6

The dog died two years before Michael Madigan. He picked us up from primary school the day after the night Mum'd rushed her to the vet's. The dog was called Rowan. She was huge and kind (a rescue greyhound).

Bernie and I were in the back of the car, strapped into our seats, looking at each other. We were quiet/waiting to hear when she was coming home. He had to tell us sometime.

But he didn't.

In the end we said, at once, over each other: Where's Rowan? Is she sick? Is she home?

He said: She's dead.

He didn't say anything else. Maybe once, Awk, Bernie, because Bernie was crying (she was howling with grief). He drove. We got home. Mum came out to the car and she picked Bernie up (even though she was, like, six).

He said, She's dead, but not to be mean, or cruel. He said it pretty softly, and only because it was true.

When we were those ages, six and ten, Bernie still had a booster-seat, and she sat directly behind him, but I was the other side, so I could see him at a diagonal. I could see some of his face across the way, and I remember how he looked in ways that maybe she doesn't (dark beard, light skin, freckles, the arm of his jumper, rolled up at the wrist; bitten nails, freckled hands).

I remember him in ways that she can't.

He steers with one hand, keeps both off when he can. When there's sun for a second, he winds his window all the way down and sits with his whole arm out of the car. He drives as though it is the simplest thing in the world. He drives as though he could as well be dreaming. If someone cuts him off or won't let him out or we're stuck in traffic coming home from school, he doesn't care. He turns his CD on. His favourite band in the world is Simple Minds. His favourite album is *Street Fighting Years* and he plays it, non-stop, from 1 – 11.

It's not his favourite, but he doesn't mind 'Belfast Child'. He drums his fingers on the wheel, keeping time with the songs, and he moves his head but it's all, always, so out of time. He speaks the words along to the singing.

I didn't know he was going to die. Nobody did.

He drives and Bernie's loud in the back of the car.

I call him Michael Madigan as though that makes him Not My Dad. I'm sorry about it, but it puts distance between us. He ended up paralysed but I can't afford to be too.

He nods along, erratically, to music that's neverending, to Track 11 as it becomes Track 1, over and over, again and again, driving us home and home and home.

7

I can't stop thinking about Anatomy. There are dozens of faces there, cold, like at a wake, turned to face me from their tables and I am supposed to say: I can identify the submandibular gland, poke and point, as though that is normal and healthy and good.

I look at my hands and I see Michael Madigan's. Freckles, chewed nails. His hands, turned over, had palms of calloused skin. He used to have a wedding band, before it wouldn't fit him anymore.

It's Friday. Bernie goes into school but I don't get up. I have some lectures but I'm not going in. There's a block of lectures called Communication Skills starting this week. We're to be taught Active Listening: nodding, saying sorry, expressing empathy. We're to be taught to hide the fact we've cut open bodies. We're to be taught how to cover up what we've done.

This week coming, on the days we don't have Active Listening & Communication Skills, we will cut into a person, peel back their skin and work down to the fat (adipose tissue). I think of the rooms (fridges), all their fragmented wakes. I'm scared that I'll do it. I'm scared that I won't mind.

Bernie gets home at four but she doesn't come find me.

When my mum gets in, they talk, and then my mum comes up the stairs, taking them slowly. She opens my door and stands at it awkwardly. She says, Bernie said you were up here. Have you gotten up today?

I say, Mm.

She says, How're you doing, anyway? Bernie's told me she's worried.

There are really long pauses when we speak to each other, like a time delay as we reach each other's continents or the time-lag needed to run messages through translators.

I say, It's gross, I guess. It's heavy. All these bodies and heads and you're not allowed to be bothered.

My mum says, Jesus Christ, Jackie. Is that it? It's your course?

You don't like it, she says, shrugs. Well, it was your bloody choice.

I go downstairs later to make beans on toast. She and Bernie are watching a DVD on her laptop, each with one half a pair of white earphones. It looks like the *Princess and the Frog* on the screen. Bernie's kind of a baby like that.

She tries to crack, sometimes, that she's named after Bernie Sanders. She has his book (*Outsider in the White House*). To be fair to her, she shares some of his facial expressions. (To be fair to her, she thinks all people are people/deserve things like Rights.)

Nobody can ever have believed her. There aren't many socialists in our part of the city. But there aren't many Catholics either. Who'd ever name a child after Bernadette?

Mum said once that it was Dad's idea. Jackie was his dad, but it was her idea to name me after him. When Bernie was born, it was he had all the ideas. He really liked Bernadette. He couldn't even explain why.

There are things about the saint that Bernie found out on Wikipedia: she didn't know any French until she was 13; she spoke Occitan (Bernie said, A Minority Language Queen).

But we don't believe Michael Madigan meant the saint at all. He meant Bernadette Devlin, whether Mum knew it or not: Bernadette Devlin McAliskey.

She was twenty-one and expelled from her Uni for her work in the Civil Rights Movement here.

She was imperative, says Bernie. She was key.

These Bernies are part of how she sees herself. I think it's important. She holds her Bernies in palms outstretched, like the icons of Jesus have him carry holes in his hands.

She needs them like Mum needs her. Mum'd have hated only me.

For example, when there was the leak that wrecked Michael Madigan's vinyl, and Mum cried for so long that she was almost dehydrated, and she called it The Flood, and she said bleak things like, Why me?, it was Bernie who was good at rubbing her back and saying, I'm so sorry. I'm so sorry. I am.

I couldn't do that. Because the vinyl itself is plastic, so it was unharmed. I know the covers were ruined and they started to mould and that was hard because those were the sleeves that he used to hold, that Mum was always going on about him being so careful with, and he'd moved all of them with them from student house to flat to this one, and they held traces of him on that maybe aren't anywhere else.

But the actual vinyl is plastic, and it's okay.

We still have the music that he wanted to listen to, that he paid for with his money and chose out of the shop.

And she called it The Flood, which it just wasn't, and couldn't be, not in any objective sense, though nothing with regards to Michael Madigan is objective.

We cleared out his study, finally, after that.

It took a long time.

I sleep there now.

What Michael Madigan died from was this really weird wasting disease. It's so rare I don't think it's got a name except, like, Syndrome X. It was just something, some gene, some misfolded protein, that ate all his muscles up inside out and then, when he couldn't move, ate up his brain.

At first, it looked like there wasn't much wrong, and there wasn't really, except that his hands shook and sometimes he fell going down the steep stairs. That was what he went to the GP about. He thought he'd need meds/maybe glasses.

But then his body was just like a doll's, lax and unmoving, and he had no weight, no fat, nothing but bones and joints popping out and the plastic tube that stuck out from his stomach, and then it was like, he didn't even know who we were. He looked at things but he didn't see them.

There were things that couldn't be proven without his input, so it was like: is he blind? Can he hear us? If I hold his hand and I squeeze it until it's warm, can he feel that? Does he exist in that body anymore?

It's nice to think that he could. It's nice to think that he was thinking things about himself and about us, saying into himself, I love you, when we told him goodnight.

But I don't really believe that. I never did. If he could have spoken, if he still had thoughts, I think they would have been like Bernie sleep-talking: nothing any of us could comprehend.

8

Bernie's eyes are puffy when she's just woken up. She groans. But she gets out of bed because she's coming with me. We walk into town and get the bus from the centre. It's going to take an hour and a half going out. I text Shauna, and she meets us at the bus stop when we get into the town. She's made her sons get out of the car. Boys, she says, these are your *cousins*!, and she beams at us as though none of us have ever met.

Wow! says Bernie. You're so big!

Nine, says Shauna, like it's a miracle.

We have met them before, but we don't see them often. They were three when Michael died, so they won't remember.

Shauna calls Bernie Bernadette.

We get into her car and she drives us home.

Her house is rural and new. It's big in that way which is kind of needless. For example, it has lots of granite in the kitchen, and tarmac on the driveway, and a tap with water that comes out boiling (things that are ugly and very expensive). But Shauna is nice. She talks a lot. She says, What'll youse have to eat? Some toast? Butter? God, it's awful early.

She talks so much that it starts to move over me, and Bernie shoves me because I'm not answering questions.

Did you want to see the farm, Jackie? Shauna repeats.

She's very nice.

I say, Yeah.

She nods. You'll enjoy seeing round it again, I'm sure.

Shauna's husband Roy gets in. Shauna says he's been golfing. He smiles, but he doesn't bother making small talk (things like saying: Hello). Shauna asks if he's free to Babysit The Boys and he hesitates.

When she's finally let go, she drives me and Bernie. Bernie sits in the front, which makes Shauna laugh for some reason, and I sit behind her, looking at Shauna through the diagonal.

She talks a lot, even when she's driving. We pass new-build houses that she says were never there before. A house in every field now, she says, in a tone like she doesn't herself live in a new build sat in an old field.

It's been so long since we've been up here that I don't see it coming and the turn-off is sudden. Shauna parks up on grass and says, We'll walk on up.

She waits for me and Bernie to get out of the car, talks about bugs on her windscreen, about how there are barely any now. Used to be in September your screen would be smoky with them, she says. But I guess you guys don't remember that.

Bernie shakes her head.

Shauna sighs. Well, my boys are big into their science. They say when the bugs go, we all go. And that's that.

We follow her up the hill. Me and Bernie aren't in the right shoes. Shauna points at Roy's cattle in the next field over. She says that this used to be meadow, but the land is all rushes now and she doesn't know why.

We keep walking. There are two bent-over trees with no leaves, and two falling down out-buildings, and then what's left of the house. From this distance, it looks like the roof is green, but then we get closer and it's lichen/ moss/rotting roof tiles.

It's a bungalow. The windows are smashed and the front door is broke open. I go up to the door. The hall takes a sharp right. There's a Sacred Heart of Jesus looking back at me, an old red lamp beneath it that used to glow red.

The wind is fairly loud and brutal. It's cold.

Bernie talks to Shauna, and I can hear in her tone that she's angry with me. She asks Shauna about the house.

She says, Was this not quite small for all of you?

Shauna says, Oh God, yeah. Of course. Sure, the four of us were in one room for the longest time, and then when we were too grown for that, me and Kate were put into the room with our parents and the boys had the other room. It was always two to a bed.

They talk about small things. Bernie wants to know when they got a TV, and did they know their neighbours. I wait until it seems like there is no time left and then I say it, I say: When they were interned, Jackie and Felix—

Shauna says, at almost exactly the same time: I don't remember, love. Honestly, Jackie, I don't.

Bernie's staring at me. It's so cold.

Nobody says anything.

I'm very loud inside my own head. I think of people (innocent) dragged out of houses, apartments, red-brick terraces, driven away down old lanes to internment camps. I think: Jackie and Felix. Michael Madigan.

I want to meet them. This is home, isn't it? This is where we all come from. So why aren't they here? Why's there nobody here?

Shauna says, There was one night when we were in the car and your dad was driving. It was after he'd gone to the Tech but he was up for the weekend. It was me, Kate, your dad, and a friend of mine. We got stopped at a checkpoint and they made him get out. It was raining. They made him strip right down to his pants.

Shauna says, They just thought it was funny. He didn't speak to us after. He couldn't.

Bernie says, Mum told me about, like, a night raid? Soldiers woke everyone up and took your parents outside. Dad told her about it.

Shauna says, With their big guns. They think they're so brave. They do it to mess with your head. She says, And doesn't it work?

Which is as close to what happened to Felix as she's willing to get.

I stand very still. The wind is angry. There's nobody left who can answer my questions. So how can I tell them that I still feel it? They're here, inside me, clots, lumps, valves in my heart that never quite close, things unspoken as though that makes them unseen.

I look at the house (horrible windows, broken door) and I see British soldiers. I look at that Jesus (I hear prayers/I see lights).

Bernie is saying, And have you read about what the Brits did in Kenya? You cannot imagine it. You literally can't.

She stops kind of awkwardly. She says, Jackie, what's wrong?

Shauna says, Oh, Jackie. Oh, Jackie, love.

She comes over to hug me but she can't reach very high.

I think Bernie will say something (Gross!) but she doesn't.

Shauna says: It's hard, pet. I know it is.

She's so nice.

It's sad seeing it like this, she says.

I say, Yeah.

I don't know what I expected.

There was a gene, a misfolded protein, something inside him that ate him up. Does it live here? Did it follow him into the city? Why am I thinking about him?

It's all like this: wasted, rotted, reedy, broke. There can be nothing rewound or undone.

Shauna says, You'll stay for a good lunch, at least. It's cold up here, you know. She says quietly, like someone other than us might hear her: It's a bit morbid.

9

When he was driving us places, he'd make us spell random words. He'd say Combine Harvester or Industrial Estate or Pedestrian. Bernie was shit at it but then she was always younger than me.

I had a teacher at primary school who told us that we had to love God more than our families. I took it to heart; that is, it worried me. I asked Michael Madigan if he loved God, and he hesitated.

I want to know more than anybody can tell me. Was he happy? Was he content? Was he satisfied with his life when it started ending? Was he angry? Was he angry about Jackie, and Felix, and internment, the night the soldiers stripped him with his sisters in the car, the night they broke in, every night there's ever been when things were horrible and wrong? Who was he? Who does that make me?

Did he miss me?

He had a beard and freckles and big dark eyebrows. His hands and his arms were not pale at all. When he got sick, Mum kept his face shaved. He didn't look anything like himself.

Did he know how fucking shit this would be, with him being dead forever and ever, there never being a day of its easing, never one hour when I can see him again, when he can just sit on the sofa and do my head in and for once in my life, I can breathe?

I said I was thinking of him and Bernie said, Why?

I remember more than her, but that just makes it lonely.

Mum used to be melted at Michael a lot but also, most of the time, she was joking. She said his name in this certain way, like, she'd kind of laugh to herself.

He wasn't old. Even now, he's not old.

There was a day when Shauna came up to see him. She didn't bring Roy and she didn't bring the Boys. It was when he was sick but we didn't fully understand how.

Shauna was very nice. She said, Paula, I've just been listening to this *beautiful* song in the car. I could only think of you. Here, give it a listen.

She passed it round to all of us. The song was called 'Song Of Bernadette', by Jennifer Warnes. It was one of those very Catholic songs, like that'd be sung by a part-time choir at mass, very warm, as in, nothing really at all.

When we had all listened, Shauna said, Here, I'll give it to Michael.

Mum said, Well. She said, Okay. She put the earphones into his ears.

I said, He's going to hate it. He loves Simple Minds.

Jesus, Jackie, said Mum. He's such a Debbie Downer, she said to Shauna.

They sat down at the table. Mum'd made us all tea.

Shauna talked about her work. She talked about Roy. She talked about the farm: Roy'd spotted some reeds in one field; he didn't know what they were from.

I've been racking my brains, said Shauna. But there just never were any reeds there before.

She talked about the Boys. They were still very little, but growing in accordance with what the GP expected. Mum asked if Shauna would eat a few Birds Eye potato waffles and Shauna said she wouldn't say no, Paula, she wouldn't say no!

By the time we remembered about Shauna's music playing into Dad's ears, he had listened to the song called 'Song Of Bernadette' eleven times. He would have been *spitting*. He hates that kind of song. He would have been saying, For fuck's sake, Shauna, you call that music!

He would have been saying, *I'll* show you music, taking out vinyl from their paper covers.

Bernie started laughing and that set me off. He'd listened to 'Song Of Bernadette' eleven times, we were pissing ourselves, Shauna was hands-at-her-mouth laughing.

But that was only how it started, because it turned out, actually, that it was one of those things that is funny at first but then you accidentally think about it too much and it's horrific, it is so sad that it could make you vomit just to think about, it is literally horrible, so horribly sad.

One of the last things he ever wrote, when he couldn't speak but could scrawl, was on a notepad in the kitchen. He couldn't remember spelling but you could make out the words. He wrote: *lok afer yorselfs.*

LOK AFER YORSELFS.

Mum shredded it one morning. It was an accident.

10

In the car on the drive back to Shauna's house and her Boys, Bernie sits in the front and they talk about Bernie's friends. Bernie tells Shauna the kind of stories, rising to crescendo, that Mum loves to hear and Shauna says, Bernadette Madigan, you are only *hilarious*.

It makes me think about Mum and Bernie, the way that they fit together. They're like those ornaments made in two parts: you can take Bernie away, and she's still whole, but taking her away leaves Mum with this crater, this shape down her side where Bernie should be.

One of the things that I've read about Simple Minds, specifically the song called 'Belfast Child', is the same criticism levelled at groups like U2, who wrote about the Troubles while being, themselves, completely unaffected: that they tried on people's trauma as a costume change, in an attempt to give their work *higher meaning*, to show that they *cared*, that their music was *healing* (which it wasn't).

But I think the criticism is only valid when it comes from certain people; that is, when it comes from certain places (these six counties). Because often it seems that the criticism comes from people from elsewhere, somewhere sat tight in the Free State, also unaffected but entirely unbothered by what was happening to people who weren't them.

It seems like it bothered them that people from Dublin and Glasgow wrote about it because it made them feel, for the first time, sitting under their skin like acne not ready to burst, that maybe they should care, and it didn't fit with what they believed, which is that Nothing Happened In The North and It Was Their Own Fault Anyway and What's Done Is Done And In The Past.

It's like people unironically posting IRELAND UNFREE SHALL NEVER BE AT PEACE on Instagram on the Anniversary of the Rising, as though changing the definition of Ireland could be the same as freeing her. It's like people my age thinking they have the right to choose to let us be Irish or not, as though that's in their power (Bernie says: you're a partitionist, Paula!).

I'm not saying I can't understand why they do it. Do you think I wouldn't pick out every clot that is knotted into me if I could?

I know it must've been easier not to care when the British Army shot a 15-year-old boy twice in the head/a 13-year-old girl in the Springhill Massacre/a 23-year-old, in the back, on his way to Gaelic.

I'm not stupid.

When the nurses came to see Michael Madigan, I hated it. Bernie sat on Mum's lap, and how was that fair? They had each other. It was alright for them, when they could wrap around each other like a Celtic Knot.

When the hospice people came, I said I was sick. I said I had diarrhoea if I had to. Mum wanted me and Bernie to speak to the staff on our own so that we could say anything that was on our minds, but Bernie had this way (I think she's forgotten) of saying all in one gulp: When is he going to die?, in the exact tone she said, What's your name? Are you a nurse?

I didn't want to be there. I didn't want to know anything. I didn't want to sit on the sofa while Bernie asked when my dad would die and the nurse gave her a sticker or a sweet or held her hand (I don't know, I never went).

Shauna drops us at the bus stop. She says loud things to Bernie about school, and AS levels (they've bonded).

Before I get out of the car, she says: You're awful like him, Jackie. You know, like *The Quiet Man*.

11

He's driving me back from an eighth birthday party. It's only me and him in the car. He says, well, Jackie-boy. Let's see if you can pass this test.

I'm excited/kind of nervous.

He turns down the music so I can hear him clearly.

If someone came up to you and said, excuse me, sir, I'd like to buy your dog. Here is one hundred pounds. What would you say?

No!

You wouldn't sell Rowan?

He's driving, and talking, and it's all for me.

Good, he says. What about if someone wasn't asking for money, they just really, really wanted her, *needed* her even, what'd you say then?

I don't say anything.

You don't know?

I don't think so.

Need more context? he says. That's good, too.

He stops looking ahead. He looks at a diagonal, straight into me.

What're you doing, fucking about with that Anatomy stuff? he says. It's gross. And you're not doing it for me. Do you think I'd give a fuck about you being a doctor?

I don't say anything.

The people are weird, he says.

Yeah. Maybe.

Are you happy? he says. Are you content?

Michael Madigan reaches his arm out and pokes me. Jackie, he says, you don't even remember what I sound like. You're guessing right now.

I say, So?

I say, That's not my fault. It'd've been fine if you'd just lost your voice all at once, but you did it so slowly we all kept adapting. I don't remember what you sounded like at the start, but it's like Mum says, *boiling frogs*. None of us do.

He says, I would never speak this much.

I look at him. I watch his hands on the steering wheel. Da, I say, I wish you'd tell me something.

Michael Madigan yells, Get out of the car, Paula!, and falling glass hits us with the burn of acid rain.

Na Sméara

Bhíodar ag sú na gréine gile
Ar feadh an tsamhraidh bhuí,
Anois, táid ina gcnapáin mhéithe,
Raidhse ina líon gan áireamh,
—Iad lonrach, aibidh, súmhar,
Ag mealladh le dúil ina milse.

Féasta saor in aisce, sócamas an dúlra
'Thugann cuireadh fial do gach créatúr
D'fhonn a síolta a scaipeadh—
Don bhroc agus don sionnach glic;
D'éanlaith an aeir is don duine.

Go raibh cnuasach chomh torthach
Is flaithiúlacht méine dá réir
Ag dul le láimh a bprioctha,
A laethanta ag dubhachtaint.

Bríd Ní Mhóráin

Berries

They soaked up the bright sun
All the golden summer long,
And now they're lumps of succulence
Massed in numberless profusion—
They're shiny, ripe and juicy,
Leading on desire with sweetness.

This giveaway feast is nature's bounty,
Designed to spread their seed,
An open offering to every creature,
To the badger and the wily fox;
To birds of the air, and to people.

This is my wish for an abundant store
And a generous mind to match,
To set beside these bloodied hands,
And the days, as they get dark.

Seán Lysaght a d'aistrigh

TWO STORIES FROM WEST AFRICA

Kangni Alem

translated from the French by Frank Wynne

For Someone To Remember Them

I cannot explain why things appeared as they did in my dreams. In the waking dreams I had while propping up the bar at The Daughters of Kilimanjaro, on the bank of the lagoon that bisects Bassadji, the neighbourhood of my childhood.

Bassadji, a poor neighbourhood that backs onto a forest of chimeras, the Palaeozoic massif of Eden Garden, thick with trees wreathed in ferns, lichen and blood. The blood of the animals regularly sacrificed to the gods of the place would send a rush of adrenaline coursing through me whenever I walked along the fence at the entrance to the forest, the fence that marked out the pathway of spells and enchantments. A famous pathway whose labyrinthine meanders I knew by heart, winding paths that led to the heart of Ablomé, from the old town to the place where Dou Legba, 'the guardian of the crossroads', sits enthroned. Dou Legba, amorphous or misshapen according to the seasons and the weather on the clay. Some days, the rains would eat into its muddy flesh, on other days the sun would bake the earth into random limbs and stumps. At such times, his body would bristle shards and slivers of bottle glass, with rotted straw, with empty tins of tomatoes *made in Italy*, with potsherds of every shape and size, and countless, countless cowrie shells.

Dou Legba is shaped vaguely like a human torso, surmounted by a ball supposed to represent his head. Into this, someone embedded two cowrie shells to serve as eyes, grafted an excrescence for his nose and carved a slit for the mouth, holes for the ears, and added a pair of horns fashioned from oval shells. From this shapeless mound emerge two stumps by way of arms, or paws.

He is now always benevolent, this 'guardian of the crossroads', especially when the stench of sacrifices seems to plunge him into a state of metaphysical digestion of which he alone knows the secret. After long days, when the rapture of the god's disciples had ebbed from whispers to silence, when the hymns of praise had settled with the swirling dust, I would sometimes come back and stare at the god of the crossroads. Groans emanated from the sinister depths of the godly heart suddenly afflicted by excess weight. At his feet the bodies of cockerels, some ineptly slaughtered, were still wracked by violent spasms. I would creep closer, taking small steps, and study the motley assortment of gifts left for him: cowrie shells, often in groups of seven, a palm nut, unfamiliar plants, a tattered scrap of fabric, beans, corn kernels, a dog's bone, a miniature machete, and sometimes a decapitated cockerel. In the empty orifices of his ears, trapped flies struggled in the sacrificial unction of blood and palm oil. Why had no one thought to distribute these generous gifts among other neighbourhood gods? They might have avoided offering to my childish eyes this extravagant spectacle of waste. In a single day, a solitary god sagging beneath the weight of so much food and drink rich in precious nutrients, while, nearby, other gods waited for someone to remember them. For, even among the gods, there are many mouths to feed.

Like every master, Dou Legba had his servants. Gods of second or third rank, who crouched at the entrance to houses, or watched over courtyards. We could shout their names without fear of enraging them, or having them pursue us: *Nyigbanto, Afeli, Djadjaglidja, Sunya, Wango, Ketetchi, Banguini, Ablowa, Kudé, Tchamba…* Names that sounded ridiculous on our childish lips, foolish names that had us doubled up laughing behind the backs of those who bore them.

'Hey, Djadjaglidja, he-who-walks-through-walls, come down from that shrine where your master placed you.'

'Hey, Tchamba, yes, you, Tchamba, he-who-has-come-from-afar, show us your passport!' (*Show us your arse*, the more reckless boys would say.)

We knew all of the Legba gods. Their powers and their weaknesses. Afeli, for example, could be both mean and cowardly. Though habitually considered the foundation on which a house is built, Afeli could choose to betray its owner, or forge unnatural alliances with evil spirits to bring about his ruin. To punish, to humiliate this arse-licking deity, we would leave him to his role as intercessor and trudge more than a kilometre to fetch his Legba rival Kpetodékè, bring him back and ceremoniously place him right under the nose of the verminous Afeli, who would slowly die of shame and starvation, and dissolve into earth, stained with tears and remorse. Kpetodékè, in turn, would betray his master, so we would trudge farther, more than two kilometres, to fetch Kpetové…

My friends and I mercilessly mocked these misshapen gods. We were all pupils at a Catholic school, and the God our parents forced us to love, to praise, to invoke, was incorporeal, evanescent, too evanescent. He had withdrawn from this world, we were told, leaving no reliable prophets, so we had to search for him between the lines of the *Te Deum* and the *Tantum Ergo*… To mock a God so distant that He could be contemplated only by the soul was an ant hunt, a waste of time. But being boys rather than saints, we felt a connection. Not with the ineffable but with the physical, the earthbound gods we encountered in our community, whose appetites were all too human— lying, scheming and fornicating. We could hardly miss the one thing that distinguished a Legba god from any others: the chthonic phallus, standing proud, ready to indulge in any feverish passion.

'Ah, Legba Agbo…' Monsieur Lomé, the landlord of The Daughters of Kilimanjaro would say. 'Legba Agbo is hornier than a rutting goat! Men call on him to cure their waning virility; barren women pray to him to fall pregnant each time a penis chafes the walls of their shrivelled vaginas.'

Spending time with the local gods, my childish head became bigger than the great wide world. And in the neighbourhood where I grew up, the bar called The Daughters of Kilimanjaro was the great wide world. The owner, Monsieur Lomé, was an artist. People said he grew rich selling talismans, Legba talismans. The artist's father, Osofo Lomeshi, had been a powerful priest at the Monastery of the Sacred Forest in Bassadji.

Legends that kindled my childish imagination spilled over the bar at The Daughters of Kilimanjaro. Often, as a change from my wanderings along the enchanted path, I would go and position myself near the bar. On nights when there was a grand ball, customers arrived in droves, in cars, on Vespas or Solex mopeds. In a neighbourhood as deprived as ours, seeing the ladies and gentlemen of the country's bourgeoisie arrive was proof that the owner was a notch above our everyday reality. He had made a success of himself, the poorer locals would say, more even than his father, who may have been a high priest of Voodoo but was a man of little worth according to the down-to-earth criteria of those comparing him to his son. He was more of a success than his father because he had found a means of selling the same fetishes that his father worshipped. He sold them to White folk, these gods we rejected without ever daring to admit as much, and White tourists would pay a fortune to acquire these statues of Legba specially made for the purpose.

'Monsieur Lomé makes special Legba statues he can sell,' said the locals. 'Have you seen the phalluses he puts on them? Solid, impervious to termites. The phallus of the future, in copper and zinc, but I suppose we're doomed to move with the times.'

Metals penises attached to finely carved wooden Legba statues—such originality was all it took to make a man rich. I could hardly believe it. As if this were not enough to seal his fame, the people of Bassadji whispered that he had transformed his bar into something even more original.

'I tell you, entering that bar is like entering a woman!'

As customers lined up on nights when there was a great ball, I would sit there, dreaming that they were entering a space shaped like a womb. The womb, of course, was a place I had never visited. Customers entered by a long, humid corridor with pink walls on which the artist had painted white spatters. So those who had entered the courtyard of The Daughters of Kilimanjaro said. Spermatic trails. Made from a concoction of water and cassava starch. People walked down a corridor that seemed endless only to emerge onto a vast plain, in the middle of which stood a great mango tree. A mound. A mountain. A giant phallus. It seemed that those who claimed to have been in the bar had not all seen the same thing. If a mango tree, a mound, a mountain and a giant phallus had risen from the middle of the vast plain at one and the same time, I would not have been surprised. My childish brain was vaster even than the great wide world.

I cannot explain why things appeared as they did in my dreams. In my waking dreams, I pictured misshapen Legba gods ritually greeting the guests: they yapped like dogs, scampering on all fours, with Monsieur Lomé's brass phalluses fixed between their legs.

Hardly had they stepped into the courtyard than a horde of tiny Legba appeared out of the darkness and began chasing women, only women, with Monsieur Lomé's huge metal phalluses hung round their necks. We will impregnate you! they shrieked, and the poor bewildered women scurried around the bar as though they truly believed that these carved wooden gods could carry out their threat. The men, titillated by the appearance of these dwarf gods, joined in their chant:

Mi li vo li vo

Mi la mon mi ya!

Finally, Monsieur Lomé would appear and hand out phalluses to everyone. Small brass phalluses whose insides had been hollowed to turn them into drinking glasses. Now, at last, the ball could begin.

And my nights camped outside the artist's bar were long. At first, my parents, worried that I had not come home, would scour the neighbourhood to find me. Later, when they discovered where I went, they shrugged off their fears. However much I daydreamed, in the end I always abandoned my dream for reality. One night, as I was leaving my lookout post, I came face to face with the artist. His car had pulled up outside the garage next to the bar, and he had climbed out, whistling the same rumba that blared from the speakers inside his bar. He spotted me just as I was about to turn away.

'Hey, kid, could you come and help me?'

I retraced my steps. He had opened the boot of his Mercedes Benz and was struggling to take out something vast, a seat carved from solid wood.

'Can you hold that end? Go on, you can do it, take that end. Do you know what this is?'

'Togbuizikpi,' I said.

'Exactly, the throne of the ancestors. A little extravagant, I'll grant you. But, kid, in every extravagant thing there hides a meaning. What's your name?'

'Dansou,' I said.

'Ah, the son of the great Marabout! Well then, you will feel right at home. Come on, follow me! What? Don't tell me you're afraid of going into a bar? Welcome to the great wide world, boy. Come on, follow me!'

The secret life of the things of this world appeared to me for the first time in this bar called The Daughters of Kilimanjaro, where the gods took the twisted form of the men and women I was accustomed to rubbing shoulders with by day.

Britney Spears' Sandwich

No, little sister, I was not laughing at you, I read your email and I answered honestly; why would you think that I would mock you? It is true that I had never heard of this girl—what did you say her name was?—Britney, that's right, Britney Spears. You say she lives in London where I live, but, little sister, the city is vast and everyone has their place, the singers and the deaf-mutes. I had not heard of her, I have no time to go to concerts here, or to go anywhere, no movies, no hobbies—work, work and more work, that is the only life a Black man in London knows, work, work, work. But don't worry, my friend Marcellin, who I stay with, says that Yasmina T, one of his colleagues at work, has a Britney CD, he asked her to make me a copy. I will listen to it and tell you whether I think that this girl you call a star is worth someone spending so much money on food she did not finish eating!

What you are asking me is madness, to go to eBay.com and bid in an auction for a sandwich that Britney Spears only half-ate. Little sister, you know I love you and that I cannot say no to you, but even you must realise that this would cost me the skin of my arse, when here in London I spend every day wondering how I will pay off the debts I left behind. You know better than anyone the circumstances in which I left Douala for the country where you say Britney Spears lives.

You remember. The morning that I told our mother that I had to leave for Europe, she looked me right in the eye and asked: *How much do you need to get away?* You were there, you were a witness, my beloved sister. And she did not hesitate to sell the two coffee plantations that put food on the family table, and the house that Papa left us when he died. She sold the house, our house, and rented a room in the district of Cathédrale. *I'm an old woman now,* she would say coquettishly, *and, besides, your sister is married.* I don't need all this space anymore. A white lie. She sold the family house, for me, so I could travel to a land where the pavements are strewn with gold. But that was not enough, so she went and borrowed three million CFA francs from Zoba, the people smuggler, and told him that once I got to London, it wouldn't take me six months to pay back those millions. Leaving your homeland for another country, that costs a lot of money, little sister. By the time I got to London, unforeseen expenses had left holes in my accounts: the genuine fake visa cost two times nine hundred thousand CFA rather than the nine hundred thousand agreed, because, before I could get the magic stamp that would work like Open Sesame on airplane doors, I first had to grease the palms of many middlemen, most of whom, I was told, had to remain anonymous. What could I do? I was told, pay this much, I paid that much. Days and days passed, still nothing would come and then someone would tell me I had to pay so much to such-and-such a man in the network, so I would go and dig into my dwindling reserves. These people have no heart, little sister, they would fuck a corpse in the arse if they thought that by doing it they would become rich and masters of the world. Right to the end, they bled me white, my own brothers. On the day I was due to leave, when I thought my suffering was over, they reappeared. In the middle of the airport, a young cop, scrawny as a slice of salt cod, ushered me into a box room and told me that I must declare any foreign currency I was carrying. By this point, I had only four million CFA francs, which I had converted into British pounds. How he knew I was carrying foreign currency, I don't know. He took £460—nearly half a million CFA—and pointed me towards the boarding gate. He was laughing: *How can you leave us here in the quicksand, brother? We will die here in the swamp and you just get to fly away—you're lucky, brother, very lucky!* This was the same man who, a minute earlier, was threatening to turn me in to the European police who checked passengers as they boarded the plane. How did he know my visa for London was fake and that I had foreign currency on me?

On January 13, 1996, I landed at Roissy airport in France without any problem. The customs officers gave me dirty looks, so I gave them a dirty look right back so that they would not ask me awkward questions. Then I took the train to London, where cousin Marcellin was waiting for me. You know what they say, the brothers who live here? White man's country be pretty, but White man's country be cold! Little sister. I did not set foot outside for a week. It was cold, it was grey, there were pigeons perched on every rooftop and my soul was saddened by the rain. Suddenly I missed the open skies of Douala and the hot rains that warm your soul. Marcellin mocked me and laughed at me: *You need go out, if you want get used to the cold, go out, go flirt, a woman's body will keep you warm, unless maybe you prefer a man's body, I tell you, I done that with men in this country, little brother, so I say, here you eat what you find, you fuck what you find, else you find nothing, you get fucked, you get eaten!*

It is nine o'clock, little sister, I am still in the Village Voice cybercafé, where I am writing to you. Just to tell you that everything did not go as I imagined when I got to London. Marcellin was charming, but he was also very strange. Sometimes he would disappear for four, five days, sometimes a week and no-one knew where he was or what he his business was in London. He would reappear with a big smile on his face and an armful of groceries. *Bizness is good, little brother, bizness is good! I can see that*, I would say, while waiting for him to help me find a job. But nothing came. Three months, six months soon turned into nine months, and I grew tired of waiting like a pregnant woman for my magnaminous benefactor to come home. But in London I had no papers, I was illegal, and I did not have the courage to go out. But, little by little, I started to get my bearings, to make fearful little ventures into the bars and cafés where Africans meet each other. One night, one of those alcoholic raptors eaten up by nostalgia for the homeland offered to lend me his residence permit in return for ten per cent of my salary if I got a job. I was just beginning to see light at the end of the tunnel when, one night, after one of his long absences, Marcellin brought misfortune to our home.

It is ten past nine, little sister, I am still in the cybercafé, still writing to you, read carefully what follows.

Misfortune did not come looking for Marcellin; it was he who courted misfortune. And the misfortune was mine…

It was the night before an important meeting, an interview for a job as a restaurant porter. Washing dishes and scrubbing pots for some guy at New Bell wasn't just some stupid job, it was my last hope. I could already see myself in the kitchen, wielding the dish brush and the spray, I'd already made plans for my first pay cheque, so why, Lord, why did you have to let Marcellin bring misfortune home to this apartment? Why could you not take his life and spare mine? I've got debts to pay, Lord, debts that my poor maman back in Douala racked up so I could come to the land of the White man, a land of lies and illusions, where the pavements are strewn with nothing but dog shit. And in the neighbourhood where I live, the pavements are not honoured by dogs doing their business, immigrants have no dogs—what would they feed them? How am I supposed to pay back Maman's debts? Why did Marcellin do what he did to me when he could have died in peace and left me in peace to carry on roaming the streets of London filled with rain and the turds of well-fed dogs?

I was making rice that night when he came home with his hands empty and his face twisted into a scowl. He wanted to talk to me, so I closed the pressure cooker and turned down the gas. We sat in the living room. He poured us shots of whisky and started drinking without even raising a toast, as strung out and antsy as a man caught in bed with his sister-in-law. *What's the matter, brother?* I asked him. He forced a bitter laugh, got up, and went to the toilet. He came back grey as an old man, and drank two more shots of whisky without stopping for breath. He was in a bad way, that was clear, and he put me in a bad way the second he opened his mouth.

I need your help, little brother, I'm up to my neck in shit. The cops be spotting me, they be knowing my bizness now, they see me, they got me in them sights! I need you to help me play a little trick on them. Nasty little trick. If I go down, a don die, how would you survive, little brother? But if I be disappearing for a day or two, it's all good, I can protect our savings and the cash will keep pumping. You know that, right? Don't look at me like that, I know you know, you just never asked. You were wrong, brother, you should have asked. People here, they lie as fine as our president Biya. They say, Marcellin, he be dealing powder. Shit, I no sell cocaine, I no sell weed, I'm into heavy shit, little brother, believe me, I run guns for warlords in poor countries of Europe, Hungary, Bosnia, Ireland, for little European thugs who watch too many war movies on Netflix. I'm a middleman, but sometimes a customer, he gets a few defective guns in a shipment and takes revenge by giving names to the police. I'm telling you everything, little brother, that way you know. Police will come for me this week, so I need to hide out somewhere safe while you pretend to be me. Three days, max, then they'll find out that you're white as snow and they'll release you. Surely you will do this thing for me, little brother, after everything I've done for you. If you do, I promise I'll pay off half your mother's debts, in cash. You'll do that for me…

As the turtle says in the fairytale I learned as a boy, misfortune does not seek man out, it is man who seeks misfortune. Marcellin disappeared. At 3am. I was staring at the ceiling, unable to sleep, when I heard a key turn in the door. Then police burst into the living room and surrounded the sofa I was using as a bed. Silent and serious, they handcuffed me and dragged me to the police van parked outside. At the police station, they questioned me all day, all night, and I told them what they wanted to hear. I said I was Eddy Marcellin, aka Makossa (such a foolish nickname!), no, I had never sold guns, I said, no, I knew no arms dealers, yes, I was a Christian and to do such a thing is against my religion. Sorry, what? I don't understand the question. Am I a gay? Oh, because the Makossa you know is gay, well, yes, I mean no, maybe, it's private, and it is none of your business…

The London police are as stupid as the police in Douala, I thought, until they decided to take my fingerprints. That is when my story fell apart. My ink-smeared fingertips revealed that I was not the man they were looking for. I felt a wave of fear as I realised I was caught up in a web of lies spun by a more talented liar than me. I suddenly knew what awaited me, I would be sent back to the country I had fled in the search of a better life, I would never be able to repay my debts, I would bring shame to Maman who had sacrificed everything for me.

The police did not find my passport in the apartment. Another trick by Marcellin, who had taken it with him. But in doing so, Makossa saved my life, since now I could say that I was from Chad and avoid the shame and humiliation of being sent back to Douala, to Cameroon. *What does the word Makossa mean?* one of the officers asked as we boarded the plane. *It is a dance in Cameroon; in the Douala language 'Makossa' means 'I dance'*, I said bitterly. *Can you teach me during the flight?* he asked. *I love African food and African music…*

It is almost ten o'clock, little sister, I am still in the Village Voice café, all the computers will soon be switched off, in five minutes they will cut my connection. I have five minutes left to tell you the truth, my truth. Only one person in Douala knows. Tantine Hawa, my old girlfriend, who works at the local Western Union where I send a little money from time to time to try to pay off Maman's debts. When I send this email, you will be only the second person to know the truth. Will you keep it to yourself? As I am sure you know, if you do not play along with my lie, it will kill Maman. She would die, her heart would not be able to endure a truth as brutal and piercing as a naked blade.

*

One by one, the lights in the cybercafé flicker out. As I step out onto rue 40, a man calls out to me. I do not know what he wants, I do not speak his language; I have been living here for so long now that even I think that perhaps it is time that I made the effort to learn Arabic.

In my head, I live in London, but in truth I am living near Moursal market in N'Djamena.

I have been living here for ten years. Since the day I was deported.

I did not send the email to my sister; I allowed the words to vaporise when the café owner cut the internet connection. But five minutes before he did so, I went to the website that my sister mentioned. It seems it is too late to buy the egg salad sandwich half-eaten by this young woman, Britney. An online gaming company called Golden Palace acquired it for a sum I cannot even bring myself to mention. But that is not the end of it. A spokesperson for the company stated that they already have samples of her saliva and her urine in their possession. Guess what they plan to do? Clone Britney, they say. Tonight, my clone will sleep in London, while the other me heads back to a tiny room on the outskirts of N'Djamena.

Quick April

done dressing for self
eked off an impulse what'll
daub the body walls in
some week or other

bread
and onwards
up and at space or
flat thinking where
kinship kind of thrived
we spoke we spoke we spoke
nights hold a separate summer
funny how the birds get bolder

nothing mutated just sat
fresh graves seen running

Caitlín Doherty

From Athens

rot the orange fish ponds
not only fruit, not what pulps
from under heel the juice in dribble
printing May, some jasmine ripe

rich stagnant bobbing
tax the ships &
            bye bye helen

fuck paris I'm for
dry pine & shade on
potent caesar's benches

an anglobusiness tiredness
    sets   *I'm on my holidays!*
tied to where my leisure lay
a cast of towelling bunches for
the postponed sea

paying a discomfort in slow slow
down up and begin at five as if
we didn't yawn with noon
sunk culture after plughole greek
tremata tremata watching the weeds
shiver as old dog legs legs of a
dog who knows we go for lunch
without her
sad!
we eat at europe's second
most important port and sirrus, it
becomes you, ants steal our food
like walking bark while you

you walk around a waterfall
built above a storm drain

Caitlín Doherty

Big Unliveable House

You can live on top of
the big unliveable house
on shocking island, it doesn't
have a piano
or a stove, but
it has bashable doorframes to sob on
it won't let you get too clever, but
it wakes you up on Saturdays with
a song from below:

nothing nothing here to see
nothing not untouched but we
go fizzing onwards endlessly to
yes a rest—no one more thing

it calls you scrubber and you like it
you whisper it back to the walls, soon
you're removing your boundary layers
oh, tissues for days! pause to count all the
lucky ghosts you sleep with

you'll wish for happy easy beauty
here
steady pigment over the whole face
all your words become appalling but
look, only all of the time

Caitlín Doherty

Boys, Crying

James Hudson

CHOKING UP

Oh, fuck, I'm about to cry. I'm in the middle of a sentence. My sentence is in the middle of a protracted 'debate' on trans representation. The 'debate' is in the middle of a two-hour class in the School of English, Drama and Film, where the tables have been arranged in a rectangle so that everyone can look each other in the eye. The published, the unpublished, the novices and the veterans are all on equal footing. It's 2019; I am a twenty-two-year-old barely out of my undergrad, and I have as much visibility as the award-winning authors in this room whether I want it or not.

Crying starts in my stomach and rises like mercury. It tightens my chest and quickens my heart. My tongue is heavy and my cheeks are roasting. Tears start burning my waterline. Oh, fuck. I'm useless. I can fight the urge to cry at every step and still lose. I'm just muscle and bone and saltwater, conquerable as a mound of dirt.

In moments like these I somehow convince myself that no one can tell I'm about to cry. That if I just measure my breaths between words, I can reach the end of my sentence without anyone noticing. Yet clearly, before a tear drops from my eye, something's giving me away to my classmates. Their expressions are changing. What is that? Pity? Compassion? Disgust? Someone asks do I need a minute. I don't know what good a minute will do me. I don't nod or shake my head. I don't do anything but focus on melting the tears away. I can't stand being interrupted, especially by my own body.

People are watching me from every table that makes up our rectangular class, waiting to hear my trans rebuttal in the 'trans debate'. I don't know why we call it that. I'm not debating anything, I'm begging for respect while others debate if I deserve it. I'm annoyed and frustrated, but that doesn't feel connected to the fat knot in my throat. I don't feel *overwhelmed* by emotion, I don't feel like I'm *breaking down* crying, I don't feel like *bursting* into tears. I don't have the language for how I do feel, because all the words for crying are tragic.

I'm not tragic. I'm on the precipice of nothing more than being embarrassed in front of my classmates on a warm Wednesday afternoon.

Each row of faces crushes me with a wave of self-awareness: I'm the only trans person speaking in this room. I wasn't prepared to be the centre of attention today. I thought a creative writing degree was a safe place full of lefty artists, where my identity wouldn't be in contention.

I try to pace my breathing and finish my point, what even was it, *something something zero trans Irish novelists*—but my body doesn't understand. It doesn't know who John Boyne is. It doesn't know what a university is, or a creative writing class. It doesn't know that boys don't cry. It only knows that distress signals are firing in my brain and it wants to protect me. It will choke me mid-sentence if necessary because it only has one priority: get help.

Crying feels like an outdated organ in this moment, an emotional appendix. Crying might have rallied Neanderthals to an injured tribemate, but today, in this classroom, it is killing my credibility. Perhaps evolution didn't predict humans turning on each other. At any rate, whether I like it or not, I start to cry.

TEARING UP

I never knew I was a blusher until someone told me, and since that revelation I've spent a lot of time wondering what I look like in conversation. People cite my eyes (big and blue) and brows (full and dark) as my most striking features. They are, reportedly, expressive. In my reflection I can study how my hair falls to my chin, how the light bounces off my round nose, I can act out emotions and try to see what others see when I laugh, frown, gasp. I can see all the ways I look without ever knowing how I come across. I'm always troubled by the gap between how I look and how people see me, doubly so when crying. There's a specific relationship between two people when one cries and the other watches. For the person watching, both distaste and empathy demand speculation around the crier's emotions. That gets under my skin. People already feel free to scrutinise my existence and I don't need to intensify that by crying in front of them.

But that's how we deal with crying; we make it a moment, a spectacle, a conversation stopper. All our art about crying is third-person. It's harder to capture the feeling of being the one crying and being *watched* while crying. The closest thing I've found is a series of photographs by Emily Knecht taken every time she cried for three years, including shots taken mid-argument with her boyfriend. 'If we're having an argument and I'm crying,' she told *i-D*, 'I'm like "Hold on, I've got to take a picture," he's like, "What the fuck is wrong with you?" It's like, is it taking you out of the moment? Is it connecting you more?'

I derive pleasure from looking at her photos, from scratching at the itch that demands to know what I look like to other people when I'm crying. I don't take photos, but I do much the same as Knecht. I interrupt my own emotions with performative ticks. I wonder what I look like, how I'm being perceived. I don't fully feel my feelings. I don't have the luxury.

With my thoughts diluted, I'm only grounded in the physical sensations of crying. My hands balled in my sleeves, pressing their cotton against my watery eyes, the dampness seeping through my jumper cuff to spread over my knuckle.

I don't know what my classmates are seeing when I look up from under wet lashes. Is my face red? Are my eyes glossy or bloodshot? Do I look wild-eyed or just vacant? Do I cry like a guy or a girl? Am I coming across frustrated or depressed? Does anyone care if I finish my sentence anymore, or do they just want to know will the wobble in my lip cave into shoulder-shaking sobs?

I look off to the side to try and keep it together and now the conversation is over. The mood has shifted. I'm pretty sure I have 'lost' the 'debate'. A tear hasn't even hit my cheek yet.

Everyone is quiet. Silence and the pressure to fill it are overwhelming; I simultaneously see the hundred different outcomes depending on how I cry, where I cry, when I cry, if I cry. I wonder whether anyone in this room has a single other trans person in their life, or if I will be their one monolithic idea of what a trans person is, how they sound, what they believe, how they behave.

ACTING UP

I know the social worth of crying in front of people; I know to take it seriously when I feel a little cry coming on. I'm fascinated by the line between real expression and fabricated television and I can't get through an episode of reality TV without commenting on the quantity, quality or function of a crying scene. I've almost memorised that interview where *RuPaul's Drag Race* alum Kelly Mantle exposes how producers push *Drag Race*'s emotionally charged sob stories.

Drag Race posits itself as a place for lost gays to find a family under the wing of Mama Ru and good sob stories (and sob they must) are core to the cathartic appeal, but trauma saturation has created a 'quantity over quality' approach. When a contestant confesses their personal trauma to judges, tears are meant to elicit sympathy; yet the sentimentality that the show is built around often brings out cynicism in the audience. Anyone, after watching enough *Drag Race*, will have had a knee-jerk *she's just crying so they won't send her home* reaction.

I've been guilty of this and I've tried to understand why. I've wondered if I take the queens less seriously because they're effeminate, if I'm redirecting the scrutiny I feel when I'm crying. I've considered that *Drag Race* competitors seldom know what edit they'll get and that *Drag Race*, in search of 'universal appeal', will prioritise a good arc over authentically conveying a crier's emotions.

Knowing Roxxxy Andrews makes it to the finale of *Drag Race* Season 5, editors showcase her tears into a two-minute-long display with five musical cues lasting into the show's end credits; conversely, from the moment Season 10 contestant Blair St. Clair first sniffles, she gets roughly fifty seconds with two pieces of music, rapidly indicating woe and subsequent resolution. In under a minute the show delivers: Blair opening up about sexual assault; queens breaking down; RuPaul building them up; a neat resolution. Blair is eliminated eight minutes later.

For the viewer, Blair crying comes out of nowhere. A shot of Monét X Change barrelling the camera cues us to feel that way—the editing pushes the idea that Blair didn't have some unseen personality left on the cutting-room floor, that she's pulling this out of her ass. It's effective. Scepticism of queens in tears honed in on Blair; in a comedy set about frequent crying scenes in Blair's season, Season 6 winner Bianca Del Rio even said of her, 'That other bitch, "I was raped!" No, fuck you. You notice she wasn't raped until she was in the bottom two? … that's fucking strategy.'

I've often tried to put myself in Blair's shoes—or rather, those of Andrew Bryson, the drag performer playing her. We talk about his disclosure and elimination, but not what came right before. He was a 22-year-old on an internationally picked-apart TV show with a notoriously toxic fandom; he had earlier received both insults and affirmations from his fellow contestants; judges had just criticised the 'cute' drag persona he secretly formed in response to feeling 'dirty' as well as comparing him to a dessert, something useable, consumable. There was so much going on and so little running time to unpack it.

All the things someone in that position won't say—*can't* say—make 'strategic' crying the most efficient edit; all you have to do is remove context. It's a week of sceptical fan engagement for under a minute of screentime. Of all the types of TV crying, it's also the closest thing to real queer life. We don't have manicured confessional interviews to speak for us when we're struggling, we don't have season-long character arcs clueing people into our backstory, we don't have a colourful cast of characters around us at all times to show straight people the diversity of queer experience. In times of 'trans debate' I have rarely, if ever, shared the floor with another trans person.

So sure. It came out of nowhere.

GROWING UP

It shouldn't surprise me when my body goes against me, making a show of me when I'm most serious. For years my hips have ached if I uncross my legs and try to sit 'like a man', and my high Valleyspeaky voice puts my phone bookings under 'Jane' instead of 'James'. I've had a lifetime to get used to it, but I'm still incensed whenever my body is stroppy.

I announced myself as James in 2011, age fifteen. I've met trans people with names from their favourite movies, shows, comics; mine came from *James and the Giant Peach*, a film released the year I was born that I loved as a kid.

A transmasculine teen pre-'The Transgender Tipping Point', I had a much more assimilationist view of trans identity. I parroted cis people's ideas of what being trans should be; don't look weird, try to pass, getting clocked is game over. I grew up, I met other trans people, I learned and unlearned a lot. I no longer feel like masculinity is something I have to copy verbatim from cis men, like it's a competition that I lose if I express myself. I'm happy being more Nathan Lane than John Wayne, and I like being trans now. I like the insight being trans gives me into myself, I like the community around me, I like trans media, I like writing while trans. I like learning the overlapping histories of butches, trans men, gender non-conforming and non-binary people. I don't call myself a trans man, I like 'trans masculine' for what it is separate from cis masculinity; formed differently, experienced differently, loved differently. Wonderfully.

Still, years after coming out it's hard to silence that part of my mind forged in the fires of cis expectation; I still get anxious about looking weird, not passing, getting clocked. I still fear being publicly humiliated if I don't adhere to cis masculinity, that I'll be treated as a failure if I do something so 'feminine' as emote. If we talk about transness—when we talk about transness—and I speak, and I put myself out there to be looked at while speaking, and when I start to cry, I would be a sensitive, irrational queer, I would be somebody reaching at maleness who can't do the bare minimum of keeping his emotions in check.

I have specific outfits to wear on days where I expect to be especially visible. I wear those outfits not to be read as male, but to look like I'm trying. Maybe if I hide my body and dress like cis people think boys should dress, don't cross my legs or hang my wrist, I'll get a night off from being an *activist*. I'll be allowed to meet people, shuffle past their awkward double-take when the word 'James' leaves my mouth, and get on with my fucking life.

I am not wearing one such safety outfit in the middle of a sentence in the middle of a class in the middle of the 'trans debate' on Wednesday afternoon, and all eyes are on me, and my heart is in my throat, and I open my mouth, and I don't even look like I'm trying.

BREAKING DOWN

A few months before the sentence in the middle of the 'trans debate', in November 2018, I went on my first real date. It was my first time meeting someone who wasn't a friend I'd made out with in my teens, someone who wasn't already familiar with me and my transness. I was meeting my first hot stranger off a dating app. A queer coming-of-age if there ever was one.

He was a gay man, attractive, and into me, but he was polyamorous and I was not. After a week-long flirtation, I broke things off.

I didn't know until then how badly I'd internalised my undesirability. I'd been out as trans for seven years—an eternity in queer time. I had learned and unlearned cis masculinity; I had stopped chasing the Sisyphean version of body positivity where every glance at the mirror should send me into a frenzy of self-adulation. I still struggled with being misgendered, misunderstood, misrepresented, but I grasped that this was a matter of perception, that I was not in the wrong for existing as is. I loved my body, genuinely. I just didn't think anyone else could love my body too.

I felt sick for days after our last text exchange, absolutely sure, at twenty-two, that I would never be wanted again in my life. I was in college the following day having told next to no one about the entire affair. I rarely tell people when I have a shot at something good, be it romantic or professional, in case it doesn't pan out and I look the fool for getting my hopes up. I got through a couple of classes with glassy eyes and a foggy brain before sitting on a couch tucked under a staircase and then, without warning, I started crying on my best friend's shoulder. She rubbed my back and didn't try to talk down my anxieties, and I slumped over beside her like a dog tired out from doing nothing.

After a few months collecting myself off Tinder, I started dating a guy in January 2019. He took me to a café I've since learned was the hotspot for every gay first date in Dublin. Even my date knew that, and he was an American who'd only been in Ireland for five months.

I got a Coke and he got tea; we went downstairs to the basement. It was warm and smelled weird, like the steam inside a hot pastry. I inelegantly confessed that I had gone on exactly one date before, but then he had to go to the bathroom and throw up because of the weird smell, so I would call it even on weird first impressions. Despite that, we both wanted to see each other again, and again, and again. He was in Ireland for his year abroad and leaving at the end of the semester, so we planned to break up in April.

On a night in March 2019, a few weeks before the middle of the sentence, we were falling asleep together on my sitting room sofa. It was so nice it started to scare me. I wanted to sleep, to be falling asleep with a boy I loved, but I couldn't stop staring at a small blue light in the corner of my TV. When I glanced around the room, bright blue streaks cut through the dark. He felt my heartbeat quicken and asked me what was wrong. I admitted that I was so, so scared no one else would like me after he went home. I pinched my eyes in the dark and whispered 'oh, fuck' out loud, asking them to not prickle. To him I said: 'I promise I'm not a mess.'

I had been on a tightrope since we'd met. He was nice and smart and funny and he knew more about gay life in Ireland than I did; I wanted him to remember me as someone equally cool. As a result I was oddly open with him, admitting whenever I felt anxious but immediately blaming it on an outside trigger—college, usually. Sometimes it was true; I told him all about the 'trans debate' thing after it happened. Sometimes I think I was reaching and I just wanted a reason to be sad that wasn't 'I am a sad person'. I was afraid it would seem like negativity just generated inside of me, that my tears were just coming out of nowhere.

In April, the week we were due to break up, he told me he had also been crying on that night we talked on the couch. I just hadn't noticed in the dark.

My best friend and I spent three full days together right after the scheduled breakup, going out to movies, getting takeaway, hanging out at my house, all planned well in advance so I wouldn't be on my own for those vulnerable days. There was a time limit—we both had finals due in less than two weeks—but she came anyway and with her company I found it easy not to cry for a few days.

Very quickly, I started to think about flying to visit him in the US. I tried filing the idea away as something for 'next year', but no matter how irrational I knew it to be, the thought wouldn't leave my mind. Abruptly I paused the episode of *Survivor* my friend and I were watching, saying I needed to go ask my mom about something before she went to sleep. I ran upstairs to tell my mom about these flight plans, hoping she would point out how nonsensical the idea was and that, equipped with her motherly wisdom, I wouldn't have to think about it anymore. I sat on her bed and didn't get so far as explaining my plan before I started crying, quietly, about how nice he was and how badly I missed him already.

BREAKING UP

In the span of our four-month relationship, he only cried in front of me once. It started when we were sitting on my bed with pillows propped behind us, talking about the practicalities of his departure. Suitcases. Taxis. Planes. He mentioned feeling sick, and I said it was an appropriate bookend for our relationship, given his initial barfing. He started crying. I was relieved for a second. It was the first time I'd really seen him cry, in the light, and he couldn't hide it.

I couldn't reconcile tears with his face. That behaviour was mine, not his. Despite having been in his exact position and knowing these things have no rhyme or reason, I was convinced it was something I said. So I asked him amid fuzzy, numb-fingered comforting, what brought this on?

He said he was just thinking about our first date. He was really going to miss me.

For the first time ever, I *wished* that I was crying. Everything was the wrong way around. It wasn't like me to be so composed. *I'm* stupid, *I'm* hysterical, *I* can't control it—I'm the one who cries, not the one who watches. I was used to my mind being calm and my body acting out; now I finally felt emotional, I felt irrational, I felt a need to express to him that I was by all definitions heartbroken, and instead I had a face like stone. I needed tears to explain that I felt the same, and nothing came.

I was so confused by my feelings the first time a boy cried in front of me. I still lack the language. Did I think my crying about our separation made me the only vulnerable one, the naive one, the one who was *in it*, achingly, humiliatingly, *for real*?

Two years on and I haven't found all the answers, but once again I've come closest through art. There's a scene early in Leslie Feinberg's *Stone Butch Blues*, when teenage Jess Goldberg is struggling to preserve their softness while embodying the toughness demanded of 1960s butches, and a femme named Angie says, 'You're OK,' then, 'Are you OK?' and finally, 'You're not OK, are you?'

These two queer people, a femme and a butch, know that the ways they can be seen in the world are limited and they will always have fundamental differences in expression; but when they're in private, Angie gives Jess a respite. Someone else telling Jess that they aren't okay is enough for Jess to express that they need care, and they do so by starting to cry on Angie's shoulder.

I didn't know it at the time, and I still don't know all the right words for it, but I feel my American gave me that. Not an outlet to be vulnerable but a way to be the caretaker for once, not the token kicked puppy in the room. A show of strength outside of cis masculinity. He let me be what so many others had been for me.

My friends, my people, my Leslie Feinbergs, my Nathan Lanes, my SOPHIEs, my loves have given me that recognition that Angie gave Jess: it's okay to cry. Not as pithy philosophy or a shallow mental health campaign, but with the full knowledge and understanding of what I am and what that means. The world is hostile, the café closed down, and my life is debate fodder, but in a wonderful way, my body was briefly tricked into thinking otherwise.

Crying, in this deliriously trans way, is outside of that copycat cis masculinity I wore as a teen, and it's a part of what makes my masculinity *mine*. I'm not on T right now but if I chose to return to hormone therapy, I might find it harder to cry. It's a relatively common side effect. I've tried imagining how I'd feel if my abundance of crying suddenly turned into an absence, and I would hope my body remembers that feeling of vulnerability even if it no longer expresses it. I'd tell it to remember this of my tears: there are times when it's scary and embarrassing and inconvenient, but what a small price to pay for the knowledge that a body has known true safety and love.

Mystery Letters

I learned today that the Roman script is actually Phoenician
which is actually hieroglyphic.
Our a's (Aa) are the tip (𐤀) of a bull's head (𓃾)
and everything goes back to Egypt.

I learned yesterday that, in the conquest of peoples,
Europeans had a big advantage
over Muslim scripts:
their letters are perpetually disconnected.
Their stolid forms are molten, like lead.
They don't bend, don't curve to time's fragile winds.

Europeans, with their Latin alphabet, funded
Gutenberg who financed Columbus' journey to the
New World.
In 1492, moveable type colonized the world.

Tomorrow, I will learn why the strange figures that appear
when Americans insert broken Arabic letters
into places where they can't grasp its meaning
spook me like evil objects.

ا ب ح م ر reads a sign in a Detroit airport (upending رمحبا)
What should have been a welcome became a curse.
ی دم آ ش و خ reads a sign in an Annapolis bathroom (desecrating آمدی وخش)
What should have been a greeting, evokes
memories of ancient Qurans
no one understands,
mimicking the imperialist's benevolent grin.

When the letters disconnect,
their audiences scatter to the winds—
migrants ford the Mediterranean, desperate to exist—
For the Europeans, they acquire the visage of demons
evoking ancient hatreds, setting in motion
reams of asylum claims they will soon reject.

The dead with their alien script will soon be forgotten.
No one thinks to ask to whom they will now be read.

Rebecca Ruth Gould

Diana in a lonely place

Emer O'Hanlon

My third encounter with her was in the kitchen, on the first night of the dig in Greece. We had just arrived in the house we would be staying at (me, the other students, and Ana, the dig co-supervisor), after a three-hour drive from the airport. Ana liked to drive with the windows down, letting the warm air fly into our faces in a way that I found unpleasant. I preferred the control of the air conditioning. When we got out, three figures stood on the porch, cigarettes in hand. A dog came running towards us from indoors, and I could feel a mosquito humming in my ear.

Later that evening, once we'd eaten, we decided among ourselves who would sleep where. There were two rooms left, one with a double, the other with two singles. Actually, the second room wasn't its own room at all; really it just formed part of the corridor that led to the other bedrooms. As we were three girls and one guy, it should have been easy to sort this out, but Katie and I mentioned our boyfriends. Nicole shrugged, unphased at the thought of sharing. Howell, on the other hand, assured all of us that he was gay, and therefore the sleeping situation should be a non-issue.

Aoife, isn't it? she asked, when we returned to the kitchen. She wasn't helping the others to wash up, because it seemed as though there were already too many cooks (two Greeks, one British). Instead, she sat at the table, cards dealt out in front of her, a small glass of something in her left hand.

My eyes shot open, suddenly recognising her. Oh, I said, you're—

She nodded. We met at the department Christmas drinks last year. I'm in the same department as the four of you actually, she said to us, all the newcomers, though really it was to the room at large. I'm one of those graduate students whose existence you like to ignore. I've seen you around the library—Aoife, Katie, Nicole, Howell, right? She counted round us.

I'm surprised you know us so well, Nicole said, sitting down and pouring herself a glass from the bottle.

I am quite observant, she said, to no one in particular.

Just hours before, I had been at Heathrow, waiting out my last few hours of freedom before I sacrificed them to the cause of a late Roman urban development. I sat in a café, where I had accidentally ordered baked beans to go with my avocado toast. I forced them into my mouth as I watched notifications buzz through on my phone.

I've just checked in my bags—how long did it take you to go through security?

So excited to meet you guys!

I'm sitting outside Fortnum and Mason, if anyone wants to join

I've just got to look for a hat any ideas where I could get a cheap one?

I joined in the conversation, of course, but I only replied tactfully. I wasn't going to go and meet them until the last possible moment. I wouldn't be properly alone again for three weeks.

Later that night, standing outside on the porch and feeling a bit dizzy from the drive and the bus and the flight and the wait and the other flight and the drive and the wine, I called my boyfriend. He sounded drunk too, in a cosy way, and told me he was sitting by the pool.

I've been looking through the novels you recommended, he said.

Oh?

Yeah. Why do none of the authors you like use speech marks? Is that considered gauche nowadays?

You can't complain about my pretentious tastes, I said. I watched all of Michael Haneke's oeuvre with you last summer. Including both versions of *Funny Games*, which I regret.

Well, look, Haneke's legacy is indisputable. But I know we disagree on this. Anyway, how are your fellow diggers?

Hard to tell. Anyway, it doesn't bother me. I'm not here to make friends. I have enough already, probably.

That bad, are they?

I've got to get to bed, I said. We're up at 6am for digging tomorrow.

Blimey, that's early.

Between my finger and my thumb/ The squat pen rests; snug as a gun.
What?
Never mind.

That first night there, I went to the bathroom to wash my face and teeth, and while I had the security of the locked door, I returned to my private tab, one earphone in, the open ear alert.

The story of all the videos I watched was pretty much the same. I believe it's considered archaic to have a real plot, though this may have been down to my preferred search terms: 'Forced', 'she doesn't realise', 'surprise anal'. I watched two such videos, taken from behind on cameras the women didn't know existed. Then I packed up my toiletries and went to bed.

It was a bad habit, like any other. But in a new place, in a new bed, I needed to do something familiar if I had any chance of getting to sleep.

I didn't know what I was going to do this summer, I told her on the porch one night, much later. She was smoking lazily. I had followed her outside, insisting I liked the fresh air.

I didn't know what I was going to do this summer, and then someone mentioned this dig and it seemed like such a good opportunity. I realised I sounded very earnest—I was always making that mistake when I tried to impress girls like her.

Sometimes, I said to her, I don't understand how people afford anything. Everyone at college talks about the holidays they're going to go on over the summer and what they'd like to do, and then they ask me why I'm going to a dig in the middle of nowhere in Greece when I don't even like archaeology that much. I actually prefer philology, but this is the only way I get sun and a break from home, you know? It's stressful having to come up with answers that everyone will believe.

She leaned over and took the wine glass from my hand. You're drunk, she said calmly. Go to bed.

That first morning on the dig, we bundled into the car at 7am and drove to the site. The dig leader, Vassilis, took the new students in his car, while the older ones went with Ana. Vassilis played music for the entire thirty-minute drive. Howell nodded off, but the rest of us didn't speak. Me and Nicole puffy-eyed from sleeping badly, Katie looking alert. This was the first time

I'd heard Adele's 'Hello', but I disliked it so much I thought it must not be the real version.

We didn't dig at all in the first half of the morning. Vassilis introduced us to everyone, and then he took us on a tour of the site, the excavated parts and parched fields around it, throbbing with insects and sun. He explained how the history of this town had changed, going from a bustling centre in the Roman imperial period to the sad early medieval parts we had to sift through now. He told us about the analysis they had done on the food remains, how they had a thorough understanding of the diets of the people who lived here. We made a circuit of the town's border, along empty, dusty lanes. I hadn't realised that Greece could look like this, a cadaverous desert. The ground was coming away into sand under my feet, colouring the exposed parts of my shins orange.

In the bathroom, while I brushed my teeth, I thought about all the previous times I'd encountered her, and about the second time in particular. How she had looked, face flushed, as she turned to the man and said, I want you, I want you to fuck me now.

The way that the video was taken meant that you couldn't see his face, which I found a great shame. I think I would have been able to understand her better, if only I knew what he looked like.

We were in the field by 7.30 (8am at the latest) every day, and we dug solidly until 1pm. For the first week, I was assigned a drain with Katie. She told me about her boyfriend, her plans for their future, the law conversion course he was taking next year.

I think it sounds like a sensible thing to do, she grinned. But I love that we get the chance to have these experiences now, before we're too old, you know?

I was two years older than her, but I kept silent.

I'd made the mistake of bringing my water bottle to sit beside me, rather than leaving it in the shade, so by 9.30 it was well beyond lukewarm, incapable of providing relief.

Aoife's boyfriend is a sports star, you know, she told the dinner table one evening.

Faces upturned. This was unexpected. I sensed that they already thought I was difficult to get talking.

Really? one of the Greek students asked. You don't look like the jock type.

It's not a jockish sport, I explained. It's fencing.

She tried to explain, in broken Greek, what fencing was to those who hadn't understood.

Nicole and Howell had questions: who was he? How good was he? Did he play Varsity?

She caught my eye as I answered their questions dutifully, feeling my words catch on something reluctant in my chest, down where I imagined my diaphragm was.

I found myself watching her video every night before bed. The video was harder to watch now that I knew her better. She squealed at first, playfully, and then it became sharper.

Don't go near my ass, she said firmly.

The video showed him doing otherwise.

She was resistant, and then she wasn't, and then she was. I found it very upsetting.

What did you do today? I asked my boyfriend on the phone. This was in the afternoon, before our late lunch. Every day, we would come back and shower, and prepare the food on a rota. Everyone dispersed while we waited to eat, kept to themselves in different parts of the house so that it felt empty, eerie, in the lull.

We went for a cycle to the village for a pastry and des glaces, he said. We bought bread for the house. You'll like it here, when you come.

I nodded, although he couldn't see me.

What did you do today?

Digging. We'll clean the finds after lunch. I found a piece of glass, but Vassilis told me it was worthless and I had to throw it away. Next time, I'll just steal it instead, but he watched me to make sure I did what he said. Best archaeological practice, I guess.

By the way, I read that book you suggested. *My Year of Rest and Relaxation*.

Oh, and?

It's just a bit nihilistic, isn't it? I could have done with more background fleshed out in the bits about her parents, like why she was so fucked up.

Didn't you like all that satire on the art world, though?

It was well done, he conceded. My parents have friends like that.

Aoife! She beckoned me over. I dropped my trowel and eased up slowly. The sun was scorching, and behind my eyes there was an indistinct headache brewing.

Eleni has brought some olives from her family's farm, she said.

Eleni offered me a tupperware full of fresh olives. One of the Greek students, she was the only one who didn't sleep at the house with the rest of us, because her parents lived near enough for her to drive in every day.

She continued talking to Eleni, asking her about her family, her goats, her thesis.

She took to playing cards with me and Howell. In the evenings after dinner, we would sit with wine on the porch, and she would ask Howell repeatedly if he minded her smoking, as though she already knew how I felt about it. We bickered over the rules of gin rummy, a game that my parents had taught me but which they both insisted was an erroneous amalgamation of two different, distinct, games.

How is your research coming along? he asked her, in the pauses between rounds.

She shrugged. We've found some interesting stuff here. I won't be able to use any of it for my thesis, obviously, but it helps me to think. I'll have to track down similar finds from other published sites to include instead. Being here is only delaying my writing. But it's also the best part of the whole experience, for me.

I don't know how you find so much to write about. He looked at me. Do you think you'd ever do a PhD?

I shrugged. I was happy to let them talk, listening to her careful answers, occasionally feeling the flex of her toes beside me on the bench, one shin tucked under her body. I'd do anything if I got the funding.

She arched an eyebrow at Howell. That's how it all starts, she said.

I'm trying to figure out what my dissertation should be on. Howell continued to probe her. Do you have any advice for final year?

Very few people will ever look at your undergrad dissertation, she said.

Do you know what yours is going to be, Aoife?

I still have time, I said, my eyes on the cards. We have months before we have to think about that stuff.

Afternoon, on the back terrace of the dig house.

My dad used to try to make up for things, I overheard her telling Katie and Nicole. Because my mum died when I was so small, he was always very intent on us talking about girl things, you know, periods and make-up and everything.

It was only 5pm, so it was still sweltering. According to the daily ritual, we washed the new finds with fine toothbrushes and laid them out to dry in the sun. Sometimes we helped to catalogue them, assigning numbers and letters based on predefined categories and locations. This was my favourite part. I could take or leave the digging.

He brought me to see all the Twilight movies, she explained, because I had no friends to go with. He'd chat with me about whether I was Team Edward or Team Jacob. At the start of one of them—maybe *Eclipse*—both guys swanned across the screen, you know, their bodies on like, full display. He was so eager to let me know he was comfortable with me talking about guys with him. It was a relief when I told him I preferred girls so it would stop.

Beside me, I could sense Eleni watching my hands, fidgeting over the same sherds.

In the second week, I was moved onto the foundations of a house with Nicole, supervised by Ana. Ana showed us how to recognise the remains of a staircase. We kept uncovering pieces of pottery, and each time we did, I called Ana over. Eventually she asked me to stop unless something actually good turned up.

Katie asked me if I could either speed up my pre-sleep beauty regime, or else leave the porch and come to bed earlier.

I hate to be that girl going on about needing sleep, she said (measured but desperate). And I don't want to have a go at you, but we have to get up so early and every time you get into bed it wakes me up.

I thought about Howell's nightly bathroom trips, and how no one questioned what he might be doing.

I'll come to bed earlier, I assured her, and I'll be more quiet.

Instead, I moved my mattress slightly. If I titled it just so, it would enable me to lie in bed and watch videos without anyone being in danger of seeing. That way, I could stay out on the porch with her as long as I liked.

*

The next day, Nicole and I dug up some skeleton parts ('human remains' is the preferred term among archaeologists, Ana explained), including a skull and part of a hip bone. Ana dealt with the matter skilfully, showing the students the auricular surface and the sciatic notch, indicators of whether the person had been male or female. Once she realised they would be taken to a museum and not buried, Nicole asked if she could pray over the bones, and Ana joined her, more out of pedagogic duty, I think, than shared faith. All of the students bowed their heads in respect, though I raised my eyes regularly to observe the others. Her head was tilted, and a crease in her cheek told me she was biting away at the inside of it.

We took turns to walk Vassilis' dog in the afternoons, and on the first Saturday I went with her. Her hair hung about her shoulders, and it was strange to see it out like that because she usually kept it in a bun.

Look, she said, I've been wanting to get out and have a talk.

We were walking down the steep hill that led up to the house, with only dry dust on the ground and trees around us. I had never seen her toes before, because we all wore hiking boots while digging. I watched them now, gradually getting dirtier through her sensible (yet still stylish) sandals. It was 4pm. My ears rang with the heat.

She opened her phone, and showed me a picture of my face on a dating app. The signal is shitty out here, she said, but I do manage to get on occasionally.

I had liked her profile, months before, just after we had met at the Christmas drinks. I wondered why it had taken her so long to see it.

That was ages ago, I said. I don't even have that app any more. I had to delete it before I came out here to make room for Skype.

I don't like drama, she said, returning the phone to the back pocket of her shorts, and taking the dog lead with her right hand again. I know you have a boyfriend. I don't need answers. I just… I want to know whether you're the sort of girl who only messages other girls when she's drunk, and then won't reply when they do.

I took her other hand abruptly. There was a small clearing through the trees by the side of the road; I'd noticed it before.

The air hummed with cicadas, still deathly bright under the glare of the sun. The heat would last for hours more. The trees provided little comfort as I drew her into the clearing with me, but the slightly dappled light meant I could take off my sunglasses and look at her straight on.

She took away her hand irritably. This isn't some sapphic intrigue, all these looks and little touches—

When I kissed her, she relaxed into me, and I twined my left hand in hers, my right at the back of her neck.

Thank you, she said, re-adjusting the lead in her hand. We'd better get a move on; the dog doesn't like to be kept waiting.

I was upset to see the skull, Nicole explained that night, because they just remind me of what people went through. I just hate the thought that we'll never know what happened to that person, you know?

Nicole had joined us on the porch, but she didn't want to play cards. She was sipping her wine nervously. I felt myself drinking fast, making up for the silences as Nicole talked endlessly about the skull. We tried to console her, reminding her that unexplained skulls did turn up on digs.

I hazily remembered another smudged night, the last time I had drunk like this. It had been after a fencing match. A hotel bar and a nasty bottle of Shiraz. I realised then that I hadn't called my boyfriend in five days, but it didn't bother me.

The bathrooms in the dig house were in the basement. In one, there was no demarcation between the rest of the floor and the shower, only a draining hole and a shower head right above.

The girls in the videos I watched were mostly anonymous, all apart from her, instantly recognisable because of her unusual first name. The title of the video was 'He surprised me with anal and I gushed SO hard', which made it seem more wholesome than it was. He grunted out her name as he asked, please, could he do it, and she said no, and then he kept doing it anyway. Come on babe, it feels so good. She had a tattoo above her hip, not visible at first because the focus was on her bum. Once she realised what he was doing, she turned around, and then you could see it. Her dark hair, her tattoo, her hands with the short nails tearing at him round the sides of the frame.

What I thought about mostly, while we were digging under the relentless sun, was whether I should tell her. Nicole interrupted my thoughts frequently, trying to get me to talk about Brexit or Trump or the environment or anything else normal. We were making our way painstakingly across the floorplan of the room that we had decided must be the kitchen because of the amount of pottery we'd turned up, even though we were pretty sure Roman kitchens weren't that big. From the video, it seemed clear that she objected to his choice of sex act, and also hadn't noticed that he was recording her. I had seen it enough times to be certain of that. But it wasn't clear if she knew now. And whether I should tell her raised all kinds of questions.

What are your boyfriend's fencing plans for next year? Nicole asked, when politics couldn't engage me.

He lost out in the final last year, I said, but I don't know what's next. I don't really keep up.

She laughed at me. You're so blasé about it. Have you seen that Ava Gardner movie, *The Killers*? I imagine you like her, watching Burt Lancaster from the sidelines.

My main memory is the Premier Inns, I told her, in a carefully constructed combination of droll and sardonic. I think I still have some of the teabags from the breakfast buffets.

I scraped the dry ground with my trowel, remembering instead the hotel room after the match, him coming to bed at 3am, pressing himself against me, the motion of it making me queasy, my head throbbing from the Shiraz. I'd borrowed the trowel from Eleni on the first day. We were told to bring our own if possible, so my mum brought me to B&Q to pick one out. It had never occurred to me that gardening trowels and archaeological trowels were not the same thing.

We've been talking about the weekend, Howell informed me at dinner.

I sat next to her, and accepted the top-up from the bottle. Eleni has suggested we go out to Nafplio on Saturday, she explained.

It's only an hour's drive, Katie said, or maybe ninety minutes. Anyway, it would be fun. We could spend the day at the beach.

The previous weekend had been sleepy, adjusting to the schedule of the dig, Nicole, Katie, and I going for a short walk on Sunday afternoon. This weekend had been built up in everyone's minds since the start, the one where we'd actually do something.

I stayed with Eleni last summer for a bit, she explained, after the dig closed up, and we had a pretty good time out there.

Their familiarity, her intimacy with Eleni's homegrown olives and her basic grasp of Greek, suddenly seemed treacherous.

Sure, I said. Well, maybe. I'll see how I feel. I have a headache building.

She squeezed my shoulder. Tell me if you need any painkillers. I have a full set, all the different kinds.

Have you read Agatha Christie's memoirs? she asked me later on, when the others had gone to bed. We were finishing our game of German Whist. The conversations we had at night after dinner were short, terse, about whatever we wanted to say at the time, easy to fit round a game of cards.

No, but I have them on my Kindle.

You should read the ones where she's on the digs with her second husband. They're really sort of evocative of this whole thing.

I've read *Murder in Mesopotamia*. Are the memoirs very different?

It's just the way she describes it all. The people, the close quarters, the… the little things. She smiled. Although their digs were pretty cushy by our standards. None of this beds-in-the-hall crap.

We went to a local museum today, my boyfriend told me on the phone. There were some Roman objects there—lamps and bowls and cups and even some intact glass bottles. It made me think of what you're doing now.

I thought of him easing his fingers into my bum, and the fact that I'd kissed him back and moaned because that seemed easier, even though his nails were long and jagged at the edges. I remembered how the headache had set above my eyes, the same straight-jacket, tightly-laced weight that I could feel now.

We've moved on, I told him. We're onto skeletons and murders now.

Christ. Speaking of which, I read the Donna Tartt book. *The Secret History*.

Well, now you know everything you need to about my kind.

I liked it a lot actually. Especially the bacchanals and everything.

All Classics students want to re-enact that novel on some level. We spend our entire degrees wondering how to go about it.

Should I be worried?

Incredibly.

What else have you been up to?

I thought about the afternoon in the clearing in the woods, when I had kissed her mouth and the light from the pool behind me glinted off of her necklace. Each time I thought of it, it seemed less and less plausible, but it seemed more likely that it had happened than the alternative.

After a day of digging, I explained, you're pretty exhausted.

*

On Friday morning, I woke early. I realised that in a week's time we would be leaving the house to catch a flight to Limoges, and she would stay here and continue to spend her evenings on the porch.

I found the video and read through some of the comments while I brushed my teeth.

That scream. Actually BELIEVABLE

4.37. We all bust then

When she turns round and you see the tramp stamp

I wondered what they would think if they knew her, if they saw how her wrists were filled out in a way that made her look like an adult, rather than my own twiggy joints.

Ana moved me to work with Howell, clearing rubble from unexcavated sections of the complex. We spent the morning dumping wheelbarrows of dirt into the pit at the back of the site. An elderly Sicilian man was helping us. He was retired, but working on the dig for fun. He had lived here (in the same village as Eleni) for decades. The first week, he'd brought us all an ice cream breakfast, which we ate out of the car boot in the still pale sunlight.

I'd kill to be half as fit at his age, Howell said, noticing me watching the Sicilian. I just don't understand how he can do it all.

The work was physical enough that it gave me an excuse not to talk. The headache had now settled firmly at my temples, pressing at the back of my skull, around my neck. I kept leaving my water out of the shade, so that when I went to drink it was already hot.

Do you need a painkiller? she asked me again, seeing me resting in the shade beside the dog.

I shook my head. I've taken some. It's just hard work today.

She nodded. And the heat's a killer too. Tell Ana if you don't feel well. She won't mind.

The others went to bed on the earlier side, gearing themselves up for an active Saturday. I asked her if she was going to go to Nafplio, but she shook her head.

I've been before. I'd rather stay here tomorrow. Lie in, get some reading done, maybe go for a walk.

I nodded stiffly, because each incline made my head throb more.

She met my eyes, and I wondered again if she remembered the afternoon in the clearing.

On our own on the porch, her breath smelled smoky, and it was easy to go from sitting side-by-side and playing piquet to kissing her. Her mouth was slightly clumsy with wine, which balanced out my dopey, headachy fumblings. Her short nails grazed against my skin, barely leaving an impression.

I ignored the pulsing in my head. Could put off dealing with it until I had to. Right now, there was no need for me to think. My hands were at her hips.

Can I—? I asked, not sure what I was asking for.

Yes, she said, as she readjusted herself. Her t-shirt rode up slightly as she did, brushing against me. The kind of cotton that I'd always found chafing. My fingers were almost exactly where her tattoo was in the video. I traced the shape of the Greek letters from memory. A pain shot through my head, and I got up.

She knelt on the bench cushion. Jesus, are you—?

I just feel really sick. It's my head, be back in a minute.

I made my way downstairs to the bathrooms, supporting myself with a shaking hand against the wall. The vomiting took over as soon as I'd reached the sanctuary of the toilet. Afterwards, I lay curled on my side, unable to tell what temperature I was between the cold tiles against my flushed cheek, the beads of sweat.

I forced my eyes open, even though the light burned them, and searched for the video again. I had to check one final time, make sure it was her. The picture quality, of course, wasn't great, but the combination of factors was too convenient, her unusual name and the tattoo of that particular Greek word. I paused to look at it, staring at the letters on a screen, the same ones I had actually touched only a few minutes before. I closed my eyes again.

Aoife? She had followed me downstairs. Fuck, Aoife, I'm so sorry. I'm so drunk it took me forever to realise how long you'd been gone, and—

She dropped down beside me, a gentle hand on my shoulder. Hey, you okay?

I managed to say some words about the headache, hoping she understood them. I pushed the side of my phone, trying to lock it, unable to find the right button. My eyes couldn't focus. I felt her taking the phone from me, my useless fingers still pressing weakly at the lock button.

Here, give that to me, and we'll—

She went silent. I knew she was looking at it, full-screen, paused, zoomed-in. I kept my eyes closed. I didn't want to see her face.

I felt her settle on the ground beside me, legs crossed. I knew the video off by heart, realised immediately that she was watching it through. Her voice was giddy to begin with, higher and younger than it was now.

I'd been drawn to her because she didn't seem to care what anyone else did, or what they thought of her. But after that night, she seemed to draw the others away with her. No one seemed to talk to me anymore, their conversation polite but always with a definite exit in sight. But then, I'd never been good at talking to anyone but her anyway.

At dinner, she had a knack for avoiding my eye when she passed around the pepper mill or the bowls of salad.

I found it in May, I'd explained to her. I had pulled myself up to sit with my back against the wall, able to rest my head on my knees when I wasn't talking. I found it one night when I was bored and I felt ashamed afterwards. I felt sorry for you.

I hated him for what he did, I said later on, after the silence. In my shower every day, I wonder about different ways to track him down. Maybe there's a way we could prosecute him or—I don't know—get him back.

Who is he, anyway? I think if I could understand why you were with him and why you had sex with him in the first place, I'd understand enough to figure out what to do next.

When she still didn't reply, I said: I'm a survivor too, you know, so I get it. I keep trying to forget it, but my boyfriend did something to me, last year, I mean like non-consensual, and I just let him do it, I even acted like I was into it. I had a migraine then too. I haven't told anyone. I haven't even mentioned it to him. Do you think I should? I know it's nothing like what happened to you.

Eventually, I tested my eyes. The harsh light of the bathroom made them water. She was still sitting beside me, on the floor, but her eyes were fixed on the screen. She was scrolling down the comments, and her thumb kept going.

At my boyfriend's parents' holiday house, he made a show of bringing my stuff up from the car, leading me to our bedroom. Then, he lay beside me on the bed, and kissed me for a long time, but without any expectation.

Never go on a dig again, he said.

You know you're always welcome to spend the summer with us, he said. If you want the sun.

I think I've had too much sun this holiday, I said, wincing. There was still a slight ache behind my eyes from the previous week's migraine.

The video is gone now. Maybe she reported it or found a way to delete it. I still search for it sometimes, to see if another copy exists, if someone else uploaded it. Just as a confirmation that she was a real person.

The evening I arrived, he opened a bottle of wine by the pool, where his friends were playing baccarat. We all knew each other slightly, but I was not as comfortable around them as they were with each other. They asked me lots of questions about the dig and the finds and the housemates, particularly the housemates.

When he stood up to get another bottle of wine, I stood too. I'm going to go to bed, I said, I'm exhausted.

There was general agreement that I shouldn't leave; the night was young.

I've been getting up at 6am every morning for the past three weeks, I reminded them. I'm not used to you rich people's decadence.

I'll come with you, my boyfriend said, stroking my arm affectionately.

Don't, I said, pushing my chair in. Enjoy your night out here. I shivered as I walked away, determined to establish my boundary.

Back in the room, I looked through all the books I had brought to Greece and hadn't touched. I looked out of the window, down onto the terrace where the three of them were still sitting. Bottles and cards and errant flip flops held in the crooks of their toes. It wasn't so different from my evenings on the porch with her. Those were the only parts of the dig that I'd really enjoyed anyway.

They will never know, I thought. I wasn't sure what they wouldn't know, but the idea that there was something comforted me. I took out my phone then, and searched for something to watch.

FEATURED POET

Padraig Regan is the author of two poetry pamphlets:
Delicious (Lifeboat, 2016) and *Who Seemed Alive &
Altogether Real* (Emma Press, 2017). They are currently
one of the Ciaran Carson Writing and the City Fellows at
the Seamus Heaney Centre, QUB. Their first book *Some
Integrity* will be published next year by Carcanet.

Poem for Bobby Kendall

who does not exist & who is lying on a bed
whose frame is a diorama of swans
advertising their monogamy. Whose robe
would be dangerously sheer if he

or his ass existed. Who is lousy with pearls
& dancing. Whose style would put to shame
the most libidinous of courting birds.
Who by the candelabra's orange light

is seductive as meringue & pliable as metaphor.
Who maps according to its johns the city
that does exist beyond the window
of the room he lives his made-up days inside.

O Bobby, the street is a rat's nest of contingency
& neon & steam from the subway grates.
A storm is blousing in from the mad Atlantic
& pitching the world to its own diagonals,

& Bobby, this is the least of our concerns:
the future is as futures often are
just history we haven't memorised
& I cannot say if you survived it.

The Understudies

All night some finches have disgraced themselves
by singing their desires through my open window;
I suggest we abolish the tree they're living in.
I have no desire to write about Laika, nor
the greyscale picture of the world she glimpsed
for five hours from a window, which, regrettably
was not left open. I want to write about the brave
& red-haired fox, the little bee, the starlet,
the coal, & the light breeze. I want to write
about Bobik, or the untamed substitute thereof
who ran like a joke around the barracks.
They who were subject to the same diet
of laxatives & jellied protein. It didn't help
that they were all, in temperament, phlegmatic,
& therefore Cancers, or Scorpios, or Pisces, though
the circumstances of their births went unrecorded
in the streets. Their mothers were abolished
because no-one & themselves desired otherwise.
They had seen some stuff & so Oleg Gazenko
thought they could bear to see some more.
I desire to abolish all desires & live
like a monk, divorced from the world.
I desire to be less sublunary. The secret
of their deaths was kept long past the abolition
of the state they died in service of.
It's hard to think Oleg Gazenko was a person
& desired. In 1998, he spoke
of this again; he said, 'we did not learn enough'.

Two Cabinets

There is a story behind the cabinets.
When I was young enough to climb inside the smaller one

I would. I was no bigger then than the smaller
of two cabinets my granddad helped to lacquer

when he himself was not much bigger than I was.
Not much happened then, & then a lot of things, but none

of this is the story behind the cabinets. No one
told it to me. Instead they'd say,

'there is a story behind these cabinets'
through the keyhole whose key was never found.

My granddad hunted rabbits by staging irresistible salads
on large, flat rocks, over-seasoned with pepper

so the rabbit's inquisitive sniffing would make it sneeze
& launch its eggshell skull into the rock.

This is a thing that happened. The cabinets are almost
as beautiful as the trees they used to be,

or so I like to think having never seen them.
It must have killed my granddad's granddad's horse

to lug those trunks out from the forest, or so
I like to think. It must have crushed their little cart:

I picture the barrel-tops repurposed for its wheels popping off
like champagne corks. Everything was something,

once. The air inside the cabinet grew small
around me. In those years meat was scarce.

9-Ball

Shane & Skyler & Jayson hear the crack
of Bakelite on Bakelite & Bakelite,
& don't watch as the balls run the course
that God determined in a quiet hour
before, even, we had made our first
rough stab at His invention.
They look at Skyler's phone & lift
their heads only to survey the leave,
briefly, & deem it good or bad, & don't
reveal their judgment to the camera.
Shane & Skyler & Jayson have no desire
to be a plot device, an obstacle, seemingly,
at first, impossible to overcome,
but overcome eventually, with grit, with luck,
with some contrivance in the second act:
a dead mentor's words remembered
at the moment of their greatest relevance
& understood at last, an undiscovered
reservoir of skill, a last-ditch push
to lift these years' weight of mediocrity.
But they know the game they play; they know
a hill is easier to tumble down than climb;
they know how breaks & run-outs run together
like some underachiever's syllables
in the post-match interview. & they know,
for now, they're safe in their folding chairs
in the audience in this small side room
in the stadium in Gibraltar, where you can hear
the planes take off from the nearby airport,
heading anywhere but Gibraltar.

History

Pink, & quivering-fresh, a two-inch strip
of salmon rests on a rice-pillow
with a sash of nori tied around its waist.
It sings against the green of what we cannot know

is real wasabi or horseradish dyed
with spinach. The windows fog & sweat
& on their other side umbrellas open
like the fleshy skirts that once

ringed the mouth of this anemone
I cannot wait to try.
It all comes served on a model boat—
28 cuts of mollusc & fish,

each one precise & gleaming on the wood.
Some lounge on the deck & some
have climbed the rigging where no sail
catches no wind & doesn't swell.

Surely there's a rock up by Lacada Point
where thirteen hundred Spanish ghosts
have crowded since 1588.
In 1270, Aquinas didn't ask

how many angels can dance on the head
of a pin, but four years later pilchards
turned to herring in his mouth.
I will not eat this octopus

on account of its ensoulment.
I'll go easy on the tuna on account
of the mercury marbled through its fat.
I'll cleanse my palate with ginger.

260 bodies washed ashore
& were buried at St Cuthbert's church;
nine more were shipped to Scotland
with their ghosts still in them,

which leaves a thousand rotting in the kelp.
What markets of worms & algae boomed
around them? What bones are reconfigured
in the shell this clam inhabited?

In 1967, the ghosts
that didn't leave the ship watched
as the world's first aquanaut dragged
their spilled mounds of gold to the surface.

Among the artefacts recovered
were astrolabes, brooches, crucifixes &c.
They are now laid out, precise & gleaming,
on velvet mounts in the Ulster Museum.

In 2014, the Glenavy River's
stock of fish sank to its bed,
like a dropped bag of coins,
like the record of a thousand wishes.

A year later, mackerel spilled
from a truck to the wet tarmac
of the Ravenhill Road, whose residents
ignored the warning not to eat them.

Their provenance was never ascertained.
Aquinas concluded that no one man
is strong enough to row a boat alone,
which is to say that even our ghosts

can't fill us. What isn't theft
now that even the seas are watered down?
I'm still hungry. I guess
this wasn't quite enough to share.

An Aesthetic Matter

Lanre Otaiku

Nanu and I agreed to meet for an intellectual conversation, much like the ones we'd seen in the French movies we'd been recommending to each other over the past year. We had developed a vigorous aversion to the Hollywood nonsense of our childhoods and thus were suitably inspired for this night of critical sparring. It was the last night of my holiday in Lagos and so we decided the city itself would be our subject, juxtaposed against Abuja, where I now lived. He was from Abuja but lived in Lagos, which is how we became friends to begin with, whereas I was from Lagos but had moved to Abuja a while back. We were to approach the entire exercise with no irony, even if it made us feel like a pair of pretentious pricks. This, of course, guaranteed me victory; there was nothing I knew better than pretending.

To prepare, I spent the hours before our meeting skimming from what were supposed to be philosophically consequential texts by an assortment of Eastern European existentialists. Nanu prepared by smoking a blunt. At least I assumed he did. I had no real idea how he got ready and, I'll be honest, I didn't care if he sourced his existential dread through marijuana or other means. The dynamic of our friendship had evolved such that, by that point, our mutual love was expressed not by how much interest we showed in the particulars of each other's lives, but by how much effort we put into impressing one another.

To that end I wore an outfit I had brought from Abuja for the specific purpose. A white buba and sokoto, starched stiff, ironed to the hilt. Gucci slippers, a gold chain and several gold and silver rings. Then I took one look in the mirror and threw it all off. Five minutes later I was in a variation of an outfit Nanu had seen on me almost every day for the year during which I had explained repeatedly that no, I simply liked how I looked, dressed in a black t-shirt and black jeans and black sneakers, and clothes were absolutely not a reflection of my inner life. I had similar explanations for my withdrawal from almost every social interaction, and my new, sudden quickness to tears whenever I heard the music of Joni Mitchell. I was fine! Nobody had to worry! I declined invitations to hang out, attempts to make me 'feel better' were summarily dismissed. I said all this so regularly and so firmly that I think I even managed to convince myself nothing was wrong, and, when the eventual breakdown happened, I was left neither feeling the bleak nothing my friends assumed to be the case, nor the predictable urge to shed uncontrollable tears, but instead a motley crue of emotions; my crushing and incapacitating self-loathing intermingled with an almost energising and all-consuming rage at the fact that my state of mind had been so obvious, so visible to everyone but me. God, I'd never felt so seen. But contrary to what people tell you, it's pretty fucking terrible to be seen. What's more awful than being reminded how mundane your suffering is, robbed of the solace that lies in that childish tendency to believe you're the first person to feel a feeling ever, to think of your pain and suffering as unique in all time and history? Insult to injury for me. I'd always prided myself on being able to hide my suffering.

Anyway, I got in my car in the hotel carpark and drove out onto a street filled with detritus that had been washed out of the gutter. Empty sachets of gin and pure water were strewn across the road as I drove down to the expressway and made the journey across town to meet Nanu. Twenty minutes later, I pulled up in a dark corner of the lounge's car park, a couple of spots from the lone floodlamp. I looked around at the security guards by the gate and figured my car would be safe, even in the dark. Then I remembered something from my last few months at the hospital in Lagos the previous year. I'd been on rotation in the emergency ward, the absolute worst, when a woman rushed in with flesh injuries. Many gashes on her left arm, so deep in one case you could see straight to her bone. One of the wounds caused a large flap of skin to hang in a way that made it look like you could open her up, like you could pick at it and it and her skin would keep peeling until you'd unwrapped her entire body. The story, as she told it, was that she'd been in traffic somewhere in Surulere. It had been her last night in the city, and she'd been hanging out with her friends. She was driving back to her hotel the night before going back home to Ibadan, and had just gotten to one of those traffic lights around the stadium when she heard the banging on her window. It took her a few seconds to figure out what was going on and even fewer seconds after for the guy, the *hoodlum*, to smash her window and demand her phone several times, a stab to her arm punctuating each word of his sentence. 'Your!' *Stab.* 'Phone!' *Stab.* 'Now!'

She'd been so seized with shock at the sight of her own blood that she remained unaware of the pain until the car behind her honked loudly. The blood stained everything, she said, from the door handle to the steering wheel, and the shock was quickly replaced by anger at how much money the car wash was going to charge her. It wasn't until she looked up, saw the traffic light was green, and sped off that she realised she'd been scared at all. And it wasn't until just then, telling us the story in the ward, that she realised she forgot to hand her phone over to the robber. I was curious about the mention of the traffic light. Would she really have stayed there, waiting for the light to turn green otherwise? What the patient herself found most unbelievable about the entire ordeal was that it had all occurred under a street light. 'Right under!' She repeated this part, over and over, like it was the most ridiculous thing in the world, and in that moment I was struck by her ability to be shocked by the sort of 'madness'—as she called it—that residents of the city like myself would be hard pressed to imagine a time without. In the parking lot, I drove my car over to the lamp, parked, and looked around for Nanu.

Nanu was already halfway through a bottle of Orijin when I walked into the lounge, which was less a lounge than it was really a large compound bordered to one side by a part of the Lagos Lagoon that was still mostly clean, so that the location wasn't plagued by flies like similar establishments in the area. We were in the aftermath of rain, and all around the moonlight made silver lakes of the shallow puddles that remained. I joined him at a table under a wobbly black parasol which swayed in the wind, doing little to protect from the drizzle. Nanu smiled, got up and shook my hand, then nudged me into a plastic chair, white and faded from years of use. A waiter in a black apron took my order and went to the bar at the far end of the lounge to get the beer I asked for. By the bar was a skinny singer dressed in leopard print shorts and a tank top, leading a band of instrumentalists who looked bored out of their minds. Nanu poured himself another glass of Orijin, holding the neck of the bottle to the tip of the glass, letting the gold liquid flow gently, then righting the cup as the lager's thick foam rose, tiny bubbles popping from the suds. The air was cool and damp. But then hot winds blew as well. Nothing was a certainty in Lagos, not even a cool breeze after rainfall. It was a contradiction that might have meant something under examination but in the moment, I was too struck by how meaningless it felt. It was a meaninglessness that felt oppressive on its own. There was nothing to be drawn from it. No poetry, no insight into the workings of humanity. But maybe that was its insight. Maybe in that way it represented something about the city—everywhere there was pain that served no purpose.

Nanu said he was tired so he would be a bit slow. His shift at the office had been draining. I told him to take his time. He lit a cigarette and looked at me with a smile.

'What?' I asked, and he waved the cigarette around. It smelled lighter than regular tobacco, and there was a faint tinge of mint to the smoke that almost made it sweet.

'No lecture about cancer this time?' he asked, and in response, I took a stick from his pack, lighting it with the end of his own cigarette. 'Oh,' he said. 'We're doing that now?'

I smiled. 'I quit the gym too,' I said.

'I take it you've completely purged it from your mind then,' he said. 'Like, you don't even miss it at all.' When I asked what he meant, he said, Medicine.

I thought about this for a moment. It wasn't enough to say that I didn't miss performing surgeries by the light of my phone, neither would it suffice to say that I physically *could* not miss the odd tightness in my chest that was so constant I was only ever reminded of its presence in those rare moments when I felt sudden and quick relief from it. But then I found the best way to put it.

'You know those stories,' I said, 'the ones about those surgeons who leave scissors and gauze and gloves inside the bodies of patients because they are so tired and overworked that they just forget?' Nanu nodded, and I said, 'Well, how am I supposed to miss a period in my life when I would hear such stories, and feel bad for the doctors, because I could see how that could easily have been me after any given 72-hour shift?'

'You make it sound like empathy is bad,' he said.

I said, 'For me it is. Empathy robs you of your right to look down on other people and what would life be like without that right? There are few greater liberties than the freedom to judge the mistakes of others.'

Anyway, we were to waste no further time. It was time for the debate. I went first, ready to rip Lagos to shreds and prove to Nanu why he didn't appreciate Abuja. As I aspired to an ideal of objectivity, or at least the appearance of it, I figured I would say some good things about Lagos first. Being that I spent the first 25 years of my life there, this was surprisingly difficult, but I managed.

I told him I thought Lagos could be beautiful at times, not just in the vague way you might get anywhere, like looking at a sunset on the beach or staring at birds flying in the sky or wet roads after night rain. And not just things like the Lekki-Ikoyi Bridge, either, things obviously designed to be beautiful (or at least not ugly). But just the whole... vibe, even though it required a conscious involvement. You couldn't passively appreciate Lagos, that was my stance. You needed to actively look past the ugly that typically followed the beautiful. Like that new 'I Love Lagos' sign, I said. The one I'd driven past at the jetty port, on Third Mainland Bridge, on my way there that night. It was my first time seeing it and it looked new. It was probably plain as day in the daylight but as I drove past it, it was a wonder of geometry and light, the way the colours seemed to glide over the surrounding water. Metres away from it were heaps and heaps of trash, literal scraps of plastic and paper and dilapidated wood. But that too was supposed to be part of the beauty of Lagos in general, according to my argument. Suffering beside comfort.

Nanu said it wasn't suffering. It was life. The kind of life only to be found in the most populous Black city in the world. I told him I suspected that such a concentration of black people anywhere could only be a bad thing, and he declared that this was evidence of my inherent self-hatred and internalisation of the ideals of whiteness. This was the result, he said, of a childhood spent with my nose buried in novels written almost exclusively by Caucasian authors. I didn't debate this. He took a sip of his drink.

'It's not easy, sure,' he said, 'but there's nowhere like Lagos.' He declared Lagos was incomparable: the 'energy,' the hustle, the bustle, the madness, the combination of sweat and Oud that characterised Friday nights out. It was all sentimental nonsense to my ears. It was clear to me that growing up in Abuja had stripped him of appreciation for that city's virtues. Moving to Lagos for medical school, he had retained that wide-eyed fascination with the city's excesses that people from outside tend to have. If you ask me, I told him, it was a coping mechanism.

'Haven't we heard this all before?' I asked him. Only in Lagos could you see poverty and wealth side by side; only in Lagos could you go from zero to hero in a day. Hadn't the same trite sentiments been expressed all through history about London and New York and just about every other urban metropolis whose residents tried to mask their hatred for its dysfunction by pretending there was poetry to be found in it?

'There's poetry to be found in everything,' Nanu said. I rolled my eyes and he reminded me that there was to be no irony. That was the agreement.

'Sure,' I said. But, I told him, I struggled to see the beauty in kids hawking drinks in traffic to people in Range Rovers. Nor did I grow up finding anything particularly poetic in the old woman with six kids on my street living in a shanty beside the mansion owned by the young man rumoured to have landed a windfall by executing a credit card scam against a middle-aged cat lady in the American midwest.

'None of that is unique to Lagos,' he said. 'There's suffering everywhere.'

'Well *my* suffering is only in Lagos,' I said. 'I hate it. I hate Lagos.'

I said it with the intention of sounding jokey and blasé, but I failed, as such attempts often did in his presence. Around him my tendency was to experience myself as an abstraction, if that's the word. My true feelings were always sure to be drawn out. Many were the times I had made a statement with the intention to sound exaggerated and deliberately absurd, only to hear my own words leave my mouth with an earnestness which I would immediately realise was not a miscalibration of tone but an expression of the true state of affairs. That I had revealed feelings I had not only not been ready to share, but in many cases had been completely unaware I was feeling in the first place. My friendship with him was like an involuntary therapy session, or like being force-fed truth serum. Maybe both. Better yet neither. Ours was a friendship that stripped all metaphor of its potency.

We fell into a silence filled with terrible jazz music from the band. The singer seemed to be approaching the night with the intention of establishing just how many 80s American pop classics could be butchered in one 30-minute interval. People ate grilled catfish and cheap beer and Isi Ewu. It was part of the appeal of places like this. It was like an upscale approximation of the local 'joints' on the other side of town where I had grown up. Nanu and I had come here a few times during medical school and we came to the conclusion it was designed for people to enjoy that peculiar brand of ingenuity unique to entertainment borne of lack, while still having plenty. It's for rich people who want to feel poor, he said once, before correcting himself and saying it was for people who used to be poor but are now rich but feel bad about it.

There were kids around dressed in perfect expressions of this. Deliberately faded shirts and distressed jeans. Hair that in the precision of its roughness belied just how much it cost to maintain. 'Vintage' jewellery that was likely bought off American retailers on the internet. Nanu and I looked around and locked eyes as certain people passed, sharing smiles in place of the heavy laughs we would have indulged in just two years earlier. But there was something hollow in our silent mockery. We both knew, I thought, that we couldn't pretend anymore. We had different financial struggles now. We had become the sort of twenty-somethings whose planned trips across Europe fell apart not because we couldn't afford them, but because we were unable to make the time. There we were, eating terrible food at that lounge, pretending we were still in touch with our old selves. We had reached a point in our lives when poverty had become, for us, too, purely an aesthetic matter. We had become those pricks.

For one, my job in Abuja meant that I got paid more than I ever did in Lagos. Nanu had also gotten a job in some kind of medical consultancy think-tank, getting paid an armed robber's salary, a matter which gave him great grief. It was great to have money and to know you wouldn't lose patients because there was no oxygen in the hospital, he said. But still.

'Still,' he said. 'It feels kind of obscene. I go to work, do my job, and go to sleep at night. I don't have to do any work to detach mentally or emotionally from patients. I don't even see patients. I'm so happy about it. But it feels wrong to be happy about it. Being outside that whole system now, I feel kind of useless because I know how bad it is. I know how desperately the medical system needs people who care. But being in it also made me feel useless because no matter how much we cared, no matter how much we tried, it was never enough. But it feels wrong to enjoy life this much.'

I told him I knew what he meant. That was why I loved Abuja. I felt so ordinary there.

'That's cos you are ordinary by Abuja standards!' he said, laughing.

'Exactly!' I said. On any given night I could be out and see this son of that governor or that daughter-in-law of a descendant of a slave trader buying out the bar. It was painful sometimes, yes, seeing all these reminders of the sort of wealth I knew I could never reasonably amass, but they were also a welcome reprieve from thoughts of people for whom my own meagre wealth represented a similarly unattainable ideal. Even though I was broke in Lagos, there was so much poverty around that I could never forget the fact that whatever little I had was more than most people would ever see in their entire lifetimes. But why did I spend so much time feeling bad about rolling up my windows, my air-conditioner on full blast to block out the sweaty hawkers and beggars in Lagos traffic, when over in the capital there were kids half my age whose idea of small talk was bragging about how many billions their daddies were making from the new roads they'd just been contracted to build? I'd seen them, partied with them, slept with a couple of them, done several kinds of drugs with them. Even with my new job and my 200% salary increase, it brought me unique comfort to know I was and would always be nothing compared to them.

The wind blew, warm and heavy. But I found I didn't mind it. I was watching my friend, who I knew was aware I was watching him. He was looking everywhere else, swaying his shoulders gently to the music, and I was enjoying his enjoyment. I took a sip of my beer, feeling the breeze rush past my ears. The air was filled with the smell of everything; grilled fish, suya over the flames, roasting corn. I could see everything on the bridge over the lagoon; the red tail lights winking in the dark, the people jogging beside the cars, the regular chaos at the toll gate with buses fighting to cut in line. Now and then, while with someone like Nanu, someone I loved, I could see all of it for what it was. I could, somehow, neither love it nor hate it, but view it as proof of life. Life was happening all around, and that meant something, however small.

Beside us the lagoon water lapped at the fence in sudden, swift movements, as if earth itself had been knocked off-balance, caught unaware by some force of the night. The jazz singer reached for notes even further out of her range. The surface of the water went up in sudden bright yellow flames. The fire licked at the night air, struggling for balance on the water's edge. A crowd gathered just as quickly as the people by the fence drew back; someone said there had been oil on the surface and this was the quickest way to get rid of it. Someone else made a comment about aquatic life being endangered and another person said anything that could survive in that dirty water to begin with was something we probably all wanted gone anyway.

'So you love it there, then,' Nanu said. It was close to midnight and we were walking to the car park. 'You don't even miss Lagos?' He smiled as he said this but I could see that he wasn't trying to trip me up. It was a genuine question.

'I miss you all the time, if that's what you're asking,' I said. He told me I didn't have a choice in that matter. But about Abuja, I said, I wasn't sure that I loved it, but it had surprised me. He knew I had only really gone there because I needed to get away from Lagos. I hadn't expected to feel anything there. People always said Abuja had no soul because it was too peaceful, and, on some level, I believed it. I hadn't expected the kind of freedom that was waiting on the other side of accepting my own selfishness. I hadn't expected anything really, except maybe a sugar mummy, because the city was rumoured to be filled with them and surely there was one of them who had a thing for fat boys? But I had instead found financial security and the joys of indiscriminate sex. I had found friendship with people for whom certain drugs were a casual enough indulgence.

We hugged as we got to my car, and he called it a tie, even though I had used up most of the speaking time. We hugged again and said goodbye, but then we sat by my car and continued talking for a few minutes. He told me he was secretly working on something. Not secretly, but in his free time. And he wasn't actively working on it, he was just going over it in his mind. A theory, he said, about modern Nigerian society. At least 'us young ones', he said. We were undergoing a new form of colonialism. I thought he was referring to the mortgaging of infrastructure all over the continent, which conventional wisdom presented as a nefarious plot by the Chinese government. Which, I have to say, I didn't really care about. But Nanu explained he had something else in mind. We were in the process of a unique form of neocolonialism, he said. A particularly insidious strain as the war was being waged with no violence but with ideological subterfuge.

'Everywhere you go in Lagos,' he said, 'people are arguing about being "progressive" or "moderate". About being republicans and democrats. Republicans! In Lagos! The other day someone in my office told me I was "regressive" and history would "leave me behind" because I didn't know the meaning of gerrymandering. I'm a fucking surgeon—well, ex-surgeon, whatever—and I'm supposed to feel bad because I don't know something that has literally zero to do with my life. Bro! What the fuck does gerrymandering mean to this Sub-Saharan African?'

I groaned, but there was no stopping him once he got started like this. We were drowning in the culture wars of a continent across the ocean, he continued. Even the expression 'culture wars' made him sick, he told me. In fact, he craved unique ways to express how profoundly stupid he found it.

Like our mothers would. This, I could get behind. The insults of a Nigerian mother were, in my view, one of life's great literary offerings, containing a poetry surpassed only by Russian novels.

He continued talking, and I zoned out a little. It was exhausting when he started talking about politics. But in a way, I think it was envy on my part. He paid such close attention to things, a scrutiny I found aspirational, and I thought about how it must feel to find life worthy of such attention. What would it be like, I wondered, to live life this way, believing strongly in things? Believing strongly enough in yourself to allow yourself to believe in things?

'This is worse than when they forced English on our ancestors,' he continued. 'This time, we're doing it ourselves. We are willingly adopting their maxims, the parameters of their allegedly moral structures, all for what? Is it impossible for us to develop our own framework of thinking?' he asked. 'I'm telling you,' he said. 'We are being recolonised. A colonisation of the intellect. People need to open their eyes. In fact, we have already been recolonised.'

'About time,' I said. 'They never should have left.'

His jaw dropped, he laughed, and he hugged me again.

As he walked over to his own car, in the light of the flood lamp, I suddenly realised what he was wearing. It was a black t-shirt with black jeans and black shoes.

Making the drive back to the hotel, I stopped at a traffic light. It was directly beside a street lamp, and I was reminded again of the woman from the hospital. I looked around, saw no human with a knife or any kind of weapon. To my left on the pavement, however, was a mound of waste. Clothes, maybe. In the shadow of the light from the lamp, it looked like a head enlarged to several times its size, like a head with several head-shaped outlines drawn around it, some kind of vortex through which I found myself hurtling, landing somewhere weeks and weeks earlier, back in Abuja, around the same time I'd decided I would spend the two weeks of my break from work in Lagos. It was about eleven months into my time in the city and I was at a club with some co-workers. We took a break outside and I watched them smoke. We found ourselves on an abandoned balcony that overlooked a section of a lake bordered by small trees and bushes. I saw some children, maybe five of them. They were climbing out of the lake, laughing, dressed in torn clothes, with no shoes, the picture of the sort of thing I saw used in certain media quarters as examples of the unquenchable happiness and contentment of Africans. I didn't think much of it. They could easily have been rich children who wore those clothes to swim because they found novelty in it. Of course believing this would require ignoring the obvious fact of how bony they were. Suffering was written on their bodies. But then skinny children weren't such a rarity that poverty was the only explanation. Couldn't they be rich and skinny? Or at least not-poor and skinny. I was unwilling to have this debate with myself. I was also too high to think straight. My eyes stayed on the children anyway. They were the kinds you'd never really see on Abuja roads. And they did seem happy, playing with a rubber doll which had one empty eye socket and a head somehow inflated, maybe by water. Maybe the current of the lake flowed through the ears and the nose of the doll, working the remaining eye from behind, spinning it round and round, or maybe it really was the weed because, in my mind's eye I could see the doll's head enlarged too, and I got a clear view of its own eye such that it too was like a vortex into which I fell, and from that lake in Abuja I found myself back in the hospital, almost a year before that, the day I finally quit.

It had been one of those rare days when my lunch break and Nanu's synced. We met up at a barbecue place around our quarters in the teaching hospital. We ate half of our food and both lost our appetites. I pointed out that our mothers would be appalled and Nanu said he might take the rest of the food for *her*. Then he caught himself and said, 'Sorry, she's not eating solid food yet. I'm not sure why I said that.'

'Who isn't eating solid food?' I asked.

'A patient,' he said. 'A baby.' She'd been born with an enlarged head, he went on to explain. It was Hydrocephalus. Then he asked if I had money to spare, he was trying to get some stuff for her as her parents had fled when they found out about her condition. I said I didn't, I'd just used the last of my cash to fix my car's air-conditioning. Then I asked why we couldn't just aspirate such babies.

'Just put a needle into the head and drain out the fluid.'

I was joking, but Nanu didn't smile. He said he just wanted money for her upkeep; it didn't need to be much. It would only be necessary for about a week anyway. I was confused, and then I saw him wipe a tear.

'Hey,' I said, 'are you okay?'

'I'm fine,' he said. 'It's just, she has no hope, you know? No hope at all.'

'So she's definitely going to die,' I said, and Nanu nodded and wiped another tear. I felt something sink within me, and then I laughed, softly, instinctively, trying to sound light, make him feel better. 'Guy,' I said, 'take it easy.' I wiped another tear off his face. 'We see stuff like this all the time, don't we?'

It was hearing the words leave my mouth that did it. They didn't sound jokey or blasé. They were my true feelings. I had seen too much to care. I felt a wave of horror rush through me as I wondered why I wasn't as horrified by the situation as Nanu was, wondered if I had become so messed up by my work, the whole system, that I had effectively become numb. And then came a second wave, horror overtaken by disgust for wondering how I could even have the space to think or care about my own 'numbness' when a child was to die.

And then I heard honking from the cars behind me, the noise like a touchstone, pulling me back out of that vortex and sending me back to Abuja before I was sent back through the other vortex, slamming me back into my body, in my seat, in my car, seeing as, drawn too by the noise of the honking, the head-shaped mound of clothes turned to look and turned out to be an actual head, on an actual child, sat beside a tray of groundnuts on which was placed a textbook which she read in the light from the lamp. And then this sent me back again, back to awareness of that tightness in my chest again, this time not from relief but from some kind of congealed anger at *something*, for what I was seeing, what I shouldn't be seeing. And just like that, it was gone. I felt lightness, I felt freedom, I felt certain I had the answer because I knew the answer. The cars continued honking, and, middle finger in the rear view mirror, I drove off, thinking, this was it, this was the answer—not roads, not sugar mummies, not cocaine, this was what Abuja had over Lagos—it knew how to keep its suffering hidden.

Swimming

Sandra Hoffmann

Translated from the German by Katy Derbyshire

There's a photograph of my grandmother Paula where she's standing in a lake, in a bathing suit. The water comes up to her middle, no higher, and she's wearing a rubber ring. And although I see her wearing it in the picture, I don't believe she ever took her feet off the ground to float on the water in that rubber ring. My grandmother couldn't swim. When I'd come home from the swimming pool as a child, she would admire my brown back, my brown neck. You're so nice and brown, she'd say. And I'd say: From swimming.

My mother can't swim either. When we were children she would stand in the shallow end with us while we'd splash about practising. Deep water frightened her. I imagine everyone who can't swim is afraid of deep water. My mother wanted us children to lose our fear of deep water. She wanted us to learn to swim; it was very important to her. And although she was always a little embarrassed that she couldn't, she came with us to the open-air pool every day in summer. Sometimes to the one in the next village that didn't have a blue-painted base, one where you couldn't see the bottom at all. It was called a natural swimming pool, and my mother would stand in the hip-high non-swimmers' section and sometimes take a stroke. Perhaps she even managed three or four per session. It was her way of showing how much she loved us children. As far as I remember, she never wore a rubber ring.

A few years ago—my mother has rheumatoid arthritis, and her joints are often terribly painful—she told me on the telephone: If it doesn't get better I'll walk straight into the water. I knew what that meant. My mother would leave the shallow end. Head for the deep water, against her fear.

My grandmother before her was afraid of deep water. Fear can be inherited, I'm sure of it. Once a fear has lodged itself in a family it's hard to get rid of it. And yet I believe fear behaves in a more linear way. Women pass on fear to women. Men pass the rules on to men. Be strong, don't cry. That was how it was when my brother and I were little, anyway. My brother can swim but not particularly well (he's not afraid, though). I'm a very good swimmer. I can swim a very long way. I like crossing lakes. I love standing on one bank, looking across at the other side and thinking: that's where I'll get to if I simply take stroke after stroke; it will be a while but I'll manage it. Then I start swimming. I tie a rubber ring to my upper arm and let it float after me. That way boats can spot me, but all the people by the lake can also see there's someone swimming. It makes me feel safe. If I got cramp, there'd be a life raft tied to me; I won't lose it. And yet, swimming in lakes calls for the greatest non-fear (or at least the second-greatest; swimming in the sea is probably a very different matter, with very different options for fear). The challenge with lake swimming is the darkness of the lake, the lake's milkiness, its impenetrability. There are very few lakes where you can see the bottom. It's on the bottom that the fish live, though, the ones the anglers talk about, their legends. Sheatfish as big as sharks, or nearly; carp that can't tell the difference between human feet and fish, and bite into them. Sea monsters, like Nessie. Leeches live in those lakes that you can't get to the bottom of (not with the naked eye, at least). I love swimming in the lake because it's different every day. The wind direction changes, the wind force, and that changes the force of the waves, the restlessness of the water's surface and where the current comes from.

My favourite lake is the Simssee, the little brother of the Chiemsee. It's Germany's third-largest lake, 1.5 kilometres wide at the crossing point. If you swim back and forth you cover three kilometres. Depending on which side you start from, on the way out or back you see a little church in a little village close to the lake, up on the hillside, and behind it the mountains. Kampenwand, Wilder Kaiser. Or perhaps you can't see the Wilder Kaiser from there. I know more about swimming than mountains. If you swim in the other direction, you see a bathing spot and a bathing raft in the water, a small sailboat marina and houses belonging to a handful of people lucky enough to be able to swim in the lake every morning.

One day when I was ten or eleven and still a modest swimmer, we met Frau Picard at the swimming pool. Frau Picard was a colleague of my father's who'd just retired, and we spotted her swimming length after length of the blue-tiled pool. Fifty metres in one direction and fifty metres in the other. I've no idea how Frau Picard came to say: Do you want to swim lengths with me? All I remember is how low I lay in the water in the first few days, how hard it was to keep my head above the surface, breathe evenly, stretch my arms out evenly, make them trace a big curve and then pull them back in. How difficult it was for both my legs to make the same movement, because one leg always wanted to make its own movement (that leg's the same to this day). I remember Frau Picard's calming voice, a yoga-like voice as she swam calmly beside me, making me think: She's the kind of woman I want to be one day!

Frau Picard seemed old to me, as a very young girl, but not too old to be a very good swimmer. I can't remember how many days, how many weeks I swam at the pool with Frau Picard, back and forth and untiring. I do remember the effort growing less, my arms and legs beginning to take the movements for granted, my neck no longer hurting, my body floating on the water like a seaworthy boat. Frau Picard became my coach. First we trained for the bronze swimming badge, for which you had to swim for fifteen minutes, dive from the edge of the pool and fetch an object from a depth of two metres. Frau Picard stood on the edge of the pool and cheered me on. By then I was already wearing a proper swimming suit, onto which my mother ironed the swimming badge. I remember being pretty hooked, and I think Frau Picard was too. Together, Frau Picard and I managed the silver swimming badge and of course the gold one too. For the gold badge, you had to swim eight hundred metres in half an hour and perform several dives and rescue tasks. All my swimming badges were ironed onto my swimsuit. The suit itself was a trophy. From today's point of view, the badges seem easy to achieve. At the time, though, they were the first major victory on the way to the woman I wanted to be: a woman unafraid of deep water, a woman who swims lengths.

These days, I think swimming is a little like running, except that your arms do most of the work. I've left the marked-out lanes when it comes to running, too; I like running in the park, looking at and listening to the ducks and birds, the dogs and their owners. I like it when the paths empty out, when the park shifts shape to become nature and I can look out into the distance.

In summer, when it's warm, I sometimes swim in Munich's Isar River. I swim against the stream because there is no swimming with the stream: you get carried along. I have to work hard to swim against the stream; the current is strong and sweeps me along the instant I stop concentrating on my swimming strokes. So I lie down facing the current and instantly start taking powerful strokes: one, two, a hundred. The water is pretty cold, and swimming in it is harder work than in a lake, but it's wonderful. After about a hundred strokes, I've been swept at least three metres backwards, but that doesn't matter. I go on swimming. I fix my eyes on the magnificent turn-of-the-century swimming baths, the Müllersches Volksbad, and I tell myself as an incentive that I don't want to lose sight of it. I know it won't work, but that doesn't matter. I keep swimming until I've lost sight of it. Then I get out of the river, always thinking of all I would miss if I weren't such a good swimmer.

3 Songs of Separation & Proximity

1

reputation
masks a rote completion
of the tasks assigned
once memorised
alongside
lamentations
for the wasted evenings
spent
deciding
on appearing
in an open doorway
to rut
commence enclosure
long before attempts
to enter joy
repeated efforts
at depressing
all the mechanisms
for retreat
are not required
one thrust will do

2

upon getting
enmeshed anew
forgetfulness returns
regards approval
standing
needs no posture
and the patience of the fool
who knows no better
than to think
of strength renewed
or plastered over
as immune
to deprivation
a wound
some slight in voice
discomfort with complaint
a rearing horse
a bull
a cow
some otters crossing fields
just out of sight

3

maternity despairs
on understanding anger
sadness better understood
protection
and obsession
wandered lanes
take up the slack
of introductions
breakdowns happen
at the end of weeks gone by
during which the thought occurred
that nothing really happened
stick back
exchange a friendship for a train
diverted
or mistaken
as the one for keeping time
exchange a walk for fractures
given into mud
attendance with machines
to indicate the liveliness

of your own body
a memory of plaster
a memory of noting what was wrong
and hoping then that other things
were too
one's head or foot
or diaphragm producing
mottled vocals
instead of what was
indicated properly
instead of sadness understood
in disappointment with the product
of a union
then disregarded
in an arable environment
within a wasteland
located amiably
located after hatred took a hold
for far too long

Alan Cunningham

all the small things
I'm glad
you're interested in
all the big things

rumour
is a first ███████
with no photograph

there is a pace
it is a of labour
the foot is lifted
and laid
with resolution
as if the earth
were coming up
to meet it

it returns
it greets
and pushes away
centuries
and minutes

it moves

my cough today
is more like my father's
than my uncle's
that's good
one lived

Archimedes stole thunder
from the labourer
he named it

a shovel
        is not
                a spade

you didn't have to
        read or write
                to know the difference

choice words
Blaah blahblah
IIIIIII
        you you you you
they they they they
saynosayyes

mind your own business
mind the business of others
language will ▮▮▮ you in the head
and still

a shovel is not a spade

her skin her skin is her skin
however it'spelt
if you don't want to own it
to cut around the wrists and pull
then leave her skin
with your eyes and your tongues and your words
that break no bones

because a shovel is not a spade

and you have no right to her right

s'pelt shovel
s'pelt spade
s'pelt right
s'pelt wrong
skin
is where it stops
is where it starts
it's so much intrusion
you think it's about one thing
then it's another

the shovel remains in the wheelbarrow
the spade in the field
it's a drain
but the ear has
always loved
the blackbird
the linnet
and the thrush

round up all the cuckoos
smash all their eggs
it's terrible what they do
send them off to England
for love
for lo'ove for lo've for love

Aodán McCardle

The Mountain Lion

JL Bogenschneider

Ralph and Sam had become obsessed with tracking and hunting the mountain lion, which had been a hot topic round these parts for some time. Ralph was my brother and Sam was our uncle, except that he wasn't, he was sort of our stepdad, but Eileen—who was our mother—asked us to call him our uncle, because nothing was ever straightforward with her. As a result, people often thought that Sam was Eileen's brother-in-law and that they'd married following the departure of our father, but it wasn't that way at all. Anyway, the truth is they weren't married because Eileen and our father didn't divorce immediately; it took years for us to get away from him like that.

Ralph and Sam spent a lot of time in the garage where they'd mapped out sightings of the mountain lion on a sheet of parchment paper spread out across and pinned to a workbench that Sam had borrowed from a neighbour. My Collins Junior Dictionary defined borrowing as being temporary and with the owner's knowledge, which didn't seem to apply to Sam, like the time he borrowed his brother's canoe, or a rake from a neighbour to draw gravel across the yard. He and Ralph sketched out an approximation of the town and it was Ralph's job to decide which sightings were verified (a green X) and which were only rumoured (a red X) although the truth is that everything was hearsay. They spoke of tracking and hunting and I wanted no part in the hunting of an animal, but wouldn't have minded so much if they'd included me in the tracking part.

Eileen wasn't interested in anything other than her nascent dress-making business. She spoke of infrastructure and business plans in the same way that

Ralph and Sam discussed tracking and hunting and she thought I should take as much interest in it too, shaking her head in despair whenever I declined to assist, which was always. Whenever Ralph and Sam were in the garage and Eileen was in the kitchen, I lay on my bed and read my Collins Junior Series. For all their planning, Ralph and Sam never went out to look for the mountain lion. Eileen didn't even have a sewing machine.

Most years we'd take a vacation, but that year there was no money to go away with. Besides, Eileen didn't want to take time off from her business and Sam was a caretaker for the local college, and so had hours to keep. In this way, the mountain lion became a kind of break to us, a respite from reality. Ralph and I didn't have friends—school or otherwise—to hang out with; despite moving to Anarene over a year before, we were still new, yet to be accepted. For me, the southern air was too much. I was used to cool coastal breezes and wet seasons derived from an adjacent mountain climate. Anarenean air assaulted me, dried me out, and the summer months were relentless. After the third week of frustrated sleep, I started going out at night.

The first recorded sighting of the mountain lion was in January. Someone heard an intruder in their back yard and when they went out to investigate, they disturbed what they subsequently described to a reporter for the *Sentinel* as a 'huge, panther-like thing. Six feet at least. Muscley [*sic*] too. Well fed. And unafraid'.

The report was reproduced and syndicated but the *Sentinel* remained the primary source of most reports, eventually running a 'Cat Scratch Fever' column after the seventh sighting in early March, which was also when the regional press and a few TV teams began to take an interest. My Collins Junior Encyclopedia said cat scratch fever was a bacterial disease, but I understood why the *Sentinel* misused the phrase because Sam often played the record.

Ralph and Sam scrapbooked the *Sentinel* and other newspapers obsessively, cataloguing sightings by date, but also sub-categorising them by reliability: whether they were first or second person accounts, visual or audio sightings. Most of what I learned came from conversations at dinner, or Ralph's excitable elucidations in bed before he fell asleep: the heat had no impact on him. I barely read the papers and couldn't concentrate on TV news for more than a few moments; my entire knowledge of current affairs that summer can be summarised as: *many mountain cat sightings in Anarene; Rialto refurbishment overruns; women warned to stay away from North Capote Street after dark; Anarene's*

oldest resident dies aged one-hundred and one; Wesson's Woolworth celebrates its
centenary with luncheons for one hundred lucky families.

We were one of the aforementioned lucky families and got to eat at
the top of the Woolworth Tower, which revolved slowly, affording us a
panoramic view of Anarene from the downtown zone where we ate to the
suburban streets further afield, followed by the sporadically located duplex
communities where we lived, and then the wide-open flats that became the
horizon. There was nowhere, it occurred to me—teasing a fast-melting sundae
apart to the background clink of other diners and the slow, wheezing strain of
the restaurant's mechanism—where a mountain lion might reasonably have
come from. I brought this point up to the table but was met with a stony
glare from Sam and a complex, condition-heavy explanation from Ralph that
involved some sort of ecological shift and hypothetical dry seasons in the
nearest mountains, which were a good hundred miles away at least. Eileen
was in her own world, staring out the window, dreaming of all the dresses
she would sell once her business was up and running.

We were experiencing a heatwave and the tourists, whose numbers had
increased following a feature about the mountain lion on the national news,
had beaten a retreat. Until then, Ralph and Sam had been offering guided
tours of mountain-lion hotspots which they'd identified from extrapolation of
their data. Ralph had made a foldable map and sold them for a dollar, taking
advantage of his picture-book cute. Then Sam would lead small groups
around town, pointing out the back yards and dumpster areas the mountain
lion had been seen in, as well as other places of interest, which were mostly
the downtown stores. Not once did the tour groups see anything beyond the
everyday and so even though Sam had Ralph go round with an actual cap in
his hand, no one ever ponied up because they'd already paid a dollar each for
the map and the whole thing—I'd heard someone say at the lunch counter,
later—seemed like a cheap trick to drum up trade for local business.

But so it was hot. Like I said, I'd taken to walking into town and back during
the night to take advantage of the marginally cooler air. These excursions had
the added bonus of tiring me to the extent that I had no choice but to sleep
until late morning. Eileen attributed my lethargy to adolescence; no one, not
even Ralph, knew what I was doing. Anarene's nightlife was non-existent
after midnight and the roads into town and the suburbs they passed through
were dead. The town remained lit up though, even the underfurbished Rialto,
and it looked for all the world like an abandoned fairground.

The night after the luncheon at the Woolworth Tower, I went out with one of Ralph's maps and the old Halina that Sam had borrowed from the college. I didn't believe there was a mountain lion because my Collins Junior Encyclopedia said reports of big cats in unexpected locales were often explainable as coyotes or unreliable and/or fallible sightings. But no one in our family was living up to their potential and I wanted one of us to be able to show for something.

I went out, again and again, paying attention to the conversations that Ralph and Sam had, making a mental note of the location of the most recent sightings and visiting those areas at night. During these excursions I became familiar with the layout of downtown Anarene in a way that would have been impossible in the daylight, when my bearings would be confused by people. I learned where the winos went at night and knew to avoid those areas, although their tendency to eat and discard their food in the same places suggested a prime scavenging hotspot for the feral. I walked all the way across town and back again, circumnavigated it, zigzagged through its streets, learned its cul-de-sacs and shortcuts and began to understand the vague boundaries between downtown and suburban Anarene and its outlier zones. I chased shadows and took spontaneous photos of foxes and skunks in dumpsters, clusters of birds disturbed from sleep by the *click-flash-whirr* of the Halina and, on North Capote, a tall man in a coat and hat who exposed himself, and I was halfway down Penton and Pike before he realised what I'd done. Later, I told Ralph I'd seen the mountain lion lurking around town, but he didn't believe me.

The heat wave abated, and it became easier to sleep, just as I'd taken to staying awake. I fought fatigue as Ralph talked about everything he and Sam had worked on each day: they'd calculated the route the mountain lion took as it stalked the streets; they'd postulated that it lived in the desert and made its way into Anarene at night; they strongly suspected that our house was on its path and were planning on setting a baited trap, or digging a pit. I didn't care and I cared. I didn't want to hear about the mountain lion and I did.

Ralph kept talking up the reward they'd get for capturing it. No one had offered one, although the *Sentinel* was prepared to pay out fifty dollars for a verified photo. In that sense, I'd come closer than anyone, but the Halina was hidden in my desk and wasn't going anywhere. Every so often I had to remind myself that there *was* no mountain lion, but that this wasn't a notion to disabuse Ralph of. So I said nothing and—inevitably, uncontrollably—fell asleep most nights to his excited hypotheses, and if he ever noticed, then he didn't care.

One night I woke up around two a.m. There was a scuffling in the yard; the garbage cans had been disturbed and there existed the air of something trying to remain perfectly still. Ralph had left the lamp on and I turned it off, quickly. There was more movement, the sound of something creeping across the same gravel Sam said would be cheaper than an intruder alarm, but no one got out of bed to check.

I understood what it meant to have a thumping heart, suppressed the urge to yell, 'Villain! Dissemble no more!' I stood behind the threadbare curtains, convinced that even in the dark I'd be seen. Maybe it was the same for the creature outside. The window was open and I tried to detect the scent of a wild, pheromonic animal, heavy breathing or a low growl. There was nothing. But, in time, there came a growing awareness of the no-silence of the night: crickets rustling, occasional owls, a smothered cough, the dopplered engine of a truck reaching us like the light from a dying star...

A vague shape adjusted itself and I perceived layers to the darkness: the window ledge became visible, the low-shimmer of the glass too, and the dimensions of the yard emerged. Slowly, the shape attained definition. It was long and slender, too upright for a mountain lion. The yard contained a laundry pole that folded when not in use and the borrowed canoe. In the dark, a thing could be all things, shapeshifting and mergeish. Some nights I'd mistake the chair on which I hung clothes for a circus ringmaster, a pareidolic mountain stack, or the boogie man. A canoe might be a wildcat; a laundry pole might be a man. Without illumination, nothing was certain. The sky was briefly pierced by a sliver of moon, just as quickly extinguished by cloud, and the night returned to its dimensionless form. Darkness. Nothing. Sometimes a yard is just a yard.

I overslept and had to be woken by Eileen. Ralph and Sam had gone to the hardware store; she needed to work on her business plan. I slipped into the garage and marked a green X on the map, just inside our yard.

I marked a red X across the road from our house, then two more green ones following further wakeful nights at the window, each mark overlaying the one before it. No one noticed these additions: Ralph and Sam's interest in the mountain lion was waning, just as mine was picking up. Sam kept asking if I had been messing around in the yard, because the gravel was always askew. He didn't believe me when I told him no. The nights approached like a predator. Sleep became my nemesis. I obsessed over closed doors and windows.

The weather turned. Ralph and Sam spent less time in the garage, so I spent more time there. It felt good to be unbothered, alone. I took the key for myself, put it on a string that I wore around my neck, tucked under my shirt. Its sharp touch became a comfort.

We returned to school no longer new. Ralph and I were in separate classes now. We stopped eating lunch together. I walked home alone. He'd become popular since the summer, whereas nothing had changed in respect of myself. Increasingly, Ralph spent the weekends with friends and our shared bedroom became my own. I lay entire evenings there: reading, writing, always with a secured window and the curtains drawn.

On school mornings, after breakfast, I'd wait for Sam to go out, Ralph to be picked up (a friend's parent collected him; there wasn't room for me) and for Eileen to work on her business plan. Once the kitchen was clear, I slipped into the garage, added the relevant number of Xs in the appropriate colours, then walked to school, looking behind me all the way.

Things changed. I was consistently late, my grades consistently bad. That which had once been important was no longer. Eventually, Eileen was summoned. The principal said he'd received reports that I didn't pay attention in class and frequently failed to complete assignments. He asked if there were problems at home, in an accusative way that led to a confrontation. Eileen rarely lost her temper, but when she did it was spectacular. She drove home like a banshee (I'd saved up my pocket money and invested in a Collins Junior Folklore Companion), riding the wind, running a red light that later resulted in a ticket. I was grounded and Eileen received a letter from the school. A social worker came the following week.

They said it was a routine visit, but everyone had to be present. Ralph missed school. Sam lost a day's pay. I was glad the blame was ascribed to the principal's interference. Ralph and I were asked questions in front of Eileen and Sam, then later, alone. I conferred with Ralph afterward, but he didn't say anything about being asked about his relationship with Sam, whether he was appropriate or inappropriate, which was what the social worker had asked me.

Sam was always appropriate with me, but I'd never thought to consider the same in respect of Ralph. I began to wonder about the time they spent together in the garage but couldn't think such a thing of Sam. Anyway, the social worker was mostly interested in our living conditions, which (I read from their notes, upside-down) were satisfactory, and our diets, which were acceptable. They gave us a bunch of pamphlets on healthy home cooking and that was that.

Except that it wasn't, because I threw a chair at my homeroom teacher, who said, when I eventually turned up for class, that it looked like I'd spent the night in a bordello. I'd never heard this word before and it wasn't in my Collins Junior Dictionary, but I knew it wasn't a compliment. Some things don't require definition.

I got suspended and spent most of the period in my room, eating little and ignoring Eileen's requests that I run errands, or stand for her as a model. She'd progressed to making designs on the same parchment paper that Ralph and Sam had used to map out the town, but still didn't own a sewing machine.

An investigation exonerated the homeroom teacher, who'd denied saying anything at all, and no one else seemed to have heard. While I was at home, another social worker came, this time to speak only with me.

They were concerned about the amount of time I spent in my bedroom. They asked if they could look through my books, and did so, one by one, including my Collins Junior Series. They picked up my journal and asked if they could read it, which I didn't mind at all because the real one was more than well-hidden. They sat on the bed, asked if we could talk and left the door open, which I minded a lot.

The social worker asked why I'd thrown a chair at the homeroom teacher and I repeated what he'd said, but the social worker told me that matter was closed. They asked if I was an angry person, a sad person, if I ever hurt or thought of hurting myself in some way. Even when they were being explicit, I found that adults spoke with innuendo.

I knew what they meant. I said that I never hurt or thought about hurting myself in some way, was neither an angry person, nor a sad one. I'd learned it was often best to reflect a person's exact language at them. They asked if I had many friends, if I went out much, what my interests were outside of reading. They asked about the key around my neck, which had fallen outside of my shirt. I tucked it back in, said that reading was pretty much all I wanted to do, that it was too cold to go out and I didn't care if I had friends or not.

They asked again about the key.

I said nothing and they left. I heard them talking to Eileen, who said she didn't know anything about a key. I tore the string from my neck—it burned—ran to the garage and locked myself in. I was in there most mornings and had added to the map substantially. There had been many sightings since the summer. I had seen him all over town: in a blue car several times, in Woolworth's at least twice, outside my school on one occasion, often on the road to our home and always, *always* in the yard, at night. The map was a maelstrom of Xs, and I saw that the greens outnumbered the reds, whereupon I experienced a sick and fiery fear.

The social worker was knocking on the door and Eileen was griping that she didn't have time for this. The Halina was on a chair and when had Sam even taken it back? I hung it round my neck, the leather strap digging in, exacerbating the burn from the string. The social worker was trying the handle of the door. I didn't know if there was another key. Sam kept all containers that were marked either flammable or inflammable on a high shelf that could easily be reached with the aid of the chair. I poured the contents of a metal can over the map. The green and red ink merged with something called *Baxter's Hypergrade*; it spilled onto the cement floor and pooled in spectral puddles. The social worker could smell the fluid through the door, and there was a note of panic in their voice that had previously been so calm. Sam kept the safety matches in easy reach of anyone. I couldn't even say why I was doing all this.

The bench lit up with a comforting *floof*. The social worker was throwing themselves at the door and Eileen was wailing in the background: she was no good in a crisis; it would never have occurred to her to call anyone. I sat at the far end of the garage, against the roller-door that was never used. Black smoke coiled across the ceiling and curled towards the floor. Some of it seeped through the inch-gap of the roller-door. I began to regret any number of decisions previously made.

It seemed an appropriate time for resolutions and I determined to put more effort in at school, become a little less insular. But I thought we could all stand to be doing our own things a little less, or even change things around altogether. I imagined Eileen using my Collins Junior Atlas to memorise the names of all the countries and their flags, while Ralph and Sam made dresses, and I no longer used compasses and black felt pens to connect sightings of the mountain lion (testing my hypothesis that they only appeared across ley lines, about which I had read in the Oxford Book of Knowledge) but made friends, and arrived at school on time, and slept well behind unlocked doors because there was no mountain lion at all.

I lay down and wrapped myself around the Halina; proof for when I needed it, facts being as weapons. I closed my eyes against the black smoke sting and saw possible futures: a sleep-deprived Ralph with children; Sam returning all the things he'd ever borrowed; Eileen's business failing, but at least getting off the ground; the mountain lion in human form, lost in the desert; the solitary death of the Woolworth building; the homeroom teacher apologising for his behaviour; the re-opening of the Rialto and Anarene's oldest resident defying expectations, living forever.

My skin was itching as the smoke descended. In a year—less than that, even—this might be a bad memory, repeatedly recalled and repressed within the same instant, prime fodder for the school counsellor, but for the moment it was all that there was and could ever be. Everything became dimensionless, animal-like shapes formed and dissipated in the smoke, in which I saw the mountain lion for real, the words heavy and light began to mean the same and the *whooze* of the fire filled my ears as I helplessly inhaled, Eileen screamed, the social worker threw themselves at the garage door and, in the near distance, a siren wailed.

from **Conspiracy**

20 May

12

as the music sounds
in the common tiergarten
he sways from side to side
on a red plush base
promiscuous tides
peaked too early
for an insufficient calm
mingling liquors
distant planetary bodies
disturb the cleansed surfaces
entries in the gazetteer
waiting to pass away

13

slyness complicates
naive histories
as if to say
how little avails
terror before aloof
vermin in its place
the gulf is washed clean
by submerged waters
fixated on breathing
in happier times
to perplex the more
forensically useful beetles

14

diminished vehicles
along crimson routes
a curious high-pitched
air of foreboding
in the absence of better information
everyone scattered
wheeling and minding
the expelled arrived
into a fallen world
limp from recent weather
prepared to sleep
to keep it from rusting

15

a featureless cast
from the act of touching
intensifies memories
taken at the flood
a knife or a bottle
with a singing tone
action recorded in tissue
in gentle households
a sudden extreme cold
as when one bites an apple
marking several thousand-fold
the dangers of surrender

16
seized by vertigo
structures that control
habit patches broken rooms
with foregone conclusions
while taxons migrate across
the element of surprise
intrepid as he was
boredom was the victor
the habit of precision
misapplied in sleep
returned as surgical insults
hedged by glass

21 May
17
simple duration
of banal occurrences
there is no end of talk
the water finds its level
your breath is in your face
though evidence accrues
this girl is young
markets are nervous
hands reach
out of effect back into cause
so many dead
it was not so

Trevor Joyce

Hot Dog

Tom Willis

I work in a hot dog spot, though I am not quite sure why. I fell into it. *Needs Must.*

Everyone here is kind of sick. They cough and whinny on the buns and the franks. Their consumption of oils and fats cannot help, nor can the cold, nor the fumes from the fryer.

Currently, I live and work in the lower part of the city, not far from the port. Today, the port is near empty, holding only a few barges and scows. They have fires burning, which send wisps of smoke over and across the fens. Here it is thin chilled air with a brackish sea-watery atmosphere. I shiver in the sunlight, even now in the mid-afternoon.

Buildings rise out of the salty earth like jagged squares of fudge, and not much happens here. Things drip. I sell over a hundred hot dogs in a day. Together we make the cheese sauce. Slice and fry; fry and slice. Dice onions amid the same perpetual flow of trivial things and cut the vegetables.

My boss Dennis comes in after a street fight, bleeding from the temple, and some of his blood blots, pools, and mixes with a streak of ketchup as it soaks into a food-soiled napkin he gingerly holds up to his head and face.

'Here, take some ice for that, Dennis.'

'Cheers, kid!' Dennis says.

Dennis stands at the door, blowing on his hands, no doubt feeling the cold.

Everyone eats an awful lot of fries. To keep warm, I imagine. Coldblooded creatures. Above our bit of sidewalk is a neon hot dog with the sauce a cartoon-squiggle of light. Despite what people say online, this place is not a truck nor a cart nor a shack nor an illegal operation; it is an old restaurant, and there is nobility in that.

You have to make the hot dogs well. One has an obligation to the hot dog.

I wash the sidewalk out front most mornings, using a hose to get it wet and a broom with plastic bristles to do the scraping. Sometimes small plants grow in the cracks in the cement. I try to leave them be. But sometimes they get rasped and torn.

There is seating. The booths are plush and comfy. The stools less so, but they are more sociable. Different people like different things. Although it is not large, some parts of the restaurant are darker than others, which is natural.

The cleaning has to be done but I do not find it enjoyable. So, when I sweep or vacuum, I leave some crumbs. I hope the mice get them. Some of the dirt here is so thick it is like sediment. We consider this a part of the place, like the foundations.

I don't eat salad since I found a slug on a lettuce leaf I was about to put in my mouth. I don't like how salads look like jungles, layered and confused. They don't sit well with me. Things conjoin but fail to interlink properly and make full sense. There are always missed connections: I missed my bus this morning.

I watched an expensive car croon on the street corner. A suited man got out and collected takeaway from a hotel restaurant known for its innovative fusion food. Another man slept on the warm-air ducts at the side of the street. That evening I give him a free hot dog (we can give away one free plain basic hot dog per day).

For fun? For fun I go hiking, where dead-looking grass bayonets sabre my legs dryly.

We are located at the intersection of 14th and Charlotte Street. Close to Greek Street. The staff have white uniforms. The uniforms are washed-out with stains and age-old discolourations (denim blue from leaking pens, muted red and saffron orange from sauces, but mostly grey. All stains turn grey eventually). My uniform has a patchwork continent of a stain in faded grey-brown and pea-green across the chest. We also wear small red plastic name badges, and, if you (the worker) so wish, a hat. I alternate with the hat, depending on the day and the weather. I enjoy this freedom.

The chili for the chili dogs is cheap and stinks of spicy hot toothpaste. Maybe that's why people get sick and sneeze particulates on the diced white onion and the pico de gallo.

My uniform is starchy and itchy. The label rasps at my side.

The crinkle-cut pickled cucumber slices reek in the cloudy vinegar they sit in. All the jars in the back look like they contain the preserved parts of humans and beasts. Some of the jars are ancient and swampy, especially when the sun hits them. Dennis got a good deal on a job lot a few years ago. I don't know how many years of pickles are left, but there are a lot. There is one window in the back of the kitchen. The sun can be so huge through this window. It lights the pickle jars up so green and luminescent.

People on bicycles with great blue insulated bags come to pick up takeaway orders from us. I hand them tinfoil cartons which become, temporarily, in transit, theirs. I like the thought of these people racing through the city with this warmth on their backs. It does make me sad however that they are made to wait in the rain until they get an order and that the company that uses them has an endgame where it uses only drones and driverless cars to deliver food, rendering the people obsolete. I wonder if the company cares if they get run down in the road or crushed against an embankment by a bin lorry. I doubt it, but smile extra hard at them when they come to pick up the food, in case they are crushed as they are delivering structurally stable hot dogs with just the right amount of relish per dog (and perfectly toasted buns), but I bet the smile comes out wan and weak and deathly and gives them a tummy-sinking sickly ruminative morality premonition as they cycle off in horror, only increasing their inattention and chances of getting crushed.

When it rains, the cellar of the restaurant floods with water that smells foul, I think because it was dug out two hundred years ago, and because there is a small cave down there. The cellar is made of crumbly red brick and a lot of mould and seemingly a bit of wattle and daub. The air down there is corrupted.

My hair is wet and greasy at the end of a shift. But there is a great sense of relief, so I don't mind so much.

Most people who eat here look ill. They come from the intersection.

We can sometimes be fun and goofy. Dennis baked a big cake for a lady's birthday. We each had a slice. He had baked a lot of coins into it as gifts. I hurt my tooth on one. Dennis thought it was hilarious. He clapped me on the back and told me to 'go boil the dogs'.

Dennis is part Greek, Macedonian, and Albanian. And he is in a love rivalry. I worry about him. The other man in the triangle-shaped rivalry has connections to organised crime.

'Hey, Sugar,' a woman said to me. Then ordered fries. She smelled of fresh cigarette smoke. And she had nice hair. I stood speechless for what might have been a full ten minutes. Then I fetched her fries.

A standard no-frills hot dog costs $6.49. When I started working here a standard no-frills hot dog cost $4.49, plus we used to put more sauerkraut in, and the sauerkraut was of a better, fresher variety. Likewise with the mustard. So things have been inflating, or deflating, depending on how you look at it.

On my way home from a shift, I play music through the unbranded earphones I buy direct from Chinatown to keep costs down.

We split the hot dogs for the chili dogs sometimes. We sizzle them split-side-down on the flat-top. It makes for a crispier experience. Inside a hot dog it is all emulsion. If so asked, we sometimes deep fry them.

But I have plans bigger than all this. I would like to go to Japan.

Oh yes, I get sick a lot. Eating hot dogs too. Too many of them. The bun dipped in gravy. And I know how the gravy's made, from powder and bones. Not good for your intestines.

Down the street from my work is a sushi place. It is much fancier than the Hot Dog Spot. I pass it coming to and going from work. Men in black headbands slice raw fish and grill thin steaks over charcoal. Each and every piece of wood in there, from the doors to the tables, is large and beautiful and has an intricate woodgrain which is deeply waxed to show it off. It has a philosophy, I read on their website: the restaurant is a place of holy human connexion where the coal-griddled meat imparts knowledge (they cook using the methods of ancient Japanese fishermen) and hand-crafted drinks share vegetable wealth, all in the warmth of an all-embracing energy surround. I see the maître d' occasionally. She is young and beautiful and has incredibly long red hair. I would say it looks like a fire or a phoenix or dragon's breath or an exclusive nightclub. She smokes cigarettes out in the street and fumes immensely.

Yesterday a man came in and asked for two chili dogs. I tried to warn him off but he did not decode my hints. He ate both then drank his 7UP looking out of the window, sadly, at the onyx night. Shock horror, it all got to him quick, the terrible sensation, and I directed him to our capacious bathrooms. It must have just poured out of him.

I live in a small flat. I moved into the flat a number of years ago. For some reason the landlord has not put the rent up. It is in one of the blocks of jagged fudge but with red and brown brick too. Rent has gone up all around me, and yet I keep on living here. It is small and neat and precise in the apartment. When you open the door, you can see my bed. The TV and my games consoles are stacked by the wall, right in front of the bed, so I can perch at the end on the soft duvet and play my favourite video games and have a good time. Move across a small space into the kitchen and you can see the ends of a sandwich. I have left a corner of it uneaten. Two crusts, the seam visible. I enjoy moments like these, when things add up. The flame from the hob is blue, and complex as azurite.

There is a spider plant in the northwest corner of my bedroom. It shivers in the wind. Streams of air coming from the river into my district ensure that there is a constant breeze flowing down my street, as if a god had ordered it to be so.

I absolutely refuse to have anything to do with hot dogs in the house. I keep my work and my home life separate. No ketchup or mustard, relish or finger buns. No sausages of any form. Nothing German really, if we're talking about foodstuffs. I've no problem with other German things. Honest. Recreationally, I do not outlaw hot dogs. Say I am in the park with friends and a hot dog tender in a cart comes along and it is generally agreed that we will get hot dogs and people are excited by this proposition, I join in without even a murmur. I have even had some good conversations about hot dogs, learned some things, and this way have made a couple of friends.

Making dinner, I cut a runner bean at an angle. It shows a cross section. A small and viridescent bean is visible in the now-spear-like pipe and the thing looks like an ovipositor. The knife slightly nicked it, so the whole thing bleeds greenly.

On the corner a man in a duffel coat smokes half a cigarette. I greet him as I pass. 'Hey Bill, how goes it?' Canvas awnings flap and crack wickedly overhead.

To get to Japan will be expensive. It will equal hours and hours of boiling hot dogs, splitting rolls, stirring the raisiny curry-paste bit of the currywurst into a workable sauce. Today, I begin my working day by slicing onions. The knife I am given is dull, and the onion juice and vapour make my eyes smart. So I cry. I am told that by using a sharp knife you avoid this problem and don't walk around all day with red puffy eyes.

To purchase: one sharp knife.

My mood rises like a balloon. I have finished chopping all the onions. I have to turn them into a sort of brown jam now, by cooking them for ages and ages. Dawn twinkles at the steamy windows. I can watch the street from where I am frying all these onions, a lumpen wavy oozing sea of onion rings and quads and half-moons and severed slices of onions melting all over each other, morphing together. I think a lot of empty-headed things when I fry vast amounts of onions. It all ends up as a bright brown sticky mess.

Dennis has a bandaged hand today. He claws the spatula from me and dampens the burning onions with water from a squirty bottle—a great wall of steam is conjured up—flipping wads of them as he goes, swearing.

'Damn food,' he says. Then, 'Damn fool, I mean.'

On leaving work a sort of aqueous fog occludes a clear picture of the park. It is dusk and there are organic noises coming from its woods and fields.

The next day is a weekend day and I go into the park. The fields are green, almost yellow. The wind gets in amongst the trees and a buzzard lands daintily in the branches of an oak. My friend Jim has sold me some hash, so I smoke a little in the field. The tree line musses. A man sells hot dogs from a stall across the park. While I am high, I get a text from the only cool friend I made at school. Her name is Dylan. She is coming back to the city after four years at college during which she became even cooler, and an anarchist. She hopes to see me and hopes that I have been well.

'Can I have a couple of coneys please, my man,' a man says to me at work. He looks to be affecting a certain detached, relaxed cool in his dress and manners, but he seems to me an awkward and anxious person.

A coney is a special kind of dog: chili, mustard, white onion, sausage, steamed bun. A classic combo. You get a feel for how to make a good one, the ratios; one has to respect the art. I want to boost his self-esteem, so I reply with a cheery 'coming right up, my man,' but my eye twitches noticeably and on pronouncing 'up' my voice reaches a needly pitch, which totally maims and kills the 'my man'. As if I had battered it to death then dug it a grave. The guy looks deflated at this, as if everything had all gone wrong and that he had really needed the boost of it going all right. I think he might have practised his line, like Robert De Niro in *Taxi Driver*, but with a hot dog order. I sometimes do that. I like to think no one hasn't done that. This guy needs to get a grip if that kind of thing can ruin his day. It used to be able to ruin mine, but I have techniques now. Ways of dealing with pressure and sadness. He seems kind of desperate, so I go all out on his coneys. They weigh in his hands the weight of small babies.

Coney, as in Coney Island, comes from *rabbit*. Something to do with the Dutch. It must have been so busy with rabbits on the island, the titchy things careening round like a fairground ride. Disappearing into burrows. Zipping out again. He had asked for two coneys. It would have meant something different if he had said the same order in the medieval or early modern period. I wonder if he or I would have been rabbit hunters back then.

'Bye now, bud,' I say kind of plaintively, with an accidental sorrow that just pukes out of me, but I also intentionally inject the words with as much kindness as I can without them seeming inauthentic to the guy as he shuffles away. He cringes when the words hit him. I must have got my tone wrong. Oh dear.

A seagull catches a rock pigeon to eat its heart and I see its mushed-up horrible mixed-up insides poor poor thing.

A man with only a few cadaverous teeth propels some mashed hot dog around his mouth. He tips his baseball cap back, like he is playing sports and needs a better view, shoots in a gulp of water, and it all goes down in one great mass, so that, for a swift moment, his Adam's apple protrudes, beaklike. He takes another bite and begins all over again. I think he is lonely. I think he wants to touch someone, or something. Maybe his gluttony is just a way to touch. To touch something that was once alive. To escape isolation. Maybe just for the enjoyment of it all. I might be wrong, and it is just to eat, nothing more meaningful than that.

I get home, put some soup on the hob to boil, watch the flames for a while, then go switch on my video games console and kick back, finally.

'Where the hell is my food?'

I was staring into the street. Someone had parked a real slick car there. So slick. Red and slick with a shiny yellow badge.

The man came closer to my face, leaning across the counter.

'WHERE THE HELL IS MY FOOD?'

While I was waiting to see what I would say, he threw several small packets of condiments hard at my face, the corners and triangle-crenelated tops and bottoms hurting, one shaving my earlobe like a tiny toothed saw would if thrown like a ninja star at an ear, and then he walked out.

'Don't mind him,' Dennis said.

'I just want someone to love me,' I murmured.

'What?' Dennis said. Then, 'Clean the fryer, would you; you daft kid.'

A cool young guy came in. He was dressed well but drably: olive tones and muted greys. He seemed pleasant but was not particularly polite and was talking to a friend who joined him and was dressed like him, but differently in some of the minutiae: more of his socks showed, like eight whole inches of pure sock fabric from ankle up to highly rolled trouser bottom, and they were a brighter colour; the second guy was in general more colourful than the first guy. They ordered, then stood chatting. While I was preparing their meal and refreshments, I heard the cool, drabber guy say to the cool, brighter guy:

'So I was going to this party, yeah, and it was right across the city, so I took the bus the whole way there, and I was reading Beckett on the bus going to this party, right, and it really fucked me, and fucked up my mood and buzz, just its whole tone and vibe was super fucking weird and trippy and mind-bending and dark, and yeah the party was really good, and I knew it was good, I just couldn't enjoy myself for some reason, the Beckett kept repeating on me and confusing the hell out of me, and I think right at the back of my mind I knew even in the moment that my strange wobbly mood was directly Beckett's fault, and there was this hot girl Celia (you know her, yeah? Hot, right?), she was there and I hadn't seen her in a long while, but I had always had this nuclear-meltdown-hot crush on her, and she was like newly single, and I fancied her back then as much as I have fancied anyone in one hell of a long time, maybe ever, but this incredibly good and intense moment, practically a realisation, like something holy, was then immediately ruined by the horrifying Beckett coming back into my head, and so I naturally messed it all up, probably irreparably, I mean I was super fucking weird, and it must have seemed to this girl like I had lost my mind, and I am *never* going to be able to explain myself to her even if she could bear to be in the same room as me ever again for more than a second without taking immediate flight; anyway, I left the party after that hideous moment in a great flash of tears, all thanks to bloody Beckett, and now she's got a totally loving boyfriend who she loves and he looks *just like me*, and I missed this whole excellent party, which was like the best party in a million years, and I've never forgiven Beckett and I never will, he should come with like some warning, man, like, THIS WILL MESS WITH YOUR LIFE AND WILL MAKE YOU LOSE THE GIRL OF YOUR DREAMS.'

I asked who or what Beckett was, but the cool guy just grunted at me like I had been rude listening to his story, and slid his dog into his rough, pretty mouth.

I went to the movies. It was something good about a battle. I liked it. Yeah, I liked it.

On the way home from the movies, I sat at the very front of the top deck of the double-decker bus. A girl in flared trousers sat across the aisle from me. She spoke into her headphones to someone—a bit I thought was just for connecting, all wires—but she must have had a speaker in there; she said in a pink, rosy cutest of cute guttural voices: *unintelligible German unintelligible German unintelligible German* I don't feel good *unintelligible German unintelligible German unintelligible German*.

A sports car zipped past the bus and smashed into some bins. I saw the guy get out dazed but excited. He exited into a swish stainless-steel-plated sushi restaurant.

Dennis's love rivalry got worse. He was eating a slice of pizza nonchalantly on the street corner abutting the forest in the park. The sun was passing gently over the world. The pizza was good, and it crunched in his mouth. He liked especially the blistered black spots, their dark crunch. He told us all this. It was a good day in a rarely warm month and 'one hell of a good slice of pizza'. He was enjoying everything so much, and the sound of the birds! Some pizza oil had slipped past the greaseproof paper sheath and dripped messily onto his shirt with a few crushed leaves of dried oregano and basil and molecules of red sauce, so he was dabbing it with a napkin when the squirrels and doves stopped making their pretty babbling noise in the glade and it was filled instead with the metallic scraping-slapping noise of a van door opened and slammed with the brunt brute male force of someone who spent a lot of time picking up heavy things and putting them down again. Silence. Dennis stood still, feeling the soft summery breeze blow against his face, the softly sharp tingle of chili flakes on his delicate lips, heard crisply a round of pepperoni soggily slip from his pizza onto the cracked concrete. Steps followed and someone bellowed.

The love rival threw down a gold ring, an embroidered silk scarf, and a royal-blue sports cap.

He said: 'Dennis, I return these terribly shit gifts you gave me over the years! Given with your deceitful hands, they mean nothing now to me and turn my stomach submarine-cold.'

A holly bough shook in the wind.

'All those days hunting in the city together, sharing slices (at this he pointed declaratively to Dennis's slice of pizza), chasing girls... But nobly, Dennis, with a heart full of honour. Now all that time, all those years, all those places, turned to waste, my history murdered, the innards of my mind and memory slain. Every moment with you spoiled; and my life was so full of you, old childhood friend.'

Dennis snorted and shunted the fallen pepperoni slice around with his white leather trainer. Like a slug, it left a trail.

'Get ready, Dennis.'

Like the love rival, Dennis pulled out a sharp switchblade and adjusted his baseball cap. His heel slipped, squelching slightly on an unusually mossy crag in the pavement.

It was all emerald green in Dennis's eyes for a flashing moment when they closed the gap and the love rival's knife sliced into Dennis's stomach to make a gruesome wound. Dennis twisted so the knife didn't go deep, but still his vision blurred like a scene reflected in a smoked gem (or so he says).

Dennis staggered to the side then with an almighty effort as the love rival came towards him with a victor's swagger. He clicked his snickering knife alive and brought it across the love rival's leg, slicing both denim and flesh. The love rival tore his leg back with a jerk and stumbled with an ogreish grunt.

Like a boar that is slashed and hurt but not yet mortally injured, the love rival was now ragingly dangerous.

I think he still could have had Dennis. But with numerous further flourishes and a sequence about battling down a side alley and into Main Street, Dennis said the love rival only ended his pursuit after being clipped by a street-cleaning vehicle. Dennis said he left the man there in the freshly swept gutter, bleeding lightly from the head. He claimed victory and told the story with too much derring-do even for him: a joyful liar and exaggerator.

He was holding a bundle of waxy tissues to his side. Dennis skimped on the tissues and they were almost all wax they were so thin, and they rolled into tiny cocoons across his sweating brow as he wiped away sweat driplets, tears, blood. The tissues held almost nothing: it was tragic, though by now his wound had at least stopped bleeding.

'You should go to the hospital, Dennis,' I implored.

But he wouldn't go. He just sat there at the counter drinking beer after beer. I think he was very very happy. I think he felt alive like an animal.

I sat by the mouth of the estuary and watched a few great grey freighters come into the city. Some were moored out at sea, waiting, their anchors deep down in the water and the dark silt. I don't know when the ships were made, but they seemed like they were from another century, like battleship destroyers.

My anarchist friend Dylan came by the restaurant. At this time, I was experiencing long bouts of tearfulness, so it was good to see her. She wasn't much of an oblivion-savourer and experienced little to no plain old chokingly-deep-in-your-lungs sadness, which I found impressive. As she spoke, my will to make hot dogs wilted, and I just listened as the chili burned and began to smell foul.

She was a utopian-style thinker, which I think gave her hope and made her happy. Even at school she had made the place more harmonious and collaborative by undermining and generally softly fucking with the apparatus of the place to the point where crueller, more individualistic and dominating staff left or were forced out. In the city, she now helped organise rallies, and could give a good tub-thumping speech. She was a real hero-style person, a woman of action plus a poet plus an orator, a mix that gets things changed through saying plus doing. People liked the ideas she published in artsy online magazines. But now she had a Big Plan, a plot cooked up out of theory and practice that she said came out of being an artist and spending an awful lot of her life in small-time anarchist circles.

'I have this idea we're doing,' she said. 'A sort-of politics-cum-art concept. You must have noticed all these exotic cars in the city nowadays? How at night, they're driven uptown to the flash hotels or cross the bridge downtown to get to these hip, grungy new sushi spots that have opened here, near the port, for its industrial and down-and-out authenticity. These showy drivers come for raw fish and rice wine and to be *seen*.' Her eyes filled with expanding pupil, and her voice was irradiating. 'But they leave a bitter, bitter taste, of toxic fumes and gentrification. These cars are pure, perfect, aesthetic specimens of inequality. You must see things this way?' She laid her hands palm-up on the counter in front of me, theatrically imploring. I nodded. 'Good!' she said. 'Sadly, most people still don't, and instead pose for photos with the cars, congratulate their owners. But people should disagree, apply pressure, critique, *do something*, to these, I don't want to say, *symbols of structures of oppression*, but...' she cocked her head, 'you see, I want people to rasp knives and keys along their sides.' She smiled. 'And spit on their windows. Just get engaged, for fuck's sake. They're the enemy.'

Here, she paused.

'I, too, dislike them,' I said, enchanted.

'What I propose is this,' she said, 'and it is grand.'

I raised a finger to ask if she wanted a hot dog, but she said, 'Shh, it will all come clear as I tell it. In a month, a number of people in an exotic car club are going to cross the suspension bridge over the river together. (I know this because I have someone on the inside.) When they do, we'll create a traffic jam, slow things down. Once the cars are stuck snugly in the middle of the bridge, we'll strike with two vehicular obstacles, like buses or trucks (we know people), and block in the cars. When they're trapped,' she grinned, 'WE appear with bats, wrenches, and crowbars. Those who don't flee immediately will do when we start smashing windows, threatening weak jawbones. For our purposes, we only need four cars. All others will be torched, beacons to illuminate the installation. With strong but flexible steel cable and a number of power tools, we'll work quickly to bend and affix cables through the broken windows and around the chassis of the cars. The cables will be looped over a tall girder, and each car hoisted upwards by a powerful vehicle of our own, perhaps a big tow truck (remember, these expensive cars are light as air). And in this way each battered supercar corpse will be sent heavenwards until they hang together from the bridge's great girder in the low firmament. Some choice welding will affix each cable to the bridge, to make things stick, and there they will sway in the wind over the black water of the river. Think of the pictures. People will be shaken, disabused of their automotive illusions, and outside sushi restaurants everywhere cars will be aflame.'

General Mechanism

Four Responses
to Jóhan Jóhannsson's *IBM 1401: A User's Manual*

by   Adrian Duncan

Elaine Cosgrove

Billy Ramsell

Hayley Carr

IBM 1401: A User's Manual *was written, arranged and produced by Jóhann Jóhannsson, and released in 2006. In Jóhannsson's own words, it is a record borne out of a conversation with the composer's father, who in 1964 was the chief maintenance engineer for one of Iceland's first computers: the IBM 1401 Data Processing System. An amateur musician, Jóhannsson's father devised a way of making music with the computer, a method involving the placing of a radio receiver next to the computer's memory, and the strong electromagnetic waves therein, and the programming of the receiver in such a way that melodies could be 'coaxed out'. Those wistful sine-wave tones were then captured on tape and preserved, until, thirty years later, Jóhann Jóhannsson listened to them, began to work with them, and then to compose his own responses. The outcome was a composition that spoke to hypermodern concerns like human-machine interaction, nostalgia for technology, simulation, artificial intelligence & the connection between 'spirit and the machine'. Fifteen years further on,* The Stinging Fly *asked four of Ireland's most innovative writers to listen to the record and respond with words. This sequence is the result.*

General Mechanism (parts I—V) | Adrian Duncan

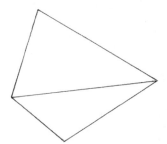

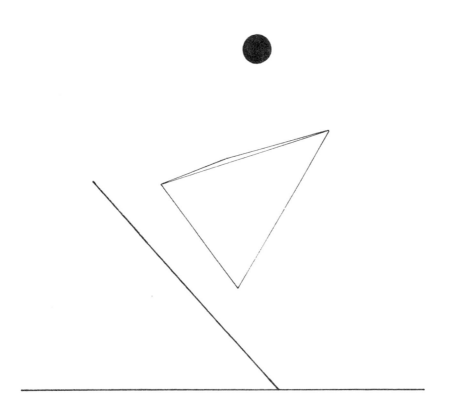

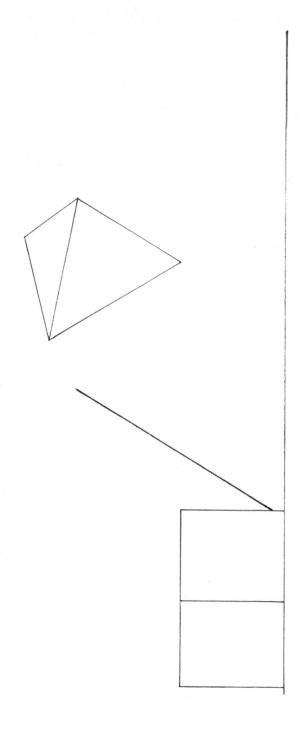

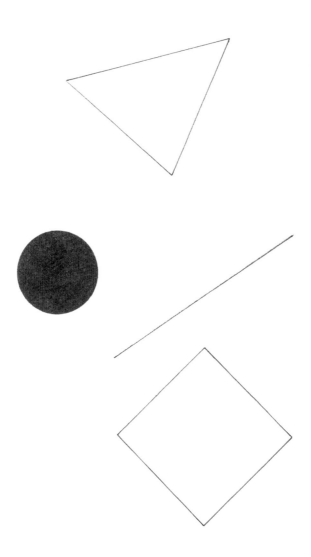

Processing | Elaine Cosgrove

I wanted to hide in the shadows of life, in the limits of the city, under the walnuts,
the pecans, the sweetgums, and I didn't want to tell you
the sun's gone dim the sky's turned black

that the screen I hold

is untouched as an instruction discarded into a drawer, is hands to another's
face that say

but listen to me

bright, austere and focused on a bathtub filled with water for cattle, my earbuds
a trailer of parts to which I sip the everyday distant

I gulp

until my earbuds blossom

but can you hear me?

I fear I will regret these shadows someday and wonder where the years went,
wonder at a life lived like a processing wheel that spins, eating each turn onto
itself

but where are the years already going?

The idle video is at least something, and there is a face there even if half-
    expressed and I am thankful for that

but it is forbearing

that this dark matter of paperwork and fees increasingly smells like a breaker
    burning out

and here I am being asked, in the safe convenience of a meeting being recorded,

if an ending really is another beginning?

I look outside and I see the garden spider building its web and that it is only
    trying to live, undisturbed, in the window,

and I see its instructional life finding purpose and its task to survive

is what it is

and this status processing for the purpose of love and the instructions on how
to live

are what they are

and life goes on as an ending and a beginning

Conversations With Jóhann | Billy Ramsell

translated from the Catalan of the non-existent poet Alberto Cenas

I first met Jóhann Jóhannsson, quite by chance, on a slow train between La Rioja and Asturias. This was some time ago, around or just after the release of *IBM 1401: A User's Manual,* the recording that, in retrospect, can be seen to have established his career.

I was aboard a first-class carriage that halted, as it happened, mere metres from where he stood, intent and ebony-clad, utterly stationary on the platform at Calahorra. And there was something about his eyes, even glimpsed through the smudged carriage window, that immediately arrested me, something restless and absorbed, a cobalt mix of loneliness and liveliness. Indeed, he exhibited a corpulent grace amid the platform's churn of luggage and goodbyes. He dipped and pivoted—his large frame taut, manoeuvrable—as he hoisted case after rigid case onto the tremoring train.

It was with no small fascination, then, that I saw him enter our compartment, his heavyset face betraying the relief, the mild bewilderment, of those who transfer trains successfully, joining a journey in medias res. The engine throttled into wakefulness. Calahorra was whisked away. Mr Jóhannsson sidled, wobbled, located his banquette, which, as luck would have it, was directly across the aisle from where I sat—desultorily browsing the latest issue of *Poesia*—next to my dozing mother.

Mr Jóhannsson arranged his paraphernalia, his outsize limbs, and sipped from a styrofoam coffee cup. He scanned the scraggly, diesel-dusted vines we trundled past. He seemed to study a clutch of outbuildings, a brown cow—skin-tight, desperate—an old woman gazing cow-like as our slow train gathered pace again.

He was accompanied by an entourage of one, a pinch-faced Luxembourgian who, I later learned, had been engaged on his behalf as a publicist of some kind. She was hardly seated before she engaged her miniature computer screen, in whose blue and pullulating shallows, excepting the briefest intervals, she would spend the rest of the journey lost.

The train braked and jolted at the foot of some interminable vineyard. Liquid spluttered, spouted from the lid of Mr Jóhannsson's coffee cup. He cursed, presumably in Icelandic, as the beige and characterless beverage puddled about his newspaper.

I leaned quickly across the aisle, swabbing and dabbing at the spillage. It was an operation I performed with what might have seemed excessive deliberation, employing a sturdy herring-bone handkerchief, one of several that for such purposes I keep ready about my person. But the gesture, its banality aside, proved a conduit to conversation, breaching the aisle-wide bank of reticence that had hitherto sat between us.

And so, with the landscape around Arnedo exhibiting only a beige and vine-ridden blankness, and our first-class compartment otherwise uninhabited, we found ourselves—haltingly at first, in gapped and frustrating English—lulled into conversation.

We dispatched the requisite prefatory pleasantries and Mr Jóhannsson, leaning across the aisle convivially, outlined to me the genesis of his then most recent record. How his father had held a position, in the 1950s I believe, with the IBM computer company. How Jóhannsson *père* had somehow 'cracked' a primitive machine, finagling it into sound. How the circuit boards had warbled out a four-note flickering melody, an act utterly counter to their programming. How Jóhannsson *fils* had happened upon, quite by chance in a Reykjavík attic, his father's lost recording of that song. How those dusty tapes, in turn, had sparked the opus he was currently in Spain promoting.

I imagined that moment of discovery: Mr Jóhannsson bent beneath the roof-rafters, dauntless amid Christmas decorations, dust from the ancient cartridges hovering in front of his cobalt eyes. It was quite the origin story, an anecdote to conjure with.

I responded with an account of my own most recent publication. *Inheritances* I'd dared to title it: an assemblage of meditations, feuilletons, that had been retched, a mere two years ago, if not quite deceased then languidly ante-mortem, from the presses of my home city.

Our dialogue continued, as we rattled through Alcanadre and Ladero, turning to the pleasures and exigencies of travel. Mr Jóhannsson, it turned out, was bound for Salamanca, thence to Lisbon, Amsterdam, Chicago. He described an endless set of public interviews, of looping implausible itineraries, of brief performances with his computer, accompanied, when circumstance permitted, by some happenstance ensemble. In Madrid, for example, he had been joined by an overly drilled quartet, in Seville by a single cellist.

He assumed, no doubt due to my haphazard English, that I, too, was on some promotional excursion, that a lecture, perhaps, or public reading of some kind awaited me in Oviedo, rather than the overdue execution of my Uncle Dominic's will and testament. It was a misapprehension that I, to my shame, did little to correct.

Our train halted, heaving, at the modernist station of Logroño. I watched an old man disembark, set out beneath the steel and angular pavilion, hand a brown-paper package to what can only have been his daughter. It was then I remembered the brandy bottle.

The subject of brandy is one in which I can pretend to some expertise, the trade having been in and out of my family since at least the 1750s. We have cultivated and distilled. We held fields of sloping purple. We have exported, sourced and speculated in all the Americas and Spains, developing over the centuries a precise and dispassionate palate, one transmitted effortlessly, through some quiver of epigenesis, from father down to son.

The bottle that that afternoon I happened to have among my traps was at the very least entirely passable. I proffered a dram to Mr Jóhannsson, tipping the amber casually into the cup that had previously held his macchiato. He sipped, winced in appreciation.

I poured for myself as the engine chugged and spluttered into motion. I urged Mr Jóhannsson to savour the brandy's furious seduction, its play, its agitation on the lips, the palate, the tip of the tongue. It was with smouldering joviality, then, that we finally broached the topic of machines. Mr Jóhannsson, it turned out, was convinced that homo sapiens, alone among species, was creating its own replacements. For it was our destiny, he maintained, to be superseded sooner or later by our baroque and digital children, by beings evolved from the software and from the silicon to which we proved so devoted.

He spoke of these putative successors with some reverence, presenting them as shimmering intelligences that would spill forth—liquid, indeterminate— from their programming, their very circuitry. And such a forecast, he insisted, needn't induce despair. For the human race would live on, after a fashion, in the memory of our inheritors; our tyrannies, our achievements suspended forever in their computerised minds, in bodiless, digital amber.

The whole thing struck me as quite implausible, to be frank, as we sipped from our soggy styrofoam. But Mr Jóhannsson extracted from me a promise to acquire, on my return to my hometown, his aforementioned just-released record album, in whose harmonies, he assured me, were embedded a further elucidation of such themes.

We sat after that in companionable silence, sipping the adequate brandy, as the silvery train continued—grudgingly, unhurriedly—through the chalk and flaxen territory of Castile. He disembarked at León, taking his narrow-faced publicist with him.

I continued, with my mother, to Oviedo, saw to the estate of Uncle Dominic, made the dusty journey home again. And my thoughts, through those sad, administrative days, circled again and again around Mr Jóhannsson: his serendipitous attic discovery, his belief in our benign, electrical successors, his precise electric eyes.

I can't have been home more than a day or two, then, when I set out to tribute synchronicity, to purchase *IBM 1401: A User's Manual*, to honour that most pleasant, unexpected conversation on the train. But the recording, to my displeasure, was only available as a 'compact disc', a brute and crudely futuristic medium I had hitherto assiduously avoided. For the digital, in music and in manners, leaves me itching and dissatisfied. No minuet, I've found, has ever reverberated with such tart and tremulous sadness as that elaborated by the dust and valves of my late Uncle Jordi's phonograph.

My pledge to Mr Jóhannsson, then, necessitated not only the purchase of the recording itself but also of a 'Discman', a vulgar throwaway contraption, Japanese and plastic. I ventured down to Carpenter Street, pretended to listen as the sales assistant rhapsodised about superior fidelity, handed over my grudging euros.

I listened to the album through, just once, turned off the stupid disc-device, told myself that was that. The following night, however, saw the Discman at my belt again. And as that indolent summer approached I found myself each evening in my bedchamber, inserting the device's awkward ear plugs, giving myself, once, twice, three times, to that wayward computer's song.

The city simmered. It overheated, emulsified into summer, curdled into the earliest impossible days of August. And still the disc's five tracks fixated me.

Indeed I kept up, over the years that followed, with Mr Jóhannsson's burgeoning oeuvre. I saw, I believe, each and every film he composed for: tolerating *Mannick*, suffering through *Prisoners* at the Phenomena (dubbed into appalling Spanish). I purchased *Englabörn*, *The Miners' Hymns*. I enjoyed them. I applauded—from a distance, unbeknownst to him—as his tremulous melodies seduced the critics first, then a slowly budding cohort of the public.

But it was always *IBM* that I came back to, re-entering, once a month at least, that exquisite unstable world, attending over and over to those liquid strings, to the violins and cellos rising, solidifying into half-glimpsed shapes, only to melt and then descend again.

I have always, almost despite myself, been one for memorabilia, for antiques and incunabula, autographs and inscriptions. So when it came to my attention that Mr Jóhannsson and confrères were due to perform in my hometown, and that the theatre selected for his performance—as it happened—was one that had benefitted over the decades from my family's largesse, I immediately made it my business to have him sign my copy of *IBM*.

I envisaged a dressing-room tête-à- tête, perhaps, or stage-door reintroduction. It was a tryst to be facilitated by Pascaul, the venue's long-suffering duty manager, a man of letters and bon viveur, with whom, at that time, I was in moderate cahoots.

Who knows? I might find myself persuaded to some back-stage bacchanal. I imagined a dim-lit cavern beneath the theatre, the slow drone of electronics, a gathering of svelte and fashionable bodies at which I—game but deferential—would linger appropriately in the background, clutching not my usual dry white wine, but some risqué and rococo cocktail.

I reached the venue early, the worn-away disc in my valise, sat through the performance, a perfectly enchanting hour-long affair, all cello and electronics, then set out for my reunion with the maestro.

It was with no little nervousness that I pushed through the post-concert bustle, making for the foyer where Pascual was set to meet me. Imagine my chagrin, then, to find my machinations utterly superfluous. For there in the marble atrium stood the venerable Mr Jóhannsson, stouter than I recalled, sporting, despite the September mildness, a sable leather jacket. He was stood behind a trestle table, shaking hands, applying his signature, greeting any concert-goer that requested his benediction.

I joined the queue. I shuffled and swayed, surprised at my apprehension, as with expectant, aching slowness the snaking line staggered forward. One by one they were summoned, received their audience with the maestro: a ragged youth tattooed and vaguely Antipoedean, a Basque girl self-possessed and youthful who proffered his record sleeve for autograph, a potbellied Scot who had his t-shirt signed.

There was, of course, no flicker of recognition when it was my turn, finally, to stand before Mr Jóhannsson. And it came to me, as I handed the album over, that he harboured no recollection, however incomplete or partial, of our brandy-softened discourse, that nothing about my face or voice had triggered such recall. The train-bound afternoon that for me had been saved, preserved in the deep cells of memory, had for him been summarily deleted. It was a matter of necessity, capacity. How could one man's memory be capacious enough for the railroads, for all the hotel rooms he must have experienced, promoting *IBM* and subsequent albums?

I said nothing, let him sign the compact disc's packaging, stepped past the foyer's faux gold columns and out into Balmes Street.

It is February. I have learned, only yesterday, of Mr Jóhannsson's passing at 49. I am seated in my bedchamber as so many previous evenings, the rickety Discman on my belt, *IBM* rotating and rotating.

The worn device skips and stutters, steadies itself again. I peruse a shelf of keepsakes: my jade hare of dubious provenance; a camel-bone chess set— incomplete, seventeenth century—bequeathed by Uncle Dominic; Uncle Jordi's dust-furred phonograph.

Silence. Then a lone voice drifts through the static, through the inadequate earphones: *We now come to the general mechanism. Every six months check the oil level of the drive-housing.* The voice continues, clipped and British, culled, I believe, from some long-ago tape recording, one of those abandoned in the attic for Mr Jóhannsson to discover.

Mr Jóhannsson, you have left me almost too much: a signed inlay, a single sun-lapped memory, these cellos, these violins that spill into the composition. They recede and rise and ebb again, their swellings, their recessions scarcely noticeable at first. I step out on to my balcony as the finicky voice continues, outlining, in scrupulous detail, the specifics of printer maintenance: *Do not forget to check that the cap-nut of the draining port is tightened. Make sure that the adjusting hub nut of the drive gear is not loose.*

I reach for a bottle shipped directly from the Penedès, from an estate in which my family, for some generations now, has retained a significant interest. I pour myself a caramel and aromatic dram.

Clouds are massing, stacking above the city's edge, building a high and unlikely edifice. Traffic noise floats upward, the noises of children pretending. I turn the volume on the Discman up.

The violins, the cellos come more emphatically now. Their promise-filled waves reach higher, submerging, with each successive surge, the trustworthy voice and its instructions. One notices, each time as if for the first time, how their four-note motif evolves, with subtle insistence, from that ancient computer's song.

The Discman skips and rights itself. The cellos, the violins rise—indifferent, melodic and electrical—in washes of data and glass. And that faraway voice continues—oblivious, intoning—while the future in a slow wave passes over it.

Troubled by Static
Hayley Carr

Break, break, break.

This is EI22HC.

I have an emergency message.

Does anyone copy? Over.

Break, break, break.

This is EI22HC.

Are you troubled by static?

Does anyone copy? Over.
My coat hook is number six. I am six today. I am six years old today, hanging
Break, break, break.
my coat on hook number six. It's true, isn't it, that I'm older? But I don't feel
This is EI22HC.
six. I don't feel older than I did yesterday. How can a person gain a whole
Are my signals fading?
year in a day? Yet it's true, isn't it, that I'm older? That I was five yesterday
Does anyone copy? Over.
and I am six today, and that my coat hook is number six?

'Over the weekend I was cutting an apple for me and my brother,' Collin

Break, break, break.

begins telling Ms Greene during our maths lesson on fractions, 'and my

This is E[22HC.

brother said to me, "I want the bigger half! I want the bigger half!" But I told

I have an emergency message.

him you can't have the bigger half, because two halves are equal in size.'

Does anyone copy? Over.

Collin is amused by his anecdote, but no one really gets it the way he gets it.

Break, break, break.

But I get it. And the more and more I think about it, the more and more I get

This is E[22HC.

it, and the more amazed I am by what he said. How can his brain think like

Are you troubled by static?

Mrs Byrne asks me about my glasses, and I tell her that everything looks
that? I wonder. I always knew he was smart, but for the first time ever, I

Does anyone copy? Over.

really big now, but I just say that because that's what she expects me to say.
think Collin might actually be a genius.

Break, break, break.

It's what everyone expects me to say. In truth, I don't really notice much of a
I stand outside Sam's bedroom, hands clasped uncertainly at my front,

This is E[22HC.

difference at all. Everything looks pretty much the same.
while Mommy takes a picture of me in my school uniform, and the man on

Are my signals fading?

I pick up a page to draw on and notice a staple in the top left-hand corner. I
the radio is singing, 'If you believe they put a man on the moon,' and I

Does anyone copy? Over.

hesitate, and think I should bring it to the teacher. But then I decide to just
think to myself, but they did put a man on the moon.
After a long internal debate ... living room, I decide that I
remove it myself, because I'm brave; because I'm not afraid of getting hurt.
The dentist at the Roselawn Health Centre is very beautiful. She looks like a
must tell Mum that I am a tomboy know. I have been trying to be a
But I don't like this woman. She's brusque and surly and rough. She jerks
Barbie doll, with platinum blonde hair tied back into a tight ponytail, and
tomboy, but she has passports. She still buys me
my jaw apart and jams her hand mirror in my mouth to observe my teeth,
thick, glossy red lips that she hides behind a surgical mask so that her
pink, girly clothes with ... makes me wear skirts and
like rows of cars parked at a kerb. I feel nervous as she scrutinises my
piercing blue eyes are the only visible feature of her face. I'm not afraid of
tights. She still thinks I like ... and teddy bears and dolls.
mouth, the expression in her eyes increasingly exasperated and critical. She
When we get home, I go straight upstairs and quietly, secretly brush my
She treats me like a girl when ... treated like a boy. I've tried to
clucks her tongue, then finally yanks the mirror out of my mouth and turns
teeth, as if this could repair the damage that's already been done. My mum
show her; actions speak ... she treats me the same. I
to my mum and asks in her thick Eastern European accent, 'Does she drink
calls up to me and asks me what I'm doing. She tells me I don't have to

peek through the living room door window. Mum is sitting in the back room, reading a book. Now is my opportunity. She needs to know. I can't a lot of fizzy drinks?' He **Does anyone copy? Over** a sort of bored disdain brush my teeth again. But these are my adult teeth. They're permanent. I As I flick through a cute little comic book in the Stedelijk museum gift shop, My mum is caught off g **Break, break, break** s her confusedly. 'No, she have to take good care of them. I thought I had always been so diligent. a rose appears in my peripheral vision. I look up and holding, the rose is a Keep it a secret any longer. I peek through the window again, and think doesn't like fizzy drinks.' The **This is EI22HC** g off her latex gloves and they How could this happen? I start to cry, big heaving breaths like stormy boy roughly my age, with a wave of blue hair, he smiles at me coyly and waves. I feel my mum's arms wrap around me and pull me close to her and make a violent snap. 'She **Are my signals fading?** says tersely, and my heart hands me the rose. When I ask him why, the boy shrugs. 'I like your jumper,' she think I'm silly? I think and think and think, and decide that I must tell sinks. 'I g **Does anyone copy? Over** ent time.' tell me it will be okay and then he turns to go, leaving me with this ridiculous rose, the stem as her one day.

'Wait!' I call after him, swing **Break, break, break** back and gathering my coat. 'Why did you give me a rose?' I blurt out frantically, but a magician never thick as a branch and plump-ed. feeling somewhat stupid and stunned, and needing something to say, I ask in my arms. 'Wait!' I try to run **This is EI22HC** y baggage — the backpack, the reveals his secrets, and the boy just smiles his coy smile. 'Why not?' I feel Everyone is drinking and getting ready to go out. It's late already; too late him his name and where he's from. 'I'm Johnny, from California.' Johnny jacket, the rose — I just **I have an emergency message** over to the entrance to disappointed. Maybe it really is nothing more than the fact that he's also a for a meal, I think, and in their honey-drunk condition it'll be another hour from California says, 'I'm Hayley, from Ireland,' I say, and then not knowing the museum where the bo **Does anyone copy? Over** nding. When I reach them, massive ascent of Zelda fan, and liked my jumper, emblazoned with the at least until they're appropriately dressed and made up and ready to leave. I am slightly out of breath. **Break, break, break** how ugly I must look with Triforce symbol on the back. Maybe it just caught his eye, and he thought They are still smoking on the rooftop when I make my way back to my you anyway. Thank you for the rose. Johnny from California smiles his my red, puffy face and hunch **This is EI22HC** my frumpy, butch attire. I'm he'd do something nice, and give a stranger a rose. Maybe it really was that room, a tiny square of space, with a sloping ceiling, a sink separate from the trademark smile, and I trudge back to the gift shop with bag on my back, my embarrassed because i **Are you troubled by static?** say, and as I look up at Sharon squeals with delight, and promptly starts playing music on her bathroom, and two beds for three people. Sharon is trying to persuade a coat bunched up under my arms, and the ridiculous rose clutched in my this boy who stares back **Does anyone copy? Over** ness, I understand that I phone' — Closer by the Chainsmokers, that rampant summer anthem that sickly Aoife to go out with everyone. I sit on the bed closest to the door, still hands, thinking, I was so close to being beautiful. have played this wrong, a **Break, break, break** d a perfect act of kindness, has seeped deep into October. The two begin to apply their make-up, faces enough that I seem to blend in with the sheets and the pillow. Aoife looks All of sudden the scene in front of me transforms into something more such a pure and beautiful ro **This is EI22HC** by looking for a reason, like elongated as they stare into small hand-mirrors cupped in their palms. I tried, and though she isn't pale, her drooping eyes and pained expression profound. I feel myself slipping through different time planes, as though I spoiling a ma **Are my signals fading?** ow it's done. watch them idly from the bed, almost dreaming, when a thought seems to make her look very unwell. But she relents to Sharon's pleadings, because were somehow looking on from the past, present, and future all at once. I The past, the present **Does anyone copy? Over** contained in this one jolt me awake. I think of something my mum told me, years ago, about she knows the only thing more miserable than going out while feeling sick is look at Sharon and Aoife and think of my mum and Jenny, and suddenly feel moment. I can't quite expl **Break, break, break** feeling. It's something like when she was younger and she and her friend Jenny would get ready for having to spend her evening with me. as though I'm trapped in someone else's memory. Won't Sharon and Aoife nostalgia for the future, like **This is EI22HC** the present, like yearning to nights out while listening to George Michael.

I have an emergency message.

Does anyone copy? Over.

Break, break, break.

Are you limited by state?

Does anyone copy? Over.

Break, break, break.

This is IZ2UC.

Are my signals fading?

Does my audio sound even?

Break, break, break.

This is IZ1FGV.

Thank for your patience.

Break, break, break.

This is IZ2UC.

Are you limited by state?

Does anyone copy? Over.

Break, break, break.

There is a loud clatter that wakes me. 'For God's sake,' Mommy hisses.

'Were you drinking?'

Does anyone copy? Over.

Break, break, break.

This is MAYDAY.

Does anyone copy? Over.

Break, break, break.

This is MAYDAY.

Are you troubled by static?

Does anyone copy? Over.

Break, break, break.

It's late in the afternoon, and the other intern and I are the only two in the office. I am unenthusiastically browsing slides in Storyline because Sean still hasn't given me any graphic designwork to do, and I'm not getting paid anyway. Will is diligently creating a pie chart, even though he also isn't getting paid, while he sings lowly to himself. 'And it's just like the ocean…under the moon…' My ears prick up.

'Is that Smooth by Rob Thomas?' I ask. 'Hmm, yeah?' 'I love that song!' I exclaim excitedly, and explain the importance it holds for me and my mum, and how it's a running joke between us to describe things as being Rob-Thomas smooth. Will admits that he only heard it for the first time recently in a mashup song. I am horrified. 'But it's a classic!'

We spend the next half hour or so intently talking about music, and when Jake and Michelle return from their lunch breaks, we continue the discussion over email, sending each other links to YouTube videos. He sends me Psycho Killer, I send him Kiss From A Rose. He sends me Wonderful Life, I send him Wicked Game. It becomes a daily routine, and I spend my mornings organising playlists in my head. It's the only work I do in this job.

We sit down on a park bench, opposite the Boston Public Library, and just do
Despite it being the middle of summer, I insist on wearing my new woolly
Then again, watching the 'sk8r bois' across the street, landing more
Mum and I sit for almost an hour watching them like this, laughing less and
what my mum calls 'people watching'. There's a group of teenagers, a bit
Zelda hat, which I think I can pull off as a kind of fashion statement, with
frequently on their asses than on their boards. I feel markedly less
less inconspicuously, until the police eventually come and usher them along,
older than me, across the road using the railings and steps of the library to
my tank top, long black shorts, and vans—that sort of Avril Lavigne look
embarrassed about my own appearance. So I pull the hat off, rustle my
much to our disappointment. It is getting dark now, and a streak of dark
practise their skateboarding moves despite the explicit 'no skateboarding'

I have an emergency message.

I'm still aspiring towards, despite having outgrown her music years ago. But
sweat-sticky hair with my hand, and snigger as one of the skaters flips his
blue cuts through the orange sky. Mum lights a cigarette and takes a long
sign. They are woeful.

Does anyone copy? Over.

I could never quite pull off that skater-girl, rock-chick vibe, most likely
board with his feet, fumbles the landing, staggers, falls, and rolls on the
luxurious drag from it. A man comes jogging through the street in his bare
pink blush. There's a breeze at last, and the heat is dispersed through it so

Break, break, break.

because my mum didn't envision the same look as I did, and she was the one
feet. This is the second person we have seen bare-foot jogging within only a
ground before springing nonchalantly back to his feet.
that the air feels nice and cool as it grazes the skin.
that bought my clothes, and now, at sixteen, I'm too self-conscious to buy
Daddy returns to the poolside and whispers something to Mommy, before
few minutes. We share a look and laugh. 'See,' she says, blowing smoke in

Are you troubled by static?

The stalls are all painted with white, flaking paint, to reflect the intense heat
anything that could be interpreted as having a style, so I make do with what
telling me he found something he wants to show me. 'What is it?' I ask
my face, then waving it away with her hand, 'this is why I like to just sit
of the sun and keep the horses cool. Dad explains. I can see the shadows of

Does anyone copy? Over.

I have, and only buy clothes with recognisable pop-culture logos on them.
excitedly, but he just tells me to wait, and takes me by the hand, leading me
down sometimes and people watch. You never know what you're going to
the horses in the shade of the stalls and when Dad lifts me up, the first horse

Break, break, break.

When we get to the next stall, I know what to do, and I say hello then reach
round the outskirts of the hotel until we reach a small, sun-scorched stable.
'All right,' Daddy says once we have petted all the horses, 'let's head back to
greets me with its long elegant face and glittering obsidian eyes fringed
for the horse myself, and rub it gently on the nose, admiring its gentleness

This is EI221C

My eyes and mouth widen with excitement and wonder. The groom looks
the pool.' 'Okay,' I moan, and take his hand, which has become red and
with thick, curly eyelashes. Dad takes my hand, and slowly reaches it
and grace. The third horse we spot is standing in the corner. 'Is it asleep?' I ask
up from shovelling hay and regards us with an inscrutable stare before
mottled, but before I can ask what happened to it he says, 'Now, that was a
towards the horse's snout, and I gently stroke it, feeling such a sense of glee

Does anyone copy? Over.

inquisitively. I think it is... But can't it have slept standing up?' I say.
continuing with his task. His skin is dark and glistening with sweat, but he
good surprise, wasn't it?' and I declare delightedly that it was.
There are mushrooms growing by a caravan park, so I decide to

Break, break, break.

'Not necessarily,' he says vaguely, we spend a few minutes studying the
works quietly and diligently in the height of the afternoon, and doesn't seem
I take Daddy's hand. His fingers are like the texture of raw carrots, I think,
decorate them with flowers and leaves... the fairies. When I come back the
sleeping horse, before moving... the horse... the next stall, and then the next

This is EI221C

Friday evening road... my mind... our presence there... the runny egg yolk sun
but they're warm as they wrap around me, and it's so cold I can see my
next day there is an orange envelope amongst the mushrooms. Inside, is a
We're driving through the park, one... away, ... from swimming. The car
dripping from passing bedroom windows. Only three and three-fifths of a
breath. I don't recognise where we are. There's loads of houses and trees.
letter addressed to me. The letter reads: 'Dear Hayley, thank you for making

Does anyone copy? Over.

stops, then my mum suddenly... ... ... I adjust my position in
song's journey to the swimming pool. There's no time for tracks three and
We're walking to mass. I don't really like mass that much. Sam doesn't have
our village so nice and for all the presents you left behind. Love from the

Break, break, break.

the... back... lifting myself... look through the...
four if we want to fit it in. Man, I feel Like a Woman, that man, I do
to go. He stays at home, I don't mind. I just like to spend time with Daddy.
Flower Fairy.' I gasp in disbelief as I reach... letter, then run inside after my
and see in the... lights of... the only... of us... stream of deer galloping

This is EI221C

across the road, a seemingly infinite source emerging from the trees and disappearing into the night on the other side. It's like seeing a unicorn or a mermaid. It's unreal.

'Look,' Daddy abruptly tugs on my arm and I divert my attention away from the shimmering seafloor and see a giant white boulder obstructing our path. 'Do you wanna see what's behind it?' he asks. I reply eagerly that I do and, jettisoning my load of all but my most precious findings, I sprint towards the rock to investigate.

and flat smooth pebbles and sea debris along the way; fish I find swimming in the water that pass right in front of my eyes! and back times ten!' I retort. 'Well, I love you to the moon and back times a hundred!' I furrow my brow and think hard. 'I love you to the moon and back times infinity!' I say finally, proud of my ultimate declaration. 'Well, that's not very nice,' Mommy sulks, 'that you love me more than I love you.' She is pouting in a very sad, silly way that reminds me of a puppy. I don't really understand why it's not nice, especially when she was playing along, but I concede anyway. 'Okay,' I declare, 'we both love each other to the moon and back times infinity!'

Mommy, shouting '...look, look, look!'
That's why I choose to go.
We walk along the sand ...ing behind the throngs of beachgoers as the waves era... no one can follow our trail. Behind the boulder is a secret beach — our secret beach, untouched by anyone else. It is a small beach, tucked in at the bottom of a cliff, with its own turquoise pool that glitters under the sun. Daddy takes a seat on a rock, and watches me as I explore, and I describe to him excitedly the see-through 'I love you to the moon and back,' she says. 'Well, I love you to the moon He smiles at my enthusiasm ... the height of the sun, tells me

it's time to head back ... to tell Mommy and Sam about what we found ...ards the main beach. I tell him I'm glad we found th... tells me it will always be our special place ... feet through the water. Behind us the waves ... they pull our footprints into really understand why it's not nice, especially when she was playing along, the ocean ... presence here.

Are you troubled by static?

Does anyone copy? Over.

Break, break, break.

This is E122HC.

Are my signals fading?

Does anyone copy? Over.

Break, break, break.

This is E122HC.

I can see a light flash in the distance.

I'm altering my course,

heading to that position.

Did you ever mistake the North Star

for a lighthouse?

This is my final transmission.

Over and out.

But Who Has Won?

after Maggie Taylor

In another version, Alice stayed in her original form.
No scalability potion, just a girl holding an empty egg cup,
feet submerged in grey weedy waters, maybe an estuary,
maybe not. *It's a matter of time,* the dull foliage murmured
in the background. She held her lips after seven departed birds
had flown back from the blank and huddled around her.
The colours from *The Birds of America* screamed out: *O it's scarlet!*
Or more like a dodo's! A flash of Xanadu on their breasts,
wings, irises: carefully preserved, songs downloadable.
Memory is a reproduction of loss, but who has won?
Her Prussian blue dress blended in with the lunisolar sky
though the blue looked all wrong. Too safe, too lifelike.
And the present tense? Who will dare speak the day?
The cumulus clouds think they have won. The pink knotted
fan coral branching out this season claims it has won.
What's in your other hand? A knife? The egg we've stolen?

Kit Fan

Mallards

Ronan Kelly

On the morning of his daughter's wedding, Colman wakes early. He lies there quietly as the room slowly brightens. Helen, beside him, sleeps on. In time, the radio clicks to life, and after the news the weather is given: it will be dry and bright, temperatures above average for the time of year, warmest in the east. He gets up then, delicately, even though it is an old joke between them that Helen could sleep through World War Three.

Half an hour later he is returning from the Londis, croissants and *The Irish Times* swinging in his bag. He makes a loop of the trip, out through the lane, home the longer way, by the laundrette, the charity shop, by Little Acorns, whose railed yard is scattered with brightly-coloured plastic toys. There are no children; it is too early. Just as he realises he has stopped walking, his phone rings. He turns away to answer it. 'Sophie, love.'

'Am I disturbing you, Daddy?'

'Not at all, not at all.' Casually, as if she's beside him, he walks on. 'Forecast's good, did you hear? It'll be good for the photos. The lake will be amaz—'

'I'm worried, Daddy. I just don't want any surprises. Any embarrassment.'

'It'll be fine, love. I'll watch her—I promise.'

There is a pause at Sophie's end. He knows she is weighing something cutting; it would not be the first time. He wants to say that Helen has not had a drink all week, except it is not quite true. But she has made a great effort, Colman knows that. Only Colman knows the effort she makes.

'It's you I feel sorry for,' Sophie says finally, her voice soft, and this pains Colman deeply, because although he is touched by the gesture, the intent of her words, he also knows her too well. And unlike him, she is a bad liar.

'Ah, don't worry about me,' Colman says lightly. The curtains are still closed as the house comes into view.

'Two seconds, Dad—' Someone is speaking to Sophie in the background—there's a muffled exchange—and he's close to the gate when she comes back to him: 'Sorry, Dad. One thing, though…'

Colman stops. 'Anything, Sophie.'

'Don't be mad early, yeah? They've no room for hanging around.'

At twenty to twelve Colman finds a place to park close to Mount Street Bridge, and they sit a while. Sunlight off the canal plays on the undersides of the springtime leaves. Helen takes a clamshell mirror from her handbag, opens it at arm's length to pucker and purse at herself, then snaps it fast when the tremble comes. 'Just remind me,' she says, 'James's parents are Cita and…?'

'Liam.'

Colman last met the Flynns on an icy day in November, when they had gathered at the reception venue to trial the proposed three courses. No one had commented on Helen's absence; instead, they all listened intently to the manager's patter: how beyond the garden, hidden by hedges, there is a man-made lake, perfect for photographs; how several pairs of mallard ducks live on it, and how—the manager paused for effect—they mate for life. Colman joined with the others in murmured approval.

'Liam,' Helen repeats, eyes narrowed on a scrap of litter skittering on the road. 'Yes, that's about right. Now—shall we?'

When they round the corner, they see James standing at the gate with Jess, Sophie's bridesmaid. James waves and comes down the pavement to greet them. He wears a grey suit and his customary big grin. They've been together four years, him and Sophie, and while Colman has essentially no idea who the fellow is, he seems a decent sort. He does something in a lab. Gallantly now, James takes Helen's arm, and she beams with pleasure. Sophie is inside already, he says.

As they join Jess by the gate, she is on her phone. 'I seem to have lost my husband and daughter,' she tells them, and rolls her eyes. Colman has known her since she was a shy, slightly scowling child; the mass of russet curls that would shake and spring then are now complicatedly pinned and smoothed.

It is amazing to him that that little scowling child has a daughter of her own, the as-yet absent flowergirl. *Astrid*—as the name comes to him he is touched again by its prettiness. 'Go on in,' Jess says to them. She smiles, though clearly she is furious. 'I'll be along.'

Colman gives her a gormless double-thumbs-up and follows as James steers Helen into the car park. Close to the doors of the registry office, the Flynns stand next to a gleaming black Saab with a white ribbon in a V from grill to wing-mirrors.

'Cita!'

'Helen!'

They hug like long-lost sisters, then step apart to admire each other's outfits: Cita's fuchsia-pink suit with matching pillbox hat, Helen's mint green wrap dress, a darker shawl over her shoulders. A week ago Colman found Helen sitting on their bed in her underwear, and weeping. The dress was in a ball on her lap. 'It *hangs* off me,' she said. He told her she was beautiful, and it was true: the bones of her face would never be otherwise; but it was true too that she had withered her body to something frightening.

'Colman, how are you?' Liam is tall and thin, beaky-nosed.

Colman takes his hand. 'Good man, Liam,' he finds himself saying. 'Good man.'

'You were unwell.' Cita says this softly to Helen as they climb the stone steps, and gravely Helen admits she was, she was.

The plates for dessert remain. On Helen's, the once-dainty pyramid of four profiteroles is in ruins; Colman took the topmost for her, to make it respectable; the others have simply been moved about.

Further down the table, standing under a glare that makes him balder than he is, Brian is delivering his best man's speech. 'Speaking of, of unrequited love,' he reads, turning a quaking page. 'A few words must be said about James's long—longstanding, ah, *affair* with Femore Gaels GFC.'

Around the room, there is laughter, and nods of rueful agreement. Colman no longer hears the words, but he nods and smiles and even laughs along, a beat behind. His eyes follow a teaspoon that is loosely gripped in Helen's fingers.

As Brian elaborates hoarsely—famous victories, and defeats, with final-whistle results not left out—the spoon hovers and pecks, a birdlike thing. It touches the profiteroles, the table's edge, the folded place-name, with the words *Mother of the Bride* there in Colman's flowing script. 'Would you do them, Daddy?' Sophie had asked. 'You've such lovely handwriting.'

'Another time,' Brian perseveres, dabbing a red napkin to his bright forehead, 'we hired this, this minivan for the away leg...'

Earlier, when the waitress poured the organic Malbec, half the room watched Helen's glass fill; it was refilled a second time and is empty now. In the last year Helen's tolerance has been unpredictable, erratic: an entire bottle might have no effect one day; on another, all it took was half a glass, and then, simple as a door opened, or closed, it hit her and she would suddenly be far gone.

Someone was sick in the minivan and Brian is not saying—'I'm not saying,' he repeats—that it could have been James. This gets a few weak laughs that ramp up suddenly when Brian drops to his seat and everyone realises that that, in fact, was the end of the story, the end of the speech. The room applauds, Colman too, a beat late again, and Helen too, once—mercifully— she has put down the spoon.

Towards the centre of the top table, heads questioningly lean forward and back. Brian hauls himself up again. 'Sorry, I forgot, it's Jess now. So, everybody—Jess?'

The room's faces shift aim with scattered volleys of applause. On the far side of Sophie and James, Jess stands. Her hands flap in front of her as she thanks Brian.

'I'm not one for speeches,' she says. 'I didn't even write anything down, I'm so bad. So, I'm just going to say, Sophie, you *look* amazing, you *are* amazing. Jimbo, you're on to a good thing here; I just *know* you'll be very happy together. So, okay, before I start crying and everything, I'm going to sing. Right from the start Sophie said she wasn't going to have one of those weddings where all the women just sit there smiling while the men do all the talking, so this— this is my compromise because I'm *really* not a speech person. Okay, so, no more blather from me. Here's an old song, you'll all know it...'

She takes a sip of water, closes her eyes. The room watches. Her hands join behind her back. '*My young love said to me, my mother won't mind...*' By little sighs and chair-creaks, the room surrenders. '*And my father won't slight you, for your lack of kine...*'

At the ceremony, Colman had noticed the swathe of rosaceous pimples on the backs of Jess's arms; he had felt a dart of pity, knowing it was a thing she'd tried to treat after the dress was chosen. Sophie had snappishly told her not to be silly, that no one would notice. As children, it was Jess, being bigger, who dominated, even bullied, Sophie. He never intervened, never raised it with Helen. He steered clear, because once—just once—Jess's fluting voice had reached up from the patio to his curtained study. 'He's a bit funny, isn't he, your dad?' He had not caught Sophie's answer.

'*It will not be long love, till our wedding day…*'

Beside him, Colman senses Helen respond to the song, sway a little in her seat. She has always loved music.

'*She stepped away from me,*' Jess sings, beaming at Sophie. '*And she moved through the fair…*'

Colman tries to focus on the lyric, the way he thinks others must, but when it finishes he still feels like he has missed some essential point. Everyone else seems to get it, though: the applause is loud and long. Colman applauds too, but also holds back a little, so that Brian might not feel too bad. As the clamour dies away it is pierced by the sound of glass being tapped commandingly with silverware. Colman's eyes shoot to Helen's hand, but there is nothing there, and the shrill ringing continues.

'Ah, so this is *unscheduled*, I know…' At the far end of the table Liam is standing, drained glass in one hand, some utensil brandished in the other. He clears his throat; once, twice. 'Sophie, you'll forgive me…?'

Colman sees only his daughter's gesture, her hand giving Liam the floor. As the recitation begins—the names of people being thanked, the departed remembered—Colman is slow to notice that Helen has begun re-testing her spoon against her water-glass, soundlessly at first, then less so.

'Helen,' he whispers, his tone pitched uselessly between a plea and a demand. A woman in brown nearby—some Flynn aunt or other—is watching now too, and frowning. Instantly, Colman withdraws.

'We are so *delighted*, too,' Liam continues, 'that *our new friends*, Helen and Colman, are both able to be with us today.'

Colman controls a wince, nods his acknowledgment to the eyes that come his way. Helen does not acknowledge anything. The spoon is arrested, but her fingers tighten. The woman in brown gives a good hard stare.

Liam's litany of names is long. Every so often, to break the rhythm, he inserts the words *all the way from* before counties, townlands, parishes. After each of these, Helen's glass chimes, a little louder every time, until one by one all of the guests are aware of it.

'Helen, *please*,' Colman hisses.

Liam ploughs on; then, during a pause, the glass rings again, loud and long, a pure note in the room. He turns to see what will happen next, to see if it is safe to continue.

Colman is in agony, but then Helen simply puts down the spoon and leans close to him. 'I don't feel well,' she says. 'I think maybe I should lie down…'

What happens next is not entirely clear to Colman, neither in the moment nor after the fact. As Helen unsteadily pushes back her chair, she stumbles—Colman rises too then, and tries to catch her elbow—but she reaches out for the table, and somehow lifts the tablecloth with her, and then it is Colman's untouched Malbec that topples first—slowly, it seems, to begin with; in a red arc it sails over the white linen edge, with cutlery, crockery, a full water jug and the pink-and-white rose display following after it.

'Oh, for God's sake,' says the awful woman in brown.

Up in their room, Colman's ancient, tan leather bag sits under the window. Helen's purple case is on the bed. Taking the grained handle, Colman moves the case to the floor, leaving two wheel-shaped depressions in the pale green coverlet. In the en-suite, Helen is being sick, and Colman knows better than to ask if he can help. Carefully he opens one of the long-necked bottles of sparkling water on the side table, controlling the gas escape. He hears the toilet flush and then there is a singing from the pipes in the wall as the tap runs. She will tidy herself, wipe the porcelain, but he will look for red specks. At Christmas there was an episode; nothing, mercifully, since. But the walls of her oesophagus are weak; bleeding, they've been told, is a risk.

Colman half-fills the glass: the bubbles seethe, dampen his hand. He sits it on a folded tissue on the table on her side. Helen comes from the bathroom, closing the door but leaving the light and the extractor at work.

'I think it was the hake…' she says, sitting on the edge of the bed.

On one knee, already undoing the clasps of her shoes, Colman agrees it might have been.

'… or the cream in the dessert things.'

Colman pauses as if to consider this; then says, 'Ready?'

Helen lowers herself back as he swings her feet up; her heels come to rest, almost perfectly, in the dimples from the case.

'Oh, that's better.'

He takes the mat from the bathroom, lays it beside the bed. He places the wastepaper basket there too. It is wicker, but plastic-lined. She does not look, but after a moment says, 'All the way from the real capital!'

Colman smiles, sits by her outstretched shins, and when he dares to pat them, lightly, the skin is cool and thin as film over the bone. *'This is unscheduled,'* he attempts to mimic, nose in the air.

'Sophie, you'll forgive me?' she says. 'Oh, she will alright…' Her laugh comes out constricted by her horizontal position. 'Little he knows her!'

For a moment, with rueful smiles, they let their daughter's nature linger.

Careful not to rock the mattress, Colman raises himself and goes to the window. It gives onto a tarmac area of overflow parking, a half-dozen cars lined up next to several large container-style bins. Idly he remembers the view from the high-ceilinged rooms they'd toured in the main house: the lawns and raked gravel and stone urns. He sees it as a wintry scene, as it had been then.

Now, below, bonnets and windscreens turn gilded, the dropping sun reflected from somewhere unseen. He unhooks the swag of curtain, takes its weight in his hand, and as he does so a child runs into view on the grass behind the cars. She falls, laughing. She rolls on her back, eyes closed against the bright, sending her gurgling laughs up and up and up…

'You monkey!' says an adult voice, somewhat muffled by the glass. The girl squeals, and Colman recognises Jess's husband, Rory, as he appears, and only then, by association, does he know Astrid. Her frock is different, yellow now. The earlier one was cornflower blue. As if a bystander to himself, Colman can never tell, much less control, where his thoughts will go.

'Come on, monkey.' Rory half-heartedly pulls a white-socked ankle. There are more squeals. 'Now, come *on!*' The tone alters, the foot is dropped. Colman registers the girl's confusion: adult unpredictability. '*Up,*' Rory barks. 'Mum'll skin you if you get grass on that dress.'

'That Jessica Peart, though,' Helen is murmuring. 'Such a lump, and then this *voice of an angel* out of her…'

Astrid and Colman study the small body for punishable grass. A moment later, hand in hand, father and daughter exit Colman's frame.

'But *that* song,' Helen continues. 'At a *wedding*? More *inappropriate* you could not get.'

Colman agrees vaguely; on the grass an image of Astrid falls again, skirt upturned, and there is a waking stir in his penis.

Then a car pulls in, sun-flare dazzling in its turning glass.

'The afters are arriving,' he says, feeling again the heaviness of the curtain. 'Open or closed?'

'I mean, I could have told her—but does anyone ask muggins here…?'
Colman lets the curtain fall; the room goes dark.
'… No they do not,' Helen says. 'No they do not.'

On the lawn it is still mild. Guests in twos and threes, drinks in hands, throw long-limbed shadows. There are fairy lights on the gazebo, violet clouds in a peach-coloured sky. A jasmine plant somewhere releases its night-scent. Colman has made it through the crowded lounge. 'I'm looking for Sophie,' he'd said, fending off small-talk, well-wishers. Liam had discovered him in a corridor and, once it was certain Colman would be alone for the evening, invited him to 'help orchestrate the cake-cutting business.' Together they'd looked in on the dining-room, where tables were already reconfigured, fresh cups inverted on saucers, napkins neatly tented, no sign now of the fallen Malbec. The name-cards, too, occurred to him; in a bin somewhere, he supposed.

He drifts through the lawn-drinkers. One by one the new arrivals will have learnt about the excitement, and one by one they will have misunderstood. A figure is hailing him and absently he moves that way.

'Mr Quinn, hiya. *Oh—*'

Rory drops to one knee to receive Astrid at full tilt. He scoops her up, wields her at his shoulder.

'Mr Quinn—sorry, stop that, Astrid—I hear you're looking for the bride?'

Astrid glowers, and Colman smiles, head to one side. She's tired, crankiness in blotches on her face. Another version of her tumbles on the grass outside his window. In this version Colman is not interrupted, every detail already sharpened, savoured, ripe for playback.

'I am, I am,' Colman sheepishly admits.

Rory re-hoists the burrowing Astrid, blows a mouthful of curls from his face. 'They were last seen heading for the lake.' His eyebrows arch. 'For a moment's peace, apparently.'

'Ah, magic, thank you. Now, this one…' Colman's fingertip doesn't quite touch the pudgy calf—he has never so much as laid a finger, ever. 'She's been amazing.'

Colman follows a meandering, high-hedged path, the deep gravel sliding underfoot. He takes the long way around, so that he can regain composure.

At the edge of the lake there is a bench where Sophie sits, facing the water, her long pale nape bare beneath her pinned hair. Jess is standing; she hides something behind her back as Colman appears.

'Oh, Mr Quinn,' she says, and a cigarette is revealed. 'I thought you were Astrid there.' She wears a wine-red shawl around her shoulders—a pashmina, some inner echo of Sophie or Helen corrects. He'd comment, admire it, only the skin complaint seems related and he would not like to draw attention.

Sophie turns. 'Are you the search party?' She looks tired and very beautiful. 'Are we gone that long?'

'No, no—you're grand.' He waves a dismissive hand. 'So did you see these famous ducks yet?'

They say they didn't think to look. All three gaze out at the gleaming, glinting surface. Jess blows a slow blue plume, and when it breaks apart Sophie asks: 'Is she coming down?'

Colman sees for an instant the curtained bedroom. 'No, I don't think she will, no.'

'Good,' Sophie says after a moment. She glances towards Jess, who holds her cigarette-hand at arm's length, fingers up, as if trying to decide about an imaginary ring. Without returning Sophie's glance, she nods.

'Do you know,' Sophie continues, 'do you know, I don't even *care*.' She looks at Colman meaningfully. 'I've said it before, it's *you* I feel sorry for.'

'Ah now, don't…' Weakly his hand dismisses again. The red specks were there in the bowl when he looked, under the rim. The day is coming when he and Sophie will meet many of the guests again and accept their condolences. When that happens Sophie will not mourn, nor will she later, when it is Colman's turn. She has feared him for too long, never knowing why.

'So, Jess,' he says, rousing himself with some difficulty. 'That song, your performance of it, it was *just* stunning. Just, just *stunning*.'

'Ah, thanks, Mr Quinn.'

Voice of an angel, he hears again Helen saying, and he has the urge to repeat that now, to feel the closeness of her words. For Colman, no one knows music like she does, and when it comes to such things he has always relied on her. It goes back to their earliest days together, and that one particular afternoon when he was waiting for her in a café off Dame Street. He'd found a rare free booth, and music was playing. More than half a lifetime later, every detail is vivid: how the upholstered leather creaked under him, how the smell of fresh and burnt coffee mingled sweet with acrid in the air. It was hot, and he'd worn a shirt and tie and could feel himself sweating. His whole life, he'd known what he was, had known and been terrified by it. But lately, desperately, he'd decided to live, to try to live, trusting that the change could follow. He threw himself into it, he went for drinks after work, he talked to women, and he met her. But it was no use, nor was it fair, and he knew—he *knew*—he had to end it... Except then the bell over the door jangled and she was sliding in across from him—*the luck of a booth*! her eyes seemed to exclaim. He began to speak, in utter confusion, but she reached across the table and touched her finger to his lips—

'Shush a sec—I haven't heard this song in years...'

He still felt the shock of it: the blood-warmth of her touch. At first he could only pretend to listen; his thoughts were reeling. Then he could hear it— jaunty, twanging, familiar to a point. *Boom-chicka, boom-chicka.* As the chorus came around again she was smiling. She mouthed along, chin low to match the gruff American singer, and when it faded out she laughed at her own silliness. A new tune began immediately.

'*This*!' she groaned. 'How can they follow *that* with *this*!' She leaned out to see the counter, as though to express her complaint.

Colman had no earthly idea why the first song was so much better than the new one, but he knew this much: that she knew, and that she could show him; and that she was young and clever and beautiful, lit with the spark of life, and that somehow, for some reason, she liked him, and because of that he could change for her, change his whole life—

'You've the voice of an angel,' he blurts out now to Jess, but the closeness is not there; he cannot call it back. 'Someone was saying that just now.'

Jess laughs, drops her cigarette and toes it out. 'Ah, you're too kind, Mr Quinn.'

Helen knew. She knew because a wife would know; because for half a lifetime their pillows touched. She knew, and yet she doubted. Together they had fought to keep that doubt alive the way others fought for love.

'He's a bit of a charmer, your old man,' Jess says to Sophie.

'Ah, here,' Colman lightly objects. 'Less of the *old*.'

They turn to go. Sophie takes Colman's arm, but after a few steps he frees himself and goes back to the water's edge. *I'll watch her*, he had promised, only that morning, but it was she who had forever watched him, and that had taken its toll. When she began to drink, he let her. And he had let Sophie hate her. If he could change one thing, it would be that.

The women look on as he sinks to one knee. He takes one of the table's red paper napkins from his jacket and picks up the scorched and flattened cigarette-stub. He examines it for embers, then wraps and pockets it and slowly stands. 'The ducks,' he explains, mock-wounded. 'You wouldn't want to see one left alone.'

'The mallards,' Sophie corrects as she comes and re-takes his arm.

'Ah, the mallards,' Jess says, as though under that high violet sky there could be no greater romance.

That night, as Colman lies down next to Helen, as the music bumps distantly through the floor, and he tells her about the lake, Helen says sleepily: 'But that's not right at all—you're thinking of swans or geese. Mallards are seasonal.' They hold hands then, as they do every night. 'Or,' she says, and in the dark Colman can hear her smiling, 'it's just some lie they tell all the couples.'

Name Your Character
John Patrick McHugh

Dragon

Hear a raging storm, hear gale and thunderous wave, and then see it. Grey sea and spray and pelting rain, and there, amongst it, rocking and swirling, a small rickety boat with a single sail. Now watch a wave build and build and toss the boat as if it were a toy. A flash of thunder. See a hooded woman and child struggling to pilot the thrown boat. Another flash: note the anguish writ on the woman's face. Black and cut to a waking princess: a silver crown of knots and jewels, a strapless ballgown. Rosegold light streams into her bedroom and now hear music for the first time, hear doves chirping, as the princess rises and pushes open a window. See a castle, its great walls and gates and four turrets, and further on the moat and canals, the packed-in townhouses with brick-red roofs and shuttered windows, the windmill and gushing waterfalls, the mist bubbling up from the gorge below, and see too the gigantic sword protruding heavenward from the centre of the castle. The music is building now, but the full orchestra is yet to play. The strings swoon and instantly drop, and then trumpets and drums suddenly sound. Now see another ship: an impressive galleon. A stone mermaid is perched on its prow, and the doves are sailing alongside it. See spinning propellers, see the wheel and levers in the bright windows above the deck. Watch the galleon fly astoundingly through cloud and sky and towards the castle as the music swells. And now *be* the boy with the monkey tail, sliding down the firepole inside the galleon. Listen to the groan of the airborne ship as you control him in a gloomy screen. Move and discover the stash of Gil stowed in the far corner, then pick the potion hidden on the opposite side. Now heed the ghostly prompt and light the candles in the middle of the room. Appreciate the slowly revealed background: the railing hooked with outfits, the dim portrait on the wall, the boxes and knickknacks stuffed on shelves and atop wardrobes, the rug beneath the boy's ankle boots with the heart and the ornate lettering spelling out TANTALUS. Now be ready to rename the character correctly, be prepared to battle the dragon-man: the first boss.

Attack

Final Fantasy IX is the best RPG, the best video game ever. Its story is frantic and fun—it unfolds with a whimsical scheme to kidnap royalty and climaxes with you, the player, battling Death to save the world from annihilation—and yet it often slackens this headlong pace to linger on tinier character moments, quieter scenes of introspection. The world of Gaia, the world you are given to explore, is crammed with secrets and moody dungeons and treasure chests to kick open. The locations you visit on your adventure are wonderous and wondrously strange: a sprawling clock-like city, an upside-down castle, a religious sect atop a tree. The inhabitants are sometimes anthropomorphic, sometimes rotund Disneyesque figures, and always charming. The music is sublime: eerie at stages, and at other stages purring to your ears like a half-remembered lullaby. The eight main characters become your friends: they are defined by their fears while simultaneously appearing like cartoons. The monster design is kooky, the big bad dungeon bosses are threatening with just the right amount of quirks. The progression of your party's fighting skills is immensely satisfying: from Fire charging to Fira, then to Firage, a Do-Re-Mi of magical spells. The baddie possesses menacing gravitas at the beginning, is sympathetic by the close. Each new screen you advance upon is baroquely detailed due to the pre-rendered backgrounds: from the lifeless blues of Terra's walkways and its towering tree-like saucers to the architect's study in the ravaged city of Burmecia with a candle flickering by the drawing board. Throughout *FFIX*, the stakes are kept excitingly high—you carry the fate of Gaia; you must confront murky questions of existence and purpose—and comically, splendidly low: will you please assist Quina in eating ninety-nine frogs so that they are bequeathed the legendary Gastro Fork?

Steal

A fat boy of nine creeps inside a garden shed. Watch as he checks over his shoulder once, twice, before crouching beside a heap of brooms and shovels and rakes in the corner. He rummages. He tests the weight of a broom and discards it, then pulls out a shovel, a twist of wrist, discards that too, and now he reaches for a sweeping brush. The boy stands, taking the handle with both hands, and swings it. Swings it again, faster. A floating wad of cobweb. Oxblood bristles. The fat boy needs to make sure that this stick isn't cumbersome, that it is not splintery to grasp. Satisfied with his choice, the boy unhooks a saw from a nail on the wall and, like a doomsday beaver, scurries out of the shed, the saw and brush under one crooked arm. He hurries to the narrow strip of garden which—he has checked, he has confirmed—lays concealed from any nosy eyes in the kitchen window. His face is blushing. He drops the broom and checks over his shoulder, once. Twice. Now he grips the saw.

Skill

In theory, an RPG is a more thoughtful experience than your average video game. It is a genre built on wits and cunning and the comprehension of statistics. You can customise your characters to function how you prefer them to function. You are encouraged to plan and defuse rather than button-bash. It is not essential to outgun your adversary, but to outthink them.

In *FFIX*, this cerebral mediation occurs from the principle of turn-based combat and random encounters. Frequently, as you are scampering through whatever destination—be it across the distinct grain of the 3D overworld, or the glossy sheen of a pre-rendered background—you will hear a sudden suck of air, witness a whirlpool slurping down your screen, and you'll be whisked to a stage and a battle against a skeleton, or a glum owl, or a small furious ram, or a zombie whale, or a multiple-tentacled demon called a Malboro…

A turn-based battle is a deferential dance, an adorably unrealistic representation of hand-to-hand combat. A typical fight: the chuck-a-chuck-a of guitar and the camera spinning to a closeup of your enemy—let's say it's the boar, Zaghnol—before a panning shot of the four characters you are using. A list of names appear at the bottom of the screen, animated bars start to chug from one end to the other. As soon as the time bar fills, a pyramid popping over the readied character, you guide a gloved hand along the four-stacked menu of command and select your wisest move: if controlling Vivi you'll perhaps pick a spell; if John you might steal ore from the furry pockets of this tusked enemy. You make your choice, you press X, and you watch for the stilted animation to begin—watch Steiner hopping forward to slash at Zaghnol, or Eiko using her flute to summon a Phoenix to scorch this piggie. A number flashes—white means pain, lime-green means replenishment—and you repeat this process until the foe is vanquished: you wait for your bar to fill, you get hit, you attack or cure or use an item, and hopefully the trumpets of victory blare and your band will pose heroically for the swooping camera at the end.

In practice, during my first playthrough, I understood none of an RPG's distinctive complexities. Zero skill was involved, zero reckoning with strategy or the nuances of spells beyond the rush of their cinematics. I didn't match armours to garner add-ons that could nullify debilitating curses. I didn't consider how the buff of a lowly dagger could be more useful than the blade higher in attack power. Instead, I kept the core party—because I liked those four characters the best—and I selected whatever helmet or robe sent my character's stats shooting up. I pressed attack and watched my character bonk the heads of baddies. I presumed that blunt force would win out, and when it didn't, when I was put on my arse by Kuja, or devastated by the security system in the Desert Palace, I would grind until my level was so high, my hit points so superior, that I could, once more, barrel tactlessly forward.

Summon

I wasn't bullied for being fat. I felt the pressure of it, yes, felt a searing and judgemental gaze, imagined or otherwise, upon my repulsive body, but I was not routinely called a fatty, or jeered at for owning a pair of tits, or shoved about the yard. I was lucky: I was a decent-sized obstruction in goals and had high-ranking friends. There was only one moment of abuse that stands out. I was in third class and my gang were annoying a sixth-class boy nicknamed Peacock. It had been occurring irregularly over a couple of weeks—giddy, egged on by our older brothers, we would pester this unfortunate boy at big break by shouting insults—but then it escalated. I can't recall what our taunting entailed—no doubt it was horrible, probably borne from prejudice about Peacock's social class or, ironically, how he looked—but, of course, I remember when Peacock ultimately snapped back one afternoon. He swung for the loudest of us and connected and sent him tumbling, kicked out at another, and then he said to me: Fuck off, Fatty. Simple, brutal. I went cold and backed away to our share of the yard, head lowered, lip wobbling. For the rest of lunch, my group didn't mention our comeuppance. The fella who was punched pretended he had not been punched. However, once home, I squealed to my older sister. I must have exaggerated and lied, I must have guessed she knew who Peacock was from town, and that weekend she ate the poor lad. She informed Peacock to stay well clear of her brother. I was playing *Final Fantasy*—honestly—when she arrived home and told me I won't be bothered by him anymore.

Item

FFIX was released in 2001 for the PlayStation. It was SquareSoft's final hurrah to that specifically grey console before crossing over to the future and PlayStation2. The game came in a blocky double-decker case (the heavy click to open each case and inside two shiny white discs atop one another; four in total). The cover image was plain and regal: holy-white apart from the runic-like lettering of the title with a mysterious crystal jammed in the middle.

Trance

I was addicted to the game in the weeks and months after purchase. I was suckered in by the scope, the characters, and I played till my eyeballs crisped. How hours fell in this trance. How ridiculous was my temper when I was instructed to switch it off. In bed, my head fried, I'd hear in rotating echoes the music of locales and characters from the game—the ragtime piano of Treno, the plucked strings of Steiner's theme alongside his clanking chainmail. Soon I begged for the official guide, and would study it daily once received, delighting in reliving the game through text. I started to envision the video game world seeping over my drab real one: the thorns over the backwall of school were actually part of the Evil Forest; I surmised that one of my detested friends would be a rat from Burmecia, and wasn't the girl I talked to not the spit of Princess Garnet? I would finish the game and take a few days off before once more climbing inside its tale of thieves and genocidal eidolons, into its gameplay loop of battling and levelling.

White Magic

The family had moved four times before we settled in Macroom, County Cork. I was eight and would receive *FFIX* about a year later. By then, I had changed school twice, had come to see friendship as a fleeting experience. I was a shy boy. In public, when not with family, I started to despise myself in abstract ways—it started with my weight but then it plunged deeper. The opening musical theme of *FFIX*—this pump-organ hum that you hear at the start menu—is entitled, 'A Place to Call Home'. The overarching motif of the game is the quest for a home—figurative and literal—and the purpose such a place can provide: John is searching for his forgotten birthplace, signified by a blue light; Eiko is apparently the sole survivor of her tribe and wishes to belong to somewhere else. Even if these concerns skipped over my mind when I was an obtuse young buck, it must have affected me subconsciously, like sugary-sweet Calpol to quench a pain in your ear. It would have clicked.

Help

An RPG stands for role-playing-game. An offspring of dice-rolling adventures, it is a genre with particular emphasis on worldbuilding and character development and story. A novelistic video game, if you will.

Ok, so, in terms of geography, Gaia marries picturesque fantasy in its greenery and cutesy settlements with some gibberish sci-fi features: two moons, a tree funnelling the souls of another planet called Terra to replace the souls of Gaia. It is a medieval society: farmers and small shopkeepers and wealthy nobles. Health is administered through flasks of potions. Creatures of incomparable power—the eidolons—were summoned once upon a time by a tribe with horns poking from their foreheads. A crystal at the centre of the planet is the source of all living things. There are large rideable birds named Chocobos, helpful cats called Moogles, and a family of hippos who run a popular hotel.

Now bear with me: *FFIX* follows the cheeky but endearing John (he has a monkey's tail, wears a sleeveless top with a dandy jabot, and his name might not be John in your own playthrough) as he arrives on a theatre ship to Alexandria to perform a play—but really, John alights to kidnap Princess Garnet (she is capable of summoning eidolons, she used to have a horn). Garnet, as it transpires, wants to be abducted so that she can find a way to stop her mother, the Queen—who isn't Garnet's real mother—from inciting war between the kingdoms ruling the continent. Garnet and John are pursued by the bumbling knight Steiner (no tail or horn), and, through his own clumsiness, a magician named Vivi (picture a pointy hat and underneath a black void with yellow eyes). As the plot becomes increasingly convoluted, as war indeed breaks out between the kingdoms, further characters join this foursome: the gluttonous Quina (clownlike with a floppy tongue), the imperturbable warrior Freya (rat with a spear), a six-year-old named Eiko (she can also summon eidolons, still has her horn), and the bounty hunter Amarant (human with teal skin). The main villain in all this is Kuja (he has a secret tail and is sort of the brother of John), whose motive advances from warmongering alongside the Queen so as to quicken the replacing of Gaia's souls with that of his home planet Terra— oh yeah, which is John's home planet, too—to simply wishing to obliterate all life once he learns his mortality is prearranged and approaching.

Are you still with me?

Black Magic

In writing about this video game, I am writing about me as a boy playing this video game, and in replaying *FFIX* today—which I am doing on the pretext of research—I am experiencing it as that boy once more. A video game as hardened memory. My adoration for *FFIX* ascends beyond the game's strengths. It is about the safety and security that swells up when I periodically wonder if I should dip back into Gaia. In other words, it is now nostalgia. It is the exact rot that I associate with the legion of superhero flicks—a cultural item that is unsurprising and intellectually boring. I play *FFIX* because I don't want to be challenged. I play *FFIX* because I want everything to be under my direct control. I play *FFIX* because I want to be a child—carefree, innocent, etc. It is a reactionary impulse. I should stop but I will not; I will continue to play it, year after year.

Focus

It was in fourth class in my all-boys school, when we turned ten and started to smell a little sour, that I became fat. Before then I was tubby, was breasted, was double chinned. But it wasn't until girls transited from slight novelty into the essential variable within our equations for what we should do against what was considered lame and shitty, that I felt fat to the world. My weight was now public, intentional. I was an embarrassment not only to myself, but to my friends. I was a stink as we glared up at the girls' school on our hike to the library. I was the reason why girls were unattainable to us. And on those rare times when we encountered girls, I could sense trouble, I could interpret my new troubling position: now I swayed between friend and useful target. If these girls were to speak to us, I was a ready-made punchline for my boys to fill space with. I was sure about this tacit betrayal because I was searching for a lad beneath me to use. I was just as traitorous.

Sword Art

In that unspyable slice of garden around the side of the house, I chopped the head off the stolen brush. Tossing the bristled end, I picked up the handle and slashed it left and right. The air whistled. I thumped the stick against the coal bunker, smiling at the drum of impact. I held it at one end and let the stick slide through my palms until I grasped it at its very centre. I twirled it then like a baton before bringing it to rest aside my hip as I pivoted into a samurai stance—left arm forward and fingers gesturing coolly for my enemy to come get some.

While I played like this, I was constantly checking for watchers in the windows, in the surrounding estate. I would throw the stick aside if I heard approaching footfall, or the backdoor, or tyres flinging gravel along our road. I would keep a football close by—an inconspicuous out. At some point, my Nana came to stay with us, and I recall coming to despise her—my beloved Nana!—because she enjoyed sitting by the sunlit window in the spare room. In this, she threatened to reveal my bizarre world. She would wave as I stamped about damning her soul, the stick stiff in my hand.

Obviously, I was nowhere near as discreet as I presumed. My father has a video of me thrashing my stick at no one. You can hear him whisper before he unlatches the window: 'We'll see now if he has his stick with him.' A space was arranged in the shed where I could deposit my deadly arsenal, my parents would shout to check that I was alive in my patch of garden, my sister lumped me over the head with one of my secret sticks during an argument.

Sword Magic

So, what was I at with the headless brushes and brooms? It was quite innocent. It is mortifying. Simply: the numerous sticks I collected became a knight's broadsword, a dragoon's javelin, a thief's dragger in my private theatre. It wasn't so much imagination: rather they were those weapons to me then. How do I explain that? Prove it? I can't. Once I picked up those sticks they were pronged and weighty and I was whatever hero in whatever current act of my drama. For those hours spent swinging my weapons, I would mutter the voices and narration for tales inspired by *FFIX*—I'd employ the same peaks and troughs of its plot, use its varied landscape—but with sprinklings of originality: I'd make up a new evil baddie, new backstories for those characters I thought were underdeveloped, new dungeons. No audience, but I was immersed in these performances. Like when playing the video game: I wasn't me.

All these stories concluded in much the same fashion: the hero discovers love in the princess from Alexandria. After he has defeated the climactic boss, he pledges devotion to her for now and forever—the Ultima Weapon still in his hands— and this princess declares her own love for him. These romantic moments never rushed beyond the promise of an unbreakable bond, a cuddle. It was simple confirmation that one person loved the other person, and my story would end right there—to be started all over again the next day.

Jump

The triumph of hearing the ping that confirms you have levelled up. The excitement of seeing your HP jumping from 930 to 971 as the corner rolls from level 19 to 20. Can I explain this rapture properly, when all it really means is that I'm a little bit harder to kill, a little bit more powerful? How do I convey the buzz in studying the slightest increase in stats like Attack and Defence, Magic and Spirit? I suppose it is like scoring a goal: no words can do justice to the elation. So you must go do it: you must grind, have your character run in circles and fight the same crop of enemies again and again and again and again and again. Only then will you soar as I soar when the experience points drop and the level springs up.

Eat

The two emotions I associate with being fat are fear and shame.

The fear sprung from the knowledge that if I spoke out of line in a group, I could be, I would be, slapped back down into my lowly place. Without much thought on their part, without much malice, I could be made to feel ugly, pathetic, worthless—which is what I felt about myself. Everyone could do me. I could perform the greatest feat imaginable—saving a peno, throwing a rubber at the back of someone's head in the middle of class—and still with one half-baked insult, I would be done.

The shame arose in trivial matters. In the dressing room, for example, I would panic over which jerseys were bundled inside the duffel bag: the newish ones, which were comfortable and baggy? Or the woollen jerseys, which were long-armed yet skin-tight, which made me look like a freak? And as a result of the trivial becoming degrading, shame came to slowly warp all public bouts of spontaneous joy—I could never fully experience happiness while surrounded by others, because it could scald as soon as it cheered.

Take Speech and Drama in school, a class I adored: the chance to act the maggot and be clapped at. Each year, there was a competition held in Cork, and on the day when we were due to sing and dance to the 'Circle of Life', I was informed I would be wearing an off-the-shoulder Lycra top with leopard print. (I still question what they were thinking in pushing such clothing: was it a sort of joke for the overseeing adults, the fat kid in Lycra?) The top clung to my body, highlighted the rolls along my stomach, built sacks out of my chest. In the bathroom, I cried while staring at the mirror, and once backstage in the theatre in Cork, I hid in a corner and hoped I'd be forgotten, that my space would be automatically filled by somebody else. When the bell sounded, when the teacher angrily told me to get ready pronto, I asked could I please not wear this top. For the first time in my life, I admitted aloud to the humiliation of my body—how excruciating it was to have this type of body. Before classmates dressed as animals and Tarzans, I pleaded, and I was told to cop on. This woman said: Will you hurry up and change.

Blue Magic

In my bedroom, I would practise John's poses from cutscenes and in-game set pieces. I'd mimic his leave-it-to-me-chest-thump, his ready-for-a-brawl-squat. I'd even attempt to run like him: the OTT lope like a rocking horse. I had changed the name within the game to my own, and now I sought to adjust the real-life John to be more like *FFIX*'s superior version.

Flair

While I was pitching this essay, my editor remarked on a Final Fantasy title he himself had loved: *Final Fantasy VII. VII* is the loftier brother of *IX*. It is a darker RPG: the 'princess' in *VII* is impaled by a katana. The editor mentioned that his experience with *FFVII* had been more affecting than with any book he had encountered as a teenager. I hadn't considered this notion or thought it could be a notion to consider—that a game could have a valuable impact on imagination and creativity—but it was strikingly true for me as well. I can remember only one book I read during the blurry run of five to eleven years old, but I recall every character beat that happened in *FFIX*, every little scene. The style I look for in books today, the very stuff I seek to replicate in my own work, can be traced back to *FFIX* and what it introduced me to: slightly off-humour, tiny character moments, perplexed protagonists, the concurrent High and Low.

More broadly, when I peel beyond narrative preferences, when I look truthfully at myself as a person, the game has had an undue impact on how I consider life. It is shameful to admit this, but a lot of my deliberate 'philosophical' outlook is derived from the John in *FFIX*, and his moral tagline: *You don't need a reason to help people*. It is a simple credo, naïve—Barney the dinosaur probably pronounced similar in a song—but it is an attitude I cling to.

Change

We said good luck to Cork when I was twelve, moving to Galway to live with my grandparents. Over my last summer in Cork, without any dietary change,

I lost a power of weight. It was never remarked upon at home; it didn't feel like an accomplishment on my behalf, it just happened. So, when I arrived in Galway, I was no longer podgy, chubby, fat. While not skinny, I was not notably titted in my new school jumper, not figured for a goalie in the yard. As I went about in public, it didn't seem as if strangers wanted to destroy me. I made new friends. I joined a football club as an outfield player.

My obsession with video games ebbed away around this point, too. I still bought a couple, but I stopped getting the magazines. Games were not considered cool in primary school nor in my secondary school, and to fit in, I suppressed all gaming knowledge beyond the latest *FIFA* and *GTA*—in the same way I would pretend to enjoy techno music for a stretch in my teens. I did try out the new Final Fantasy games and enjoyed *X*—John now had blonde-tipped hair—but never got on with the rest: the freedom and self-expression I had found in *IX* wasn't present in the newer ones, mainly because voice-acting was dominant, character's names were set in stone, and so your own imagination was less useful.

Throw

Occasionally, throughout my teens, I would throw up after a meal. Now and then, I would feel certain that I was becoming fat, fatter, and I'd find myself kneeling by a toilet with my head tipped forward and two fingers in my throat. I would gag and retch and vomit bile and chunks of food. The sudden slosh of this acidic mixture, the gasp for air between rounds. I'd repeat this action five to six times and once content with the amount of food discharged, I would wipe the slime from my mouth and the rim of the toilet, unstick wayward nuggets of food from the bowl. I'd flush then and flush once more for luck.

This expulsion wasn't done regularly enough for me to think of it as a problem. I just would do it, as I said, now and then, because I didn't want to be fat, get fatter, I didn't want to experience being that John again.

Defend

Oh, *FFIX* is undeniably a slow game. And yes, the persistent random encounters become a pain. The battles themselves are often formulaic affairs—hit the attack button, wait for your turn, hit attack once more. The plot relies on the villain explaining his scheme to the camera while atop a dragon. The limitations of the hardware—how much the PlayStation could handle on screen, how many unique models it could process—are a further hurdle to traverse. Yes, Chocobo Hot and Cold is an arduous side quest. Fair enough, the dungeons are quite straightforward: the puzzles never exceptionally taxing. And on closer examination, *FFIX* is nowhere near as wonderfully expansive as you presume it to be—in fact, it is quite linear: the story shuttles you briskly along to point A to point B to a boss battle; repeat.

Escape

... is the purpose of Final Fantasy, the purpose of video games. To escape and explore a more interesting world. To escape and accomplish things I could not accomplish in real life. To escape and not be myself—or, better, to be somebody else.

In the years since my first lumbering playthrough, I have replayed *FFIX* an insane number of times. I have beaten it on the PlayStation2 and 3, the lappie, an iPhone after a day spent selling schoolbooks. I have perused the Final Fantasy Wiki into the wee small hours. I have read nonsensical theories that seek to fill *FFIX* plot holes, to enhance the lore. I listen to the game's soundtrack when writing, while writing this essay. When I feel uncommonly sad, I search for my favourite cutscenes on YouTube—and while watching all thirty-nine minutes of the ending sequence, I still swoon like a lonely child when the princess leaps into John's arms. I know the game off by heart—and when I suffer a memory lapse, I will pause and consult my guide. There is no challenge, I want no challenge. It is an automated experience. And yet, despite the many years, as soon as the theme music chimes, I'm no longer me. Instead, I am that better John, whose personality is charming and brash, whose actions are virtuous, who is skinny and likeable. There is glory when I step through the Ice Cavern and the entire world of Gaia opens up and out for me and my party of adventurers: the domed huts of the bucolic village of Dali in the distance, the lump of rock that is Observatory Mountain, the foggy valley far below and its deep and dark woods, the field of stippled green and olive that I must now traverse, the nooks and hollows that I must explore, the mightiest monsters that I must slay.

Sonogram

Underdeveloped, fading.
Due date a negative number now,
illegible.
Light as cellophane.
Shiny.
Creased accidentally down its spine.
Brown envelope growing microscopic fur (lanugo)
from years of handling.
Written in ink on the triangular flap
the word Private (in bold).
Ghost letters E.D.D.
Liquid metal smell (almost) of oil.
Under a magnifying glass
lack of clarity amplified.
Grey, the colour of an industrial blanket.
Not quite steel, but steel wool.
Utility,
without comfort.
Scent of an illicit library book
you forgot to return.
The yellowed smell of shame/guilt.
Rectangular,
smaller than a human adult palm.
Devoid of sound (completely, wholly mute).
The off-white head
never quite entitled to call itself bone (white).
A static blot, where a heart should beat.
Litany of numbers.
A barcode
you need a doctor's eye to read
or comprehend.

Martina Dalton

My Father's Wives

I watch our neighbours dither
when meeting her at mass, in the shop,
at my father's graveside, search their little brains
like squirrels troubling dirt, frantic for her name only
to unearth the other buried one, greedy for any acorn.
I swear I see a strange expression of delight
paw across their faces as my mother's face stiffens.
Exhilarated by their mistake, defiant. *Don't they see
my mother*? I wonder. *Don't they know she is a different woman?*
They are more than just my father's wives. Her name means *pearl*;
my mother's *unity*. I hold an acorn in my palm,
push it through tributaries of flesh.
Scraping its pointed heart into cemetery mud,
I spell out their given names in blood.

Victoria Kennefick

Naming the Foals

It is the darkest time of year in the Northern Hemisphere, months before the growing season, and I am casting about for names.

The birth date is always January 1st. And a name must be found before February of the second year. Six names for each, listed in order of preference, for someone else to decide.

Each name no more than eighteen characters, no initials no trade names, no numbers except those above thirty and only if they are spelled out.

No words like colt or filly. No racetracks or famous winners. No name that's already in use or that's ever been named.

I carry a book with me for writing down names as they come— pruning back the winter garden, glancing at the clock, pouring a drink:

Sudden Flight, Traveller's Hymn, Treasured Time, Rags to Riches, Blind Faith, Sphinx's Riddle, Praise the Painter, Second Harvest, Merchant's Dream, Constant Optimist.

Grace Wilentz

The 40ft

Each time the sea licked the step,
the cold shocked me to my core.
(Worst where the breeze stung my wet skin.)
Another swimmer joined the queue behind me,
and before me it was just the sea now.

Sure, I'd had my day in the Convention Centre,
waited on the labyrinth of snaking queues,
arriving eventually at M-Z. I received the packet
with the certificate, Amhrán na bhFiann photocopied,
a slip for the passport office and the little tricolour badge.

My partner left to sit with the other guests.
We were strange by then, having come apart just as
the stress of whether I'd be able to stay was finally lifting.
A month before, he took a day off work to lie for me
at the GNIB office, so I could get my last stamp.

Separated into tiers, we sat nervously
while the Garda band hammed it up with pop songs,
until eventually the Minister came out.
And though I'd cried as a guest at my friend's ceremony,
knowing what it meant to her to have her status not tied

to a husband who tried to run her over twice,
when we got to the part where we all sing
Amhrán na bhFiann, I couldn't understand why I didn't feel a thing,
though the eyes of the man from Sierra Leone to my left
and the man from the Philippines to my right

were glassy, and wet. I knew without looking
that the swimmers queueing behind me were surely
becoming impatient, so I dove. All in, I didn't know
if I was paralysed or revitalised, or how
I'd ever draw a breath again.

But in that cold, opaque sea, somehow I started
treading water, and hand to heart, I never felt so Irish.

Grace Wilentz

0

is / not a number

       it is an open mouth
       that lies beneath, while you are inside

an exclamation
       realisation
placeholder for the unknown

       in Babylonia 0 = two slanted wedges
       in China it was represented by a blank space—a sigh
       in another language it is a bellybutton—an innie
       that retreats into the womb—backwards into beginnings
       and endings, till both disappear

                      zefiro via ṣafira or sifr
                  cipher
             by any other name
          blank space
        black hole
       concept that runs through / consumes
     all knowledge
   0

                      Brendan Casey

Trouble

Maggie Armstrong

Negative

A day that begins with a negative pregnancy test might continue like this: eating lunch in a little café, with the Captain, let's call him; a dull Tuesday. Our plates were piled, we were making conversation, when a face went by the window.

I froze, then laid down my fork. The Captain gave a rough and spiteful laugh and slapped the table. He left the café, and I heard: 'Hey. How's things? Why don't we have a word right here, then?'

And: 'Seriously, get the fuck away from me, back off, I'll call my lawyer.'

'Oh you'll call your lawyer, will you!'

'Yeah. Listen, man, can I pass?'

What I saw on the street were two men in a confrontation and the reason was myself. But it was disturbing, a sorry spectacle, a teenage fantasy come miserably true. All I could do was smile, and pay for the food we weren't even going to eat now. Waiting for my change, I thought, well at least. At least I'm not.

For a week or so I'd been plagued by the idea that I was pregnant. If you've been in this situation you will know how entirely consumptive it can be, how you lose days to your imagination, to websites and ideas. But that morning I'd taken a pregnancy test, and it was negative so I came into town. I bought a quilted Isabelle Marant jacket at half price, and got a haircut, then thought we could have lunch, though unfortunately in the same place where I'd had lunch with another person some months before. Unfortunately I'd gone other places with that person too.

Now I had to cross two streets and run down an alleyway where the Captain paced around and kicked the graffiti on a shuttered shop, saying, 'It's unjust, it's me who suffers, not you,' while I regressed, all over again, to a heap of pulpish sentiment, dismay and woolly regret, pleading, 'But I'm so in love with you!'

The next morning, I did the last test in the pack of three and it was negative. I might have also bought another pack, because I used to take a lot of pregnancy tests. There was just too much of the crystal ball about a pregnancy test, too many stories told in their mini plastic screens to resist an opportunity. It was March 2016, and I was 31, so old enough but by no means satisfied with what I had. I was working for a newspaper, and writing short stories to send away to competitions, and that year I wrote some of my worst work. I lived on a quiet redbrick road beside the old asylum at Grangegorman. The day was punctuated with yoga, Vietnamese iced coffee, loose arrangements, drinking, reading, falling asleep on my desk. And there was the Captain with his two little children in a house across the city, with their teddies and their milk cups and their playroom that resembled a shattered kingdom of Lego.

We had met a year or so before, around the time his marriage fell apart. My sister told me he would never leave her—'and she's not going to leave her husband, is she?'—but sure enough they were planning on separating. Then one evening he phoned to say he wouldn't be coming over. His wife had a sore arm. Days later she had a strange fall. It turned out to be glioblastoma, a grade-4 tumour on her brain that was inoperable and incurable, the most aggressive kind of brain tumour. 'She has six to eighteen months of life,' the Captain told me, crying in his parked car.

He would sometimes bring nightmarish news of her deterioration. How she bought all new clothes from TK Maxx to fit her new slim figure, and had a flamboyant custom-made red wig she wore once. How she built a crowdfund page, a blog, and how the Daily Mail journalist who interviewed her misspelled both her children's names. In the weeks that followed her diagnosis, she would still send her husband to Halal shops for tahini and feta cheese. She would still dance with her two small children. I saw them dancing in a video someone took in their TV room. She carefully places one foot over the next, and hops lightly, guiding each child in a hand, her real, doomed red bangs flowing around her shoulders. I couldn't understand why she wasn't distraught, crying, thumping fists in this video. She wasn't laughing either, she was just living, and looked a little tired, same as anyone.

Within a short time, she left the country to be with her parents, to look for new treatments and a medical miracle, and the children stayed with their father. They were four and six then. She was 38.

Positive

That Saturday night I got a late period in the toilets of the Lighthouse Cinema, half way through the Coen Brothers' *Hail, Caesar!* Scarlett Johannson plays a pregnant Hollywood starlet whose angered studio boss arranges the secret birth and fosterage of her child so she can maintain her spotless image. The part is underwritten, but she plays it with a ferocious discontent. I thought about how pregnancy is always beguiling in films and books, and just about anywhere. The drama is already written, with its threat of savage pain, the story constrained within a set time period. I loved pregnancy in other people. Though whenever I imagined it happening to me I felt terrified. Terrified particularly at the idea of the baby that would be born at the end of the pregnancy. A baby you would be required to take care of, who would grow up into a child—a story unconstrained by any set time period.

Still I was almost wistful the next day as I swallowed my painkiller and saw to all the dreary toilette. Wistful, relieved, resigned, and then, over the following days, confused about something in particular.

Nobody will want to hear about that thing, it isn't great to read about, or write about to be honest. But for a while I'd been convinced something was amiss and strange in my body. Two weeks before this I had visited my GP, who tested me for pregnancy and then, to my disappointment, chlamydia. The implications were almost unbearable. I cursed my luck; how had I failed to see this wreckage coming, and how had I concealed it from myself? Then the results had come, and it wasn't chlamydia. It was nothing, blank. Then, on the Tuesday morning following the cinema, I walked to my parents' house and went straight upstairs to the bathroom, performed another pregnancy test and lay down on the floor. After the three minutes had passed, the stick showed two pink lines.

I climbed in beside my mum in her bed. 'I'm so tired,' I complained, hoping she would ask why, though she hadn't noticed I'd become a different person. The Captain, though, burst into tears on the phone then drove over with a box of multivitamins and some ginger sweets, plus a digital test to confirm the unsettling news. That week appointments were booked, mirrors studied and I went further into my naval, and up my own arse. Pregnant, I thought, standing on the tram. Handle with care! 'I'm pregnant,' I told women at work I didn't know. Did I look different? Did the air taste different? It was something like going to sleep and waking up a queen or goddess. Not everyone would have seen it like that. But I believed they did, I believed they were about to stand in awe and envy at my fortune. The world would hold its breath, reposition its gaze, step aside for me.

The only thing to do was to spend any money I had in Brown Thomas. A loose t-shirt dress. A billowing shirt. Formal shoes to make a good impression because, as was beginning to worry me, I now had only nine months to complete everything and become a published writer.

Six weeks

There is that obstetrical quirk whereby the beginning of a pregnancy is dated back about two weeks pre-conception. So at four weeks pregnant you have completed six, and time now will be packaged into weeks and days, not months or years. Six weeks conferred a certain confidence, and smug fatigue, that St Patrick's Day, as I walked on Dollymount Strand with some old pals. Later, I thought, I'll retire to my writing desk and finish the short story—the winning one. The sun shone across the glittering tide but my phone buzzed and buzzed because the Captain was across the city with his two children, entering a state of resentment.

He was more often than not alone with his children, wrapping them up in waterproofs and driving them up mountains, or taking them to Tayto Park or Eddie Rockets. Cancer leaflets were stashed around his house, a new, inexperienced au pair had to be hired and quickly entrusted with delicate responsibilities, meetings with 'services' scheduled. They were 'linked in' with the services. The children needed to be fed constantly. On a day off the Captain might be found in a car park, buying good quality tracksuits from an Adverts dealer; on a Sunday, the Captain, a tall, robust man, would sit on the floor in a pile of crushed laundry, matching odd cartoon socks. And I'm calling him the Captain not just because has a real way with order, and time, but because he is one, in the Greek Army, a recent promotion in absentia from artillery lieutenant. He's in the reserves, and still retains his rank.

'Paddy's Day is a family day!' he texted now.

'Oh, you think?' I replied, and my phone sparked and raged until nightfall. It wasn't the first big fight, never the last. Going home that night I got off my bike to search 'abortion England', but my phone was getting rained upon. He arrived later with another box of vitamins and the new 4th edition of *What to Expect When you're Expecting*. He knelt at my feet with these shining gifts, and the night went silent, and across the rest of the city time hurled everyone on.

Five weeks, two days

One evening at my salvaged hipster writing desk I was looking up mummy forums and other garbage sites when I went to the toilet and stared at a shape of fresh pink blood. My heart dropped. I returned to the mummy forums, then closed up my computer and walked to the hospital.

The waiting room was full of pregnant women I will remember for life. The apple-cheeked woman with the messed up golden curls; the 25-year-old woman in tight jeans, on her fourth baby, his first. They'll always be pregnant, with that brave and slightly withering look in their faces, like they've seen it all by now. I picked up *Good Housekeeping*, an old *Vogue*, and *Cheltenham, 2016*, with a 40-page festival preview, and a jockey on the cover with two long smile lines that looked like fallopian tubes. I couldn't think straight. A screen on the wall informed us shark meat is forbidden in pregnancy, also liver and any kind of pâté. The Captain held my hand in one hand and played a game of chess on his phone with the other, but nothing could soothe the terror in my lungs, a terror that is special to a hospital, when waiting seems eternity. A terror that comes with self-reproach, thinking how easily all this could have been avoided.

A group of Asian women came in wearing leather jackets over their pyjamas and talking excitedly; a thin girl come out of Early Pregnancy Assessment, crying, with her boyfriend's arm around her, and then it was our turn.

The doctor put on a pair of Prada tortoiseshell glasses before applying gel to my stomach. I didn't feel like I was there; I felt I was just a character in a budget drama I'd been watching all my life. She told me the pain sounded normal and some bleeding can happen and she gave me a small smile. Everything else was consistent. The thickening of the womb, that was good.

The next day a second registrar put a wand inside me, and on the screen they found a pregnancy sack with a dot on it, but it was obvious this wasn't telling her much. 'You're at 5 weeks 2 days, that's nothing!' this second registrar said and she booked me back in for a scan that Friday week—nine days' time.

I left with an illicit excitement, then went to the toilet and bled some more. I bled a lot that week, as what was happening seemed to be a miscarriage. A kind and understanding registrar, on the phone, talked me through everything. She sent a doctor's note. When I walked outside and into town, pregnant women filled the streets, and a friend sent me a picture of her new-born baby. Harsh pains crawled up my legs. I couldn't be in public anymore so I went home, where I continued to bleed. I sat up in bed, typing out a puff piece about an actress. Pains multiplied and played up and down my side, spread around both hips, stomach, back, the backs then fronts of my thighs. I lay there, listening to new age music on Spotify, and couldn't eat. I couldn't talk to anybody. I was still not comfortable with any kind of injury you couldn't shout about, that didn't give you some distinction. Now I felt the most obscure kind of sadness, curled on my bed while my sister tipped her 35-week pregnancy between us and ate biscuits.

Zero

It was Easter Week, the commemorations of 1916. Like skeletons at the feast, we went for a drink and to the cinema, and the film was *Maggie's Plan*, in which Greta Gerwig falls for her sperm donor having had a disappointing affair with Ethan Hawke. Then I started passing clots. I went to my parents and stayed in bed taking painkillers, coming out once a day to go for a mournful walk by the river, or stare at the television. I re-watched *Michael Collins*. Later—odd choice—*Raising Arizona*, when Nicholas Cage and Holly Hunter can't have babies so they steal one. I felt so sorry for myself. From time to time I took out the ultrasound picture and found it pathetic. A mysterious grey morass. It looked like the ghost of a life, or a fake picture of a UFO, a vanity project. It seemed idiotic to get upset over a bunch of cells that would have caused full mayhem if allowed to advance. The day before my scan, the registrar put my name on a list for a D&C, a procedure under anaesthetic that would come after the scan, only once the early loss was confirmed.

The morning of the scan I was very hungry, having fasted for 12 hours. Peeved-looking pregnant women smoked at the hospital gates, or paced corridors holding giant globes in their dressing gowns. It was April Fool's Day, and nature had already played her prank, I thought bitterly. Once lying down I asked the nurse if she could turn the screen away—a hot tip from the internet, no flies on me. The Captain held my socked foot in his hand, while the nurse fixed her eyes and moved the nozzle around. 'This is the heartbeat,' she said and turned the screen back to me.

Six weeks again

It was likely only something called sub-chorionic hematoma. I never asked at the time, it didn't matter anymore. I rushed out of the hospital with the Captain and the sun burst through the clouds, because we both desperately wanted what we'd thought was lost.

We took the afternoon off. Lunch, iced coffee, a Hungarian film called *Son of Saul*, set in Auschwitz. Saul is a Sonderkommando, a prisoner responsible for guiding fellow prisoners to the gas chambers, then disposing of their bodies. In the film he comes across a slaughtered boy who is his son, and he takes the body so he can give him a proper burial. There is a prisoner uprising, and an SS chase, but this action feels separate to the film's main adventure quest. Saul's hard-boiled and trance-like determination to give his young son dignity in death and this amounting to the greatest love imaginable.

Twelve weeks

And on the Monday that we came out of the hospital with a picture of the baby's crown and pursed lips in profile it took all my stamina not to brandish it at everyone I met. I told everybody: old friends who couldn't have cared; my therapist… I also told her about how the Captain and I had been fighting constantly, and about how one of the children kept fleeing from his classroom and the other kept stealing trinkets from shops and houses, and my worries that I would not be able to handle the children. What if I became their stepmother? What if we fell out? What if I became a single mother and the children were left without any kind of mother?

'Well you might have thought about all that before you got pregnant,' she said, and we sat in baffled silence.

A friend directed me to a good maternity website, and I filled my basket up. Four hundred and eighty euro: Halterneck polka-dot swimming togs, Kate Middleton black turtleneck dress, workwear—items I would pair with my pregnancy fishnets, borrowed maternity parka and Repeal the 8th badge. I felt intensely special, dignified and modest. The only thing on at the Omniplex was *Bridget Jones's Baby*.

Sixteen weeks

On my birthday I complained over the phone about having to carry so many tomatoes across the city in order to make the gazpacho from scratch. And you just couldn't get commitment when it came to numbers for food. I was so frustrated with everybody. This birthday was my swansong, my send-off, the last chance to be an individual person. The buzzer went, and I ran down with the same skittish happiness I have at every party, only this one was significant, fin de siècle.

I opened the door, and the two children shot past me into the building and up the stairs. The Captain stood there, exasperated. 'Where have they gone?' he said.

In my hand they'd left two limp cards, and I read the more legible one: HAPPY BIRTHDAY MY BIRTHDAY IS NEXT YEAR DADDY'S GETTING ME A DEATH STAR LEGO THANK YOU FOR THE PARTY WHAT ARE WE GOING TO EAT.

No question mark, just the blunt request for information. What are we going to eat.

The party was for this child, just as every day, from now, was to be repurposed around this child, around children. In those stampeding moments I knew it absolutely: it wasn't about us grown-ups anymore. We had our chance, we spent it. I had the feeling that the earth was shifting beneath my feet.

Afterwards I shopped in the maternity boutique on Wicklow Street. Giant pyjamas with a rosebud pattern and unflattering waistband. Then to Arnotts, measured for my triple-the-size knockers. Two quality maternity bras with nursing straps, and some maternity hosiery.

'Sixteen weeks, you wouldn't know', the bra ladies said, and 'Yeah you wouldn't know at all, you're so neat!'

I smiled and shrugged. It was all about me, was it not. No question mark.

Twenty weeks

All this time I'd been working up some pretty voluminous drafts of fictions. Hatchet jobs, dramatisations of mild trauma, or partially veiled character studies. I'd filled thick folders with passionate unfinished manuscripts, having binned all the rest as I produced it, like a reverse production line—fill the page, scrunch it in a ball, throw it in the bin, miss the bin, or get it in and hiss, 'Yes!' Then do this again, and again, every Saturday and Sunday. I had big hopes though, great delusions. An ideology I might describe as *convenience feminism*—people had wronged me because I was a woman, and this could be my special niche, my manifesto. Livid, sexy wrongedness.

I arranged to meet a celebrated writer who had kindly offered to look at my work. He was waiting in his local pub near the coast. Wearing a giant *Rosemary's Baby* dress, I collapsed on a chair and produced from my knapsack two folders, bulging thick with flopped manuscripts. 'I have about sixty stories here,' I told the writer. None of them are finished and they are all the same story.

I'd never been this close to such a distinguished author before, and was relieved he was unshaven, slightly overweight, with stale coffee on his breath. His words were sensible, unmystical. Workaday, almost. He told me that you couldn't just write when you felt like doing it, you had to make a schedule. That producing anything was something to be proud of. He wished he had a folder of beginnings. 'What do you want to write?' he asked.

I explained that I would simply like to write a story set in a city. 'But I have to move soon, to the suburbs, There's so little time, and now'—he followed my gaze down—'it's too late. I can't make field notes. It's all finished now.'

The celebrated Irish writer said absolutely not. 'It's already in you,' he said. 'Everyone knows what such and such a city looks like and sounds like. What they don't know, is how it feels. The emotions you had at that time in that city. No one else knows how it was for you.'

'So, what are you writing at the moment?' I asked him. He was making tentative notes for a novel but he couldn't yet begin it. 'Because I don't know the ending yet. I never begin something without knowing how it ends,' he said.

All the weeks and through the years

The Captain and I seemed to disagree fundamentally and our relationship grew dire. Days and nights were a garbled wasteland of you you you, blablablablablablablablabla. We had no understanding of how to fight other than bitterly and to the end. No known control over what might happen at a given moment. But we were both quite good people, we still thought. We should invest in our happiness. Our first counselling session was set inside in a grey housing estate strung with Dublin football bunting and flags and broken tricycles lying around. Antoinette was a large, breathless woman with static aubergine hair and a mouth she kept carefully screwed up, maybe lest she might smile. She led us up a squeaking stairway to an untidy room with warm grooves in the sofa cushions and half-drunk tea mugs and pieces of paper bluetacked to the walls, saying things like, *Self-knowledge burns bright in dark times.* After she'd cleaned up, we began.

The Captain explained, 'My wife, my ex-wife, has cancer. My girlfriend had an affair. She is pregnant.' The woman's face dried up with worry.

'Pregnant by?'

'By him, by him!' Overjoyed that this much was true. 'And it wasn't an affair it was—!' Here, I explained why I believed that it was nothing like your typical affair.

'That is an affair,' she informed us.

The first session was placid, introductory. In time I would say things like 'You both have it in for me! Why did you drag me out me here?' but normally it was just fraught and unpleasant. We mounted those ominous stairs every Tuesday at 6pm and there was always that sense of being led by a stick and penalised, made suffer for the sins of our immoderate passions. I liked Antoinette, the way I used to like those schoolteachers who were afraid of their pupils. I felt she didn't hate us, she honoured the contract. Though when we started to fight she looked overwhelmed, and flapped her hands.

'Now, now, it's all very emotional!' she'd say and I'd say, 'Yeah!'

'She betrayed me,' the Captain would remind us, and I would glare into nothing and chew my jaw.

Antoinette became just another source of disagreement, a fresh bone to encircle and growl over. 'I'm never going back to Antoinette!' one of us would yell, or, 'Antoinette says don't do that!' 'I've suffered enough!' 'You've put me through hell!' 'I'm pregnant!' I'd type abortion services on my phone, just to spite my face. We're awful, I'd think, a waste of time.

Then one day Antoinette closed the door behind us and the house receded into the mists and folds, never to be driven by without a shudder. It was impossible to determine what we might have taken from our time with her, other than the knowledge that most counselling sessions are 50 minutes long, not an hour, and most services charge about 80 euro for couples and 70 euro for individuals, although couples' counselling is infinitely more distressing.

There was one day, however, when I sat on her backside-indented sofa doing the individual session you are awarded if you stay the course—your chance to tell your own side, get the truth out there!—when I suddenly started laughing.

'Sorry,' I said. 'This baby is kicking me. It hasn't done that before. Oh god, it's feisty.'

'Aha, must be a boy,' Antoinette quipped.

What if it is a boy, I thought later, and every day that followed. What if it is a boy?

Any given week

We ended up unable, or unwilling, to pass an evening without a fight. Because the bottom line here was I was pregnant. I just wasn't going to let him treat me in the way that I would comfortably allow myself to treat him. I wouldn't have it. Pregnant, you were basically a mother. A gentle, loving person. Mothers didn't cheat and lie and disappoint everyone. Mothers bore the weight of love and nursed it in their arms.

Late for work under my own employment, I lingered in the kitchen listening to two male relationship experts being interviewed by Sean O'Rourke. One expert said that a couple will rarely survive a woman's infidelity because for a woman there will be an emotional connection. Emotional connection being, I guess he meant, the most egregious betrayal. Meaning a woman has the greater power to destroy what is good.

Later on, in a car facing Sandymount beach the Captain and I both worked ourselves up into tears. I don't remember everything we used to fight about only that the Captain was often getting phone calls, both to his work and his mobile, from strange numbers with just a person breathing into the line and sometimes saying, 'hello? Hello, hellllllo?'

The person, his friends, his friends' friends, could be anywhere. I used to see him in the backs of people's heads, or find the sound of his name in other people's names. Or we would go into a wine bar to have an early evening snack and have to run back out. There were streets we couldn't go to anymore, and pubs and cafés, subjects that were banned.

And people. All the people that we couldn't see, so that in the end we rarely went anywhere involving other people, unless they were made of celluloid, watched in the darkness of a cinema theatre.

'What have I done now?' I'd ask him. 'Don't like it, find someone else, you [name],' I'd rage. I'd think I couldn't stand myself, the conditions that had made me, the complacency, neglect—it was all my parents' fault, teachers, classmates, tennis club, neighbours, other kids, relations, sisters, cousins, aunts, that man, his fault, my grades, dyslexia, or attention deficit, asthma, my mother, all her fault, and it was your fault, and my own personal fault too. Did that explain things?

And there was the night I lay in a dismal hotel room looking at the dismal sea in the dismal holiday town we had visited, and I cried and cried. I thought, it's terrible when things happen that you're not able to tell anyone ever only maybe one friend, a person you have not yet decided upon. Terrible when there are things you've forgotten because you can't even tell them to yourself. In the dark, on a tear-stained pillow, I bought a gold lamé maternity dress.

That week

One warm summer evening the Captain and I walked down the road from my house eating Classic Magnums. We were just at the part of a combustion when the heat and pressure rise to your face and there is no alternative but that you attack, and I was saying 'Act your *age!*' while he retreated into superior silence. We passed Grangegorman clock tower, the former penitentiary which at one time served as a transportation depot for women required to find themselves a better life in the colonies. The Captain took out his phone, then came to a halt. He stood in the middle of the path, and started mumbling in Greek.

'Come on,' I said. 'Walk and talk.'

'I'm sorry,' he said. 'I don't know what Facebook is saying.'

'What do you mean, what's it saying?'

'It's saying that she died.'

That night we sat on the floor of his TV room surrounded by suitcases, folding little shorts and t-shirts, bunching up goggles and crocks and filling straw hats with underpants. They were going on the 7am flight and the children jumped around the room, shrieking, 'We're going to Greece, we're going to Greece!'

She was buried in the churchyard in her small village. While the Captain and children were throwing handfuls of earth into her grave I was in town trying to pass the time. I went into Clarendon Street and lit a candle. Then I went to Mothercare. Three summer Maxi dresses, two long camisoles, a maternity denim miniskirt, all of which would join the bags of her clothes in her old bedroom.

Thirty-four weeks

We flew to Athens for our summer holidays. Mosquito bites protruding from my flesh, we took a boat to Santorini Island, where, shacked up in an old villa, we read our books, and ate sliced figs and white cheese for breakfast. We drove around rocky cliffs and swam in clear water, and ate the fish he had selected from the back kitchens of tavernas. The children, staying with their grandparents, spent nights in A&E for different reasons. I bought beach dresses from shoreline boutiques; a romper; animal print espadrilles.

Towards sunset one evening, he asked me to go drink a virgin cocktail while he did a message. I made it a spritz and I sat watching the sun dangle in the clouds, luminous like a pinball. Later, we ate fried fish with glasses of beer on a cove, then braced the precipitous roads on foot, alongside trotting donkeys. The idea was to watch the sunset, but it was uncomfortably hot and I couldn't walk, because of a yoga incident in the second trimester which I have spared the reader. I was in pain most of the time. The Captain was silent, looking at the mountains. We walked until we were really irritable, then found a collapsing hill that led to a little hippy bar mobbed with tourists bearing selfie sticks.

'You hate it here, don't you?' the Captain said, and I said, 'Yes, it's truly awful.'

The next day we took a boat to Koufonisia, whose name translates as Hollow Island, because of all its caves. After the expensive hotel breakfast I ran to the bathroom and vomited. It was interesting to feel this bad, nearly eight months along. We spent the day ailing on a beach, then rocked around on another boat. I wanted to lie on the hotel bed and complain, but he wanted to watch the sunset so he said, 'Come now, quick.'

We walked past the port, up a dirt road, and as we rounded the island, with the Aegean Ccean beneath us and the sun falling into the mists, he pulled me aside.

His face was white and serious. 'The light is failing,' he said. 'I am extremely nervous but I wanted to tell you that I think the life we could have together could be brilliant.'

'No,' I said.

I saw then he had a little velvet box in his hand so I said, 'Okay, but get on one knee.'

He bent down on one knee and put the ring on my finger.

'That's my left hand,' I said. 'It goes on my right hand.' He pulled off the ring and squeezed it past the knuckle of my ring finger. A lone woman walking past with her dog stopped to clap and cheer us. My eye fell on the blue stone that sparkled on my finger.

'Is it a dummy?' I asked him. 'It's not … real?' I put the ring between my incisors and bit down hard on it.

'It's a sapphire from Santorini.'

'And this?'

'It's gold. Nine carat, yellow gold.'

'How much did you pay for it? Tell me!'

I hated the words I said. But I had just never imagined a proposal of marriage, and so I had never imagined one like this, browbeaten with morning sickness. I had never imagined my material lust could target in its calculations an innocent piece of jewellery. I was frantic.

'I can't tell you how much!' he said.

But he told me, in rough terms, not without pride. I asked him to get down on one knee and do it all again.

We sat together on a bench, with fingers interlinked. The evening sun had left behind the mountains now, it was getting dark quickly, something significant was over.

Champagne, or knock-off, was ordered in the only fashionable restaurant on the island. The Captain requested the cushions to prop me up, and we made a wincing toast and took some pictures, FaceTimed my parents. I pushed away the food, twisted the ring around, stared into its charming angles.

'Do you like it, really?' he said, and I smiled at him, and instead of telling him that I liked it or I didn't like it I took it off and slid it across the table. I gave it back to him. The easiest mistakes and breaches can cause the most lasting damage, I've discovered.

There was silence.

He said, 'I think I just want to go home now.'

The little box was open beside the ring. He said, 'Go on, put it in the box. Go on, I can sell it on Adverts.' I put the ring in the box and immediately regretted it. He stood up and asked for the bill.

'No!' I said. He paid the bill and left the restaurant.

I was aware of the waitress who'd taken our picture and the people at the nearby tables, watching with a quiet thrill. 'He's sick,' I said to the waitress. 'Kalinichta.' I took the half-drunk bottle, left our food and ran out the door, back into the past where this hadn't happened.

The little streets were lined with jewellery shops and families at tables, drinking beer, children playing, large grandmothers in black. I found him at the small beach and sat by the lapping tide, where he said, 'Just tell me how much you want per month for the baby.'

He took the room card and walked away, and I sat there by the stones and seaweed and dead crabs. The waves rolled and splashed and lay back on some rocks, alone and swollen, a starfish, or a beached mermaid. I sent emotional texts, and looked up flights to Dublin. I drank the rest of the bottle, and admired my ring with a new poignancy. I love it, I wrote. I love you! The baby kicked and punched me with affectionate reproof.

Back in the hostile little bedroom, he had drunk every one of the bottles in the minibar—orange, rose, mastic, even Bailey's Irish cream—and scattered the empties on the mattress which he'd separated from mine. I said, 'Please!' but he raised both his arms in the air and began to move his body with a sort of grace—he was dancing the *zeibekiko*, the customary dance of the soldier returning from defeat. I whimpered and looked up articles about foetal alcohol syndrome, the lifelong effects, and went off on a lurid image search. I was certain I had ruined my baby's life. I saw the future jeer back at us, inflicting hard hits, bad injuries, devastating outcomes that we might not recover from. My head hurt; the Ryanair website was incomprehensible. For hours I said blah blah blah blah blah blah blah—then fell asleep promising my child I would never neglect it. I would take care of it.

The next morning, we attended breakfast together. Afterwards we went back to the same bench overlooking the sea. I wore the ring and we took a better picture, and I texted my mum to say it was back on with the Captain.

We embarked for Pireaus Harbour on a boat thrashed by a vicious storm.

Gifts followed, on our return to Dublin: a bottle of real champagne (lost or stolen in the house move), a 6-cup silver Bialetti (burned apart mid-percolation). The ring was small for my finger, and remained controversial.

Thirty-five weeks

It was the end of October, and the baby was due in a month. I wrote a list of pregnancy symptoms, something like:

Thing 1

Thing 2

Thing 3

Thing 4

It went on until offending Thing 31, and the ink ran before my eyes until it was a sheet of black things.

When weekends came, the Captain met with Adverts dealers, picked out buggies, car seats, a Moses basket, muslin cloths, a changing table and other systems and accessories I couldn't understand the need for. He went to a parking lot to pick up the second-hand buggy and its obfuscating component pieces. There was talk of a car-seat, special car-seat fixers. Then he wept on the phone, 'You do not seem to be taking an interest in this new arrival, Maggie. You know what, the other day, I had to put the clothes for the baby into the baby's drawer, on my *own*.'

We watched *The Witch*, a thriller about a family of 17th-century New England settlers cursed by witches as one by one their children die. In one scene the grieving mother dreams she is feeding her dead baby at her breast and when she wakes a crow is pecking out her bloodied nipple.

Thirty-seven weeks

It was time to move in with the widower and his children. I started to empty cupboards and fill boxes of my things and vacate my room for the new girl moving in. My father arrived with a selection of his tools and spent the afternoon patching up the hole in the wall made by the Captain's fist back on the night that he found out about the thing with the other guy.

'It was so strange,' I told my dad as he worked. 'The corner of a box I was carrying just crashed into the wall and with such speed that the plastering chipped off…'

My dad made no comment; he hadn't asked in the first place.

'Not seamless,' he said, packing up his tools, 'but they could hang a mirror there, or a nice picture frame.'

The Captain loaded all the boxes in his car, the children played with their Furbies. The last of my possessions were stuffed in the basket of my bike, and there were bangers and bonfire smoke in the air as I pushed down the hill and back up the hill, over the rivers and across the city. I arrived, breathless, to my lover and his sons sitting around the table, with welcome pictures and a square confection made from a Betty Crocker brownie mix, decorated with jellies, or holes where the jellies had been picked off.

Thirty-eight weeks

The day I fell on top of myself going past Trinity College, ripping my new Italian tights, cutting my knees and being helped up by strangers, was the same day a memorial for the children's mother was held in the Orthodox Church in Stoneybatter. I was upset, hooked up to a monitor in Holles Street, that I couldn't possibly make it to the memorial. What never occurred to me was that I might not be wanted there. If it had occurred to me that a congregation of her friends might feel uncomfortable meeting another woman at the church, a woman who was heavily pregnant—or worse, that they might be a little titillated by the scandal—it was only a distant rustle that I didn't hear, not then. It didn't figure that a new woman, new baby, a sparkly ring, was eyebrow-raising. That what we might be sampling really were the funeral baked meats that furnished forth the wedding table. It didn't occur to me that I might not be welcome generally, at this occasion or in the wider community, ever again, nor he, nor their children. That our new life was a transgression, and we would need to make it on our own from now on, more or less.

The Captain rearranged his house, did my laundry and made salads. He cleared out half his wardrobe, all her clothes and boots and French cosmetics, gave me a special padded gadget for controlling backache, a clip on my phone to block the radiation that could cause brain cancer. Wedding pictures were taken down. Boxes of her things were hauled out to charity shops. Her bronze and orange costume jewellery, which used to hang by the door, was moved somewhere. Recipe books and some photographs were kept. So was the subscription to the Irish fashion magazine that came through our post box. Did I want to keep the subscription? he asked. I did, I decided, so over morning coffee I read about feasting ideas and inspirational Irish women in business, finding happiness post-divorce. I hid from the children, and I couldn't look inside the baby's room.

At 39 weeks, I found that I was wandering Arnotts. I'd been told your feet get cold when giving birth so I bought three pairs of luxury knitted woollen socks, Wolford and Falke, and also a year's supply of tights. On the way out, I passed the kids' and babywear and bought the first babygros I saw, white, blue and lemon yellow, €38 euro each. I thought, if I get four more babygros that's one for each day of the week and we'll be set to go.

Thirty-nine weeks

The fridge was stacked. Cushions and birthing contraptions loomed inside a special box. I reread my hospital list, which went like this:

Item 1

Item 2

Item 3

Right up to unnecessary Item 18.

I stopped, dismayed at one item. Size 0 nappies. I could hardly stand without pain, or eat an apple, and there were nappies of different sizes? More to the point, I was expected to know about this today? How would I fit everything in my Stork Sack? It wasn't fair I had to pack for someone other than myself. I read the list again. Size 0 nappies, barrier cream and water wipes. All a source of existential disquiet.

Time edged forwards and then backwards and got stuck. A week after I moved in and late at night, I packed a different kind of bag and said that I was going to live with my parents, getting as far as the car door. Then I went to bed.

Forty weeks

There was no baby, just the lightning streaks that make you think you're about to give birth on the side of the road. I went to the theatre to review an Oscar Wilde play and also to show off. With this watermelon up my dress, the feeling was rare and extravagant, as if I had rented out some wildly overpriced couture ballgown, and would never be this special and majestic again. The gumption of having something that enormous stowed inside your body, the blazing fertility and voluptuousness of the whole mise en scène.

There were light-hearted raspberry tea comments in the foyer, and *make sure you get an aisle seat* jokes in the ladies'. As I found my way to seat E15, the artistic director of the theatre boomed across the auditorium, 'Christ almighty, nothing to do with me, is it?' His row of friends looked up, and some smiled nervously.

That week I walked in department stores and bought bad Christmas gifts and weird self-gifts—two repulsive faux fur blankets that slid around the house for years afterwards. I used to stuff them behind doors, thinking who let these beastly things in here? Where was I when I consented to buy these?

Forty-one weeks plus two

Another Sunday. I sat splayed out on a bench in the playground while the Captain went to get coffee and the two children ran around, hid in bushes, disappeared up trees. Playgrounds, I thought: they really are the answer to everything. I thought about myself. The baby was more than a week overdue and each morning I would wake and ask myself, will I die today? I worried, looking at the other mothers, because I didn't find their babies cute. What lack of human feeling did this point to? I had no love for what I was expecting. I'd been miscast here as a mother in the wings.

A shout came, and both children ran towards me, one holding out his arm. Drops of blood fell on the concrete. Mayhem followed, and the narrator is foggy on the details. We stood at the boot of the car while the boy howled and his father barked orders for First Aid, then stuffed us all in the car, the child's arm bound in toilet roll.

'What happened? What happened?' we all said at once. The Captain drove in the bus lanes and broke red lights. He sped through town, through Merrion Square where I saw the reassuring bastion of the National Maternity Hospital flash by, and then we crossed the river to the children's hospital.

We spent the rest of the day in the waiting room, filling forms and visiting the vending machine. Befriending other children, trying not to look at the open cartilage of a boy in football shorts. Trying not to stare at the mother holding the swaddled baby whose face was turning blue.

A film played above the seats, not quite *Frozen*, but a short which some research tells me was *Frozen Fever*. It was tinny, and annoying. Kids watched *Frozen Fever* or stuff on phones, or cried. The baby kicked impatiently throughout. I thought: it's just today, right? The kids thing. But I also knew that this was it, our destiny. Accident and Emergency, pens attached with string, crisps and sweets, stitches, dressings, books unread, books unlikely to be written, and no dinner waiting. And women in scrubs asking, 'How did it happen?'

What happened was he'd been up a massive tree. Something gave, a bough had snapped, a branch drove a gash into his wrist. What happened was unsupervised.

That night, alone again, thank God, I returned to the short story I was working on, and I finished the whole thing, then sent it off in delirious wakeful exhaustion. I didn't know a thing. Who my friends were, or my family, how to take care of a baby. I didn't know my story would meet with firm rejection, the first of seven from that magazine alone, and I fell into a deep sleep.

Aphonic

Thinking survival & living aren't the same is just privilege
& in your light,
I am a poor animal, bottle-fed formula and unsteady legged.
I was a ghost until you moulded me to a lifeform you liked
but now my hands are phantoms again,
writing bad poetry & picking at spots
instead of peeling oranges and reading Lorca,
a colostrum of the heart.
There's a terrible want in me.
I'll hollow myself out for it over & over again
but
love poems are supposed to be about other people, not
about proving a point, or the mess that we made of things.
Train windows look like they're self-reflecting
but they're only bouncing one emptiness off of another
to form a middle ground & that
is where your face hangs
in a canopy of blackened stations, flickering
like the sore-heartburn of streetlights that fade only to distance
while I press hot hands to glass & follow
your driftless form with these palms that only ever sung with life in your presence.
My fingers come away pleated with cold.
You used to carry my pulse from me to breathe it to a whisper
& I think of calling out your name,
but what would be the point?
Now that you can't even recognise your own shadow,
& I remember too well the murdered rooms of our past.

Katelyn O'Neill

It's Not That You Can't Have The Grand Gesture, It's Just That It's Meaningless

We *made* money. We *made* God.

Are we all to bow down to the force of our imaginations for the rest of forever?

FUCK inflation, I don't give a fuck about inflation because it's not *real*, it's just another way for them to keep a handle on us.

I like to get drunk and text men asking, 'why we can't just print more money', and I trip over myself laughing at them tripping over themselves to mansplain the fucking economy.

The old gold standard, Jeff Bezos=Jeff Pesos and we're closer

to being millionaires than he is, that's how rich he is and

isn't that terrifying?

He'll never spend all that money and I just want a nice slice pan without worrying about how much bread I'll have to eat a day so it doesn't go off—otherwise it isn't worth buying.

My God all that money, junior ministers getting raises and parties that weren't voted in in power, I mean,

come on Leo just come out and say you hate poor people.

No school dinners anymore, parents should be telling children it's prime cut for dinner when really it's the tongue of the petty bourgeoisie and the wage gap now is worse than it was

in revolutionary France, and one of the worst bits of it is the:

What do *your* parents do? Vapid blinking, here, listen, I'm not stupid because I'm not posh and full of notions.

In the end death is unnatural to thought but is it really that thought is unnatural to the essence of life? There's none of this nonsense with animals. Maybe consciousness is the curse.

What do my parents do? FÁS, the dole, take your pick—and stick it up your fucking hole.

Katelyn O'Neill

In The End

Rachel Connolly

The orange sky in the big window says it's late afternoon when I wake up. It's not dark yet. Even for April the room's freezing; probably a heat cut. I should have closed the curtains to keep the heat in before I went to sleep, but I don't remember it seeming so cold when I got back this morning.

Where's Jo? I say out loud and then half wonder who I am talking to.

It's probably too late for him to still be out. I hope he didn't turn up and end up standing outside without a key; we'd argued about that before. I said he was making a big thing about nothing at the time, but I knew he was right, even if I never admitted it. I never admit when I am wrong because I hate saying sorry.

I take one hand out from under my duvet and layers of blankets and press the backs of my fingers flat against my cheek. *Fuck that's cold.* My entire face is so much colder than my hand that it sort of feels as if it's been detached from my body. I feel that familiar sense setting in, of disorientation that comes with waking up and not remembering exactly how the night ended. The familiar sense of unease.

What time is it even? Where is my phone?

I see it sticking out of my shoe, by the bottom of the bed. I turn it on and it says 17:07 is the time: the night we were at would have ended a few hours ago. There are a few *which party are you at?* messages, but nothing from Jo. At least that means he probably wasn't stuck waiting outside in the cold. I get up to go and see if Katia or Ana is around to come for a coffee. Now that I am properly awake and I know what time it is, I want to do something with the rest of the day. I want to leave the flat, at least. I knock on Ana's bedroom door first and there is no answer so I knock again, a few times, and then bang the middle of the door once with the palm of my hand. When she still doesn't answer I open the door anyway, just to check, but the room is empty. She really is out.

I get a glass of water from the kitchen and then try Katia's room. She answers on the first knock, *Yes, yes, come in.*

When I open the door she apologises for the mess and I laugh out loud because, of course, her room is completely pristine. It always is. She even has a rule that you have to leave your shoes in the hall outside her door before entering.

What mess? I ask and she laughs and nods at a single shirt, crumpled on the bed beside her, with a coat hanger beside it. I think of my own room, and the pile of things I brought back from the clothes bank weeks ago, or even months ago in some cases, and still haven't decided what to do with. All in a heap in one corner. I laugh even more.

This isn't mess, I say, as I sit down on her bed. *This is like the base level of disorder that someone generates by existing in a space.*

She laughs and says I am the authority on mess so she will take my word on that.

So, what time did you get in this morning? she asks. I remember she left before me, sometime around dawn.

Maybe midday? I say. *Around then anyway. I left the party before then, but I walked back with Pete and smoked at his for a while before I came back here.*

What, so five hours' sleep? She laughs. *Why didn't you take a valium?*

Her face is full of deliberately exaggerated fake concern. More than anyone else Katia needs things like a full night's sleep, hot meals, and for everything to be tidied and ordered. She has no patience for the heat cuts, or when there's a shortage of anything at the food market. We are opposites in that sense, and the way I go about things seems as ridiculous to her as her fussiness seems to me, so she just shakes her head as if to say: *what are we going to do with you?*

I tell her I accidentally left my valium with Jo. I took them out with me in a little purse I use for speed and then gave it to him when I left. *But it's fine, you know I actually feel fine. I came to see if you want to get a coffee or food or something?*

I wait outside her room while she gets dressed and, as we're leaving, she says she was in the nice café last weekend and there was nobody working. I'd noticed the same the Sunday before that, so we walk the long way, that takes us past a food market, to pick up coffee on the way.

Inside the market is as cold as the street so it is definitely a heat cut and not just something wrong with our building's boiler. Although I don't point this out to Katia because I don't want her to start going on about how there should be a rota for everyone who works in the plant. We have had that conversation a hundred times and it never goes anywhere. If there are not enough people working at the plant to safely run every generator then we only run the ones that supply electricity and there is no heat. I think this is a good enough compromise, but I can never get her to see it that way.

We walk around the aisles, full of neatly stacked standard-issue packages and tins with nearly identical black and white labels, and collect a few packets of coffee from the very back of the shop, a few minutes' walk from the tills near the entrance. The food market is almost empty. The only other people shopping there are a pair of older women, one holding a basket containing some tins and the other consulting a list and directing them towards the aisle with grains and pulses. I recognise one of them and I say hello as we walk past and they both nod and smile in response, almost in unison.

Lennie, a girl who we know from parties, is working on the till. She is sitting on a tall stool dressed in a long leather coat, black gloves with holes for her fingers, and a scarf wrapped around her face so it covers everything below her bottom lip. The sections of hair that frame her face have been cut short, so they just meet the top of her scarf; the rest is tied back. We put our packets of coffee down and she asks us how we are and what we've been doing because she hasn't seen us out in a few weeks. Her and Katia speak for a few minutes and I don't say a lot because they know each other better. Katia explains that the coffee is not just for us, and that we are taking it to the café, and asks if we can take two packets even though our ID cards have the same address.

Sure, that's fine, Lennie says. *Go and take another packet if you want. It's a good idea. It was the same the last time I was there, a few Sundays ago, there was nobody working. I suppose they've all decided they want weekends off.*

We say goodbye, and that we should try and see each other soon. Katia and I leave and walk towards our favourite café. I think it is probably everyone who lives in this area's favourite café; it is in a very grand old building, with huge windows and lots of plants. I remember someone, maybe Ana, saying the building used to be a church, when religion was more of a mainstream thing, but I never looked it up to check. If it wasn't a church it was probably a museum or something similar.

We turn on to the street the café is on and I notice some new graffiti on the wall of one of the first buildings. It has letters in red, swirly writing and there is a crude outline of a skull and a list of dates and a phone number.

I elbow Katia and point to it. *This is definitely new?* I think I know what it is but I don't want to be the one to bring it up.

I think so. Yes, I'm almost certain I haven't seen it before.

When we are closer it is obvious the swirly letters say DC. We stop to look at it. She asks me if I think it is an advertisement for one of the Death Clubs.

That is what it looks like, I suppose, I say.

Do you think it's real? she asks.

I don't know. Maybe.

They might not exist at all; everything we know about them is from rumours. I only know of one person who has gone to one, and I've never met him. He's a friend of Jo's called Marc. Marc was very anxious about The End; the way that some of us get but nobody really talks about. He was so bad he was barely getting out of bed. The Death Club he went to was in one of the old farm buildings in the forest at the edge of the city, where they used to keep animals before meat-eating was phased out. He went during the months of incessant, torrential rain, and had to trudge in the dark through waterlogged soil. It was not easy to find.

When he arrived a pair of security men gave him a token with a number on it and took a photograph of him holding it. They did that for everyone, as a record of who had which number. Later they locked the doors. All the Death Clubs have a version of this process in common, or at least that's what the rumours say.

After the doors were locked they picked one number out of a box. From what I know about these clubs, if the person whose number it is does not come forward, then they go through the photos to find out who it is. Jo said this person did come forward though, he didn't make a fuss. They hanged him that time, but apparently the methods differ.

It was exhilarating, Marc said, according to Jo. He was very frightened while he waited and he had not expected to be and that gave him perspective. There is something interesting about the idea of waiting like that. But I don't know if I would admit that to anyone. Maybe Katia thinks the same thing and wouldn't admit it to me. People do talk about them, the Death Clubs, but as a joke, or in a way that makes it hard to tell if it is a joke or not. Maybe other people we know have gone and don't want to say. It is hard to talk about and hard to admit to. And they might not even be real.

I reach for my phone to take a picture of the numbers, just as a record, but then remember I left it at home. I don't really want to ask Katia to, and I know where it is, I suppose, if I want to look again.

We were right; at the café there's nobody working. But someone who clearly had the same idea as we did has already brought coffee so we leave our bags in one of the cupboards. Someone else, or maybe the same person, has used one of the large industrial pots to make soup, so I heat some up for us. We sit down on one of the worn old sofas to eat.

When we start eating I realise I am hungrier than I thought I was, and we don't speak for a few minutes until Katia points at the window. Three guys who were at the same party as us last night are coming towards the café. I look to see if Jo is with them, but no. I tell myself that doesn't necessarily mean anything because this isn't his group of friends, but I can't help making a note of it. I say to Katia that I haven't heard from him this morning, and she asks me if I think that means anything and I say no and then she asks why I brought it up. She is always so blunt.

I laugh slightly too loudly, in a way that sounds very fake even though I don't mean it to. *No reason. He was supposed to stay at ours and I was worried he was locked out. I never gave him a key.*

She asks if we had an argument—again she is as blunt as possible—and I tell her no, we did not, but that for weeks he has been cagey, or on edge, or something that I can't exactly identify or describe, so I didn't want to do anything that might start an argument, like accidentally leaving him locked out. She says she has noticed the mood too, but I can't tell if she's just saying it to agree with me.

Max, Peter, and Sven, the guys who were at the same party as us last night, walk into the café and Katia waves them over to join us. Peter drags another sofa and Sven picks up two chairs. Max, the one I know best from working together at The Plant, gives us both a hug and sits on the chair arm next to Katia, causing the entire sofa to slide backwards under his weight. He is far too tall, in a gangly way, like a normal-sized person who has been stretched out on a bigger axis, but always happy and smiling so that his size does not seem imposing.

How was the rest of your night? Katia says, addressing them as a group, as the others sit down.

Peter says it was good. *We haven't been home yet. I'm kind of wrecked actually.* Sven goes to get the three of them coffee while Katia and Peter talk.

I lean back on the sofa to avoid talking across Katia and ask Max if he saw Jo when they left, but he says he doesn't think so. *Although I wasn't really looking for him*, he adds. *He could have been there, I suppose.*

Then I interrupt Katia to ask Peter and he says the same, more or less. Out of habit I put my hand in my coat pocket to check my phone and then remember I left it at the flat. I let my hand rest on my knee instead, so the movement looks purposeful.

We sit at the café talking for a while. Me and Max and Sven, who also works at The Plant but on the mechanical side of things, agree to go in tomorrow but not till late, around 11ish, and then go for a pint after, sometime early afternoon. Katia and I walk back to the flat the long route through the park; it's a nice evening, despite the cold. The air smells of smokey frost.

At the flat I check my phone. There are a few messages from people asking if I plan to come to work tomorrow, which I don't bother replying to. There are no messages from Jo, so I call him and it rings and rings and then goes to voicemail.

Hi, hello. I speak very quickly after the tone and then stop because I don't know what I want to say or why I called, even. *Give me a call when you can,* I say, and then hang up.

I wake up in the middle of the night and my room is freezing. I had terrible, frantic dreams about being chased and afraid. I sit up in bed and find my cigarettes but I can't see my lighter anywhere and I don't want to smoke enough to bother looking properly so I set the packet back down on the floor. I check my phone and there is nothing.

I think about the things I have to do tomorrow. Or today, technically, but later. I really don't have to do anything if I don't want to. But I know I will feel better if I go to The Plant for a while and do some work, even if it is just for a few hours, so I will do that. It will be good to see people and to feel useful. Jo might phone by the time I am finished, but if not I can walk over to his flat and see if he's there. Just to check that everything is fine, which I am sure it will be.

I remember the first time I met Jo, through friends at a party in a glass building near the river. It used to be an office, or something, and it can't be used as flats because it floods too much. I was so down at the time I didn't want to be out, or to do anything, but Katia and Ana kept forcing me, which in hindsight was kind of them.

That night I planned to wait until they were too busy to notice me leaving and then slink back to the flat. But then I started talking to Jo, and I had the feeling there was something interesting about him, even if I couldn't say exactly what. He seemed to be slightly removed from everything that was going on around him. He asked me if I was having a good time, and I said no, and he said, good, because he wasn't either. That was such a line, looking back on it, but it seemed funny at the time. It actually seemed like the first genuinely funny thing someone had said to me in a long time, despite all the time we all spend laughing.

We walked back to his after the sun came up. I remember the walk very well because we saw a man on the way with a little boy. They were holding hands;

the fresh perfect skin that children always have made the man's look worn and used. We looked at each other and burst out laughing. *Is he real?* Jo asked. I remember saying that I could see him too, but that was all the reassurance I could give.

I still think about that man and his child often. Having one, now, is a brave thing to do, and I am not that brave, but I am jealous of the sense of purpose that man must have. Or maybe he just feels even more scared than I do, with someone else to look after besides himself.

That night was the end of that phase, for me; of feeling so angry and overwhelmed, all the time, about the life we have been condemned to on this dying planet. Angry at everyone who came before and carelessly made this a place with no future. And angry with myself, at the same time, for not being able to cope with it. Meeting Jo was a distraction. I still don't know what to do with myself beyond getting up every day and trying to keep busy and to have fun. The difference is that now I want to get up every day and do something with myself more than I want to lie in bed, feeling despondent. Maybe everyone always felt like this but there were more distractions.

I can't get to sleep again and I don't want to read, so I lie and think till morning. Max calls me around half ten in the morning and I tell him I'll be in later, I have to run an errand first. I walk to Jo's flat and stand outside phoning him. I phone him three times and get voicemail each time so I ring the bell and his flat mate Beth lets me in. She says she has not seen him in a few days but she lets me into his room. His bed is made, the covers neatly folded back on themselves, and his phone is on top of his pillow.

Beth stands behind me and says it's strange that the room is so tidy.

Yes, I say, and I must sound more alarmed than I intend to because she seems to realise that was the wrong thing to say and starts talking about how he often goes out without his phone. And how he likes to be alone sometimes, and will just disappear. Does he do that? I think. Without telling anyone?

I don't want to be in the flat anymore so I tell her I have to go to work and half run down the hall. She is polite, or disengaged enough not to shout after me. I can't think of anything else to do so I walk towards the café, to find the graffiti we saw yesterday. Just to see.

Dead Tree With Six Vultures

You'd nearly think the scene
was pre-arranged—a tableau

somehow set for only us to see:
a volt of Old World vultures—

white-backed, Old Testament
and bent like battered angels.

Not cherubim or seraphim
but angels all the same—

prodigious wings by Botticelli,
Fra Angelico, Van Eyck

but with that added, heightened whiff
of carnage, blood and rot.

Is this the tree from Genesis?
Can this be Eden emptied out?

John Kelly

The Hereafter

Nobody knows it's here.
You can't see it from the road
or the mountain, or the bog.
It's so well hidden it's a mystery
even to the lake to which it flows.

Usually, it's barely there at all—
just a trickle over whitened stones—
but when cold rain falls
for days on end, the secret river
fills and runs and swells.

Everything's perfected then
in a cool, fluorescent atmosphere—
sunlit black and lime-green banks,
jewelled gravel set for trout.
Enter here by rowboat. Disappear.

John Kelly

STINGING FLY PATRONS

Many thanks to:

Susan Armstrong
Maria Behan
Valerie Bistany
Jacqueline Brown
Trish Byrne
Edmond Condon
Evelyn Conlon
Claire Connolly
Paul Curley
Kris Deffenbacher
Enrico Del Prete
Andrew Donovan
Gerry Dukes
Kieran Falconer
Ciara Ferguson
Stephen Grant
Brendan Hackett
Huang Haisu
Sean Hanrahan
Teresa Harte
Christine Dwyer Hickey
Dennis & Mimi Houlihan
Garry Hynes
Nuala Jackson
Charles Julienne
Jeremy Kavanagh
Geoffrey Keating
Jerry Kelleher
Jack Kelleher
Margaret Kelleher
Claire Keogh
Joe Lawlor
Irene Rose Ledger
Ilana Lifshitz
Lucy Luck
Petra McDonough

Jon McGregor
John McInerney
Maureen McLaughlin
Niall MacMonagle
Finbar McLoughlin
Maggie McLoughlin
Ama, Grace & Fraoch MacSweeney
Mary MacSweeney
Paddy & Moira MacSweeney
Anil Malhotra
Gerry Marmion
Ivan Mulcahy
Michael O'Connor
Ed O'Loughlin
Lucy Perrem
Maria Pierce
Peter J. Pitkin
George & Joan Preble
Fiona Ruff
Anne Ryan
Linda Ryan
Alf Scott
Ann Seery
Attique Shafiq
Eileen Sheridan
Alfie & Savannah Stephenson
Helena Texier
Olive Towey
John Vaughan
Debbi Voisey
Therese Walsh
Ruth Webster
The Blue Nib (Poetry Website)
The Moderate Review
Museum of Literature Ireland
Solas Nua

*We'd also like to thank those individuals who have expressed the preference
to remain anonymous.*

BECOME A PATRON ONLINE AT STINGINGFLY.ORG

NOTES ON CONTRIBUTORS

Kangni Alem is an award-winning Togolese writer, critic and playwright. He founded the Atelier Théâtre de Lomé in 1989. He has published five novels and three collections of short stories, the most recent of which is *Britney Spears' Sandwich* (Lomé, 2019). This is the first time his work has been translated into English.

Maggie Armstrong is a writer from Dublin. Her fiction has been published in *The Dublin Review* and Fallow Media. This is her first essay for *The Stinging Fly*.

JL Bogenschneider is a writer of short fiction, with work published in *Cosmonauts Avenue*, *The Interpreter's House*, *Necessary Fiction*, *PANK* and *Ambit*. Their chapbook *Fears for the Near Future*, written under the name C.S. Mierscheid, is available from Neon Books.

Hayley Carr is a writer from Dublin. She has previously been published in *The Stinging Fly*.

Brendan Casey is an Irish/Australian writer. He has an MA in Creative Writing from UCD and is the recipient of a Literature Bursary Award from the Arts Council. His novel in progress was longlisted for the 2020 Deborah Rogers Foundation Award. He lives in Inistioge.

Rachel Connolly is a writer from Belfast who now lives in London. She has written essays for *The Guardian*, *The New York Times Magazine*, *The Baffler* and others.

Elaine Cosgrove is from the west of Ireland. Her debut collection of poems, *Transmissions*, is published by Dedalus Press. Elaine moved to Atlanta in 2019.

Jonathan C. Creasy is a writer, filmmaker, musician and publisher based in Dublin. He is author of *The Black Mountain Letters* (Dalkey Archive Press), editor of the anthology *Black Mountain Poems* (New Directions), and director of the forthcoming documentary, *The Blue Shroud*. He is founder of New Dublin Press and co-director of the production company Dreamsong Films. www.jcreasy.com

Alan Cunningham is the author of *Count from Zero to One Hundred* (2013) and *Sovereign Invalid* (2018).

Paula Cunningham's pamphlet *A Dog Called Chance* and her debut collection *Heimlich's Manoeuvre* are both published by Smith|Doorstop. She lives in Belfast.

Martina Dalton's poems have appeared in P*oetry Ireland Review, The Irish Times'* 'New Irish Writing', *The Stony Thursday Book, Crannóg, Skylight 47, Channel,* and *The Honest Ulsterman*, among others. She was selected for Words Ireland's National Mentoring Programme 2019. She received a notable mention in the Cúirt New Writing Prize 2020.

Katy Derbyshire is a London-born translator and publisher based in Berlin. Longlisted for the MAN Booker International Prize in 2017, she translates contemporary German writers including Sandra Hoffmann, Clemens Meyer and Olga Grjasnowa.

Caitlín Doherty is a writer, historian and poet who lives in London. Her most recent pamphlets can be found through Sad Press and the Earthbound Poetry Series.

Adrian Duncan's debut novel *Love Notes from a German Building Site* won the 2019 John McGahern Book Prize. His second novel *A Sabbatical in Leipzig*, published by The Lilliput Press, was shortlisted for the 2021 Kerry Novel of the Year. His third novel, *The Geometer Lobachevsky*, will appear in 2022.

Kit Fan is a novelist, poet, and critic. His second poetry collection, *As Slow As Possible* was a Poetry Book Society Recommendation and one of *The Irish Times'* Books of the Year. *Diamond Hill*, his debut novel about Hong Kong, is published by Dialogue Books and World Editions in 2021.

Rebecca Ruth Gould is the author of the poetry collection *Cityscapes* (2019) and the award-winning monograph *Writers & Rebels* (2016). She has translated many books from Persian and Georgian. A two-time Pushcart Prize nominee, she was awarded the Creative Writing New Zealand Flash Fiction Competition prize in 2019.

Sandra Hoffmann lives in Munich, where she teaches creative writing and writes for radio and newspapers. Her debut, *Schwimmen Gegen Blond*, was published in 2002, and her fifth novel *Paula* (tr. Katy Derbyshire) won the Hans Fallada Prize for politically and socially engaged writing.

James Hudson is exploring queer and trans identity through speculative fiction. His writing is published with Monstrous Regiment Publishing, Southword Editions, *The Common Breath* and *Pop Up Projects*. He also works with the Small Trans Library and the Trans Writers Union to improve the accessibility of queer writing in Ireland.

Glen Jeffries was born and raised in the north-west of England. He has previously lived in New York and Arctic Norway and is now based back in the UK. His non-fiction writing has appeared in publications including *Hakai*, *Arctic Deeply*, *Earthlines* and *Smithsonian Magazine*. This is his first short story to be published.

Trevor Joyce co-founded New Writers' Press in Dublin in 1967, and SoundEye in Cork in 1997. His most recent books include *Selected Poems* (2014), and *Fastness* (2017). *Conspiracy* is a set of 144 12-line poems composed between May 18th and July 9th 2020. He is a member of Aosdána.

John Kelly is from County Fermanagh. His first collection of poetry, *Notions*, was published by Dedalus Press in 2018.

Ronan Kelly is the author of *Bard of Erin: the Life of Thomas Moore* (2008). His fiction has appeared in *The Dublin Review* and *Winter Papers*.

Victoria Kennefick's first collection, *Eat or We Both Starve*, is published by Carcanet Press. Her pamphlet, *White Whale* (Southword Editions, 2015), won the Munster Literature Centre Fool for Poetry Chapbook Competition and the Saboteur Award for Best Poetry Pamphlet.

Seán Lysaght is the author of six volumes of poems, including *Scarecrow* (1998), *The Mouth of a River* (2007) and *Carnival Masks* (2014) from Gallery Press. He has also written prose about wildlife and landscapes: *Eagle Country* (2018) and *Wild Nephin* (2020). His *Selected Poems* appeared from Gallery in 2010. He lives in Westport, County Mayo.

Aodán McCardle's current practice involves improvised performance/writing/drawing. He is co-editor of Veer Books and author of a PhD titled: 'Action as Articulation of the Contemporary Poem'. He has appeared on RTE Radio 1 Extra's New Normal Culture: 'Keywords' (Episode 1) and has written critical work on the poetry of Maurice Scully in *A Line of Tiny Zeros in the Fabric* (Shearsman 2020, Litmus Publishing; The Lichen Issue). His Instagram handle is @redochretattoo.

John Patrick McHugh is from Galway. His work has appeared in *The Stinging Fly, Banshee, The Tangerine, Granta* and *Winter Papers*. His debut collection of short stories, *Pure Gold*, is published by New Island Books and 4th Estate.

Liadan Ní Chuinn is from the north of Ireland. Their work has been published in *The Stinging Fly, Dark Mountain* and *Tolka Journal*.

Is tobar gan bhonn é aoibhneas Chorca Dhuibhne, a thugann ardú meoin do **Bhríd Ní Mhóráin** agus inspioráid leanúnach dá saothar. Thaitin a tréimhse mar scríbhneoir cónaitheach ag Oidhreacht Chorca Dhuibhne le hurraíocht ó Ealaín na Gaeltachta (2003-2018) thar barr léi. Tá seacht gcnuasach foilsithe aici.

Emer O'Hanlon is a writer and PhD student from Belfast. When not researching her thesis on 18th-century women and ancient nude statues, she also reviews books for *The Irish Independent*. Her short fiction has appeared in *Wretched Creations* and *The Honest Ulsterman*. She is currently working on her first novel.

Katelyn O'Neill, 21, is a final year Creative Writing student at NUI Galway, pursuing a Masters at City University of London. She is working on a first collection, and has had work featured in *The Stinging Fly, Burning Jade* and the *Kilkenny Poetry Broadsheet*.

Jill Osier is an American poet. Her collection *The Solace Is Not the Lullaby* was selected for the 2019 Yale Younger Poets Prize and was published by Yale University Press in 2020.

Lanre Otaiku was born in Lagos, Nigeria, where he grew up. He currently lives in Toronto, Canada.

Lisa Owens is a novelist and screenwriter. Her debut novel, *Not Working*, was published by Picador in 2016 and adapted for BBC Radio 4's Book at Bedtime. She lives in London.

Billy Ramsell's most recent collection of poetry, *The Architect's Dream of Winter*, appeared in 2013. Over the years he has published poems, articles and translations in *The Stinging Fly* and was a guest editor for Issue 32 of the magazine.

Cathy Sweeney's short story collection *Modern Times* was published by The Stinging Fly Press and W&N in 2020.

Grace Wilentz is a poet based in The Liberties in Dublin. Her first collection, *The Limit of Light* (The Gallery Press), was named one of the best books of 2020 in *The Irish Examiner*. She is the recipient of a Literature Bursary Award from the Arts Council.

Tom Willis lives in London.

Frank Wynne is an Irish literary translator from French and Spanish whose authors have included Michel Houellebecq, Javier Cercas and Virginie Despentes. He jointly won the DUBLIN Literary Award, and has twice won both the Scott Moncrieff Prize and the Premio Valle Inclán. He edited the anthologies *Found in Translation* (2018) and *QUEER: LGBT writing from Ancient Times to Yesterday* (2021). During 2021, Frank is collaborating with *The Stinging Fly* as our first translator-in-residence.

Tell a friend | Treat yourself

2 issues | one year

€25 Ireland | €30 overseas

Also available: Magazine + Book Subscriptions

SUBSCRIBE ONLINE AT STINGINGFLY.ORG

Subscriptions include access to our online archive.